MURDER AT BARKER STADIUM
A MARGARET AND MONA GHOSTLY COZY
BOOK II

DIANA XARISSA

Copyright © 2024 by DX Dunn, LLC

Cover Copyright © 2024 Tell-Tale Book Covers

ISBN: 9798325926419

All rights reserved.

No part of this publication may be reproduced, distributed, or transmitted in any form or by any means, including photocopying, recording, or other electronic or mechanical methods, without the prior written permission of the publisher, except as permitted by U.S. copyright law. For permission requests, contact diana@dianaxarissa.com

The story, all names, characters, and incidents portrayed in this production are fictitious. No identification with actual persons (living or deceased), places, buildings, and products is intended or should be inferred.

First edition 2024

❦ Created with Vellum

I

"I'll just have water," Margaret Woods said.

"You're American," the waiter replied.

Margaret laughed. "Is it that obvious?"

He nodded. "But you have to tell me why you're on the Isle of Man. I've always wanted to visit America, but I can't imagine very many Americans want to visit a small island in the Irish Sea."

"My father was born here," Margaret explained. "He and his family moved to the US when he was a teenager. His mother's sister, Mona, stayed on the island. When she passed away, she left her estate to my aunt, Fenella Woods."

The waiter's jaw dropped. "You're Fenella's niece? Everyone on the island has been talking about you."

Margaret flushed. "Oh dear."

He shook his head. "It's all good. We weren't certain what to expect when Fenella came to the island. Most people thought she'd just sell everything she'd inherited." He looked around the room and then leaned closer to Margaret. "I heard that she inherited over a hundred properties around the island."

"I have no idea what Aunt Fenella inherited."

"Of course, she's off on her honeymoon now, isn't she? We were all surprised when she married an ordinary police inspector."

"Daniel is a wonderful man."

The waiter nodded. "And now you're involved with a police inspector, too."

Margaret smiled at Ted Hart, who was sitting across the table from her. "How does anyone do anything illegal on this island?" she asked. "Everyone seems to know everything about everyone."

Ted nodded. "It often makes my job easier."

The waiter laughed. "Sorry, Inspector Hart. I didn't mean to talk about you as if you weren't sitting there."

Ted nodded. "It's fine."

The waiter turned his attention back to Margaret. "I know it isn't any of my business, but I heard that you're working for Park's Cleaning Supplies. Is that right?"

"Yes. I'm a chemical engineer, and I was fortunate that Park's was looking for someone with my qualifications at just the right time," Margaret replied.

"I'd have thought, with all of Mona's money, that you'd never have to work again."

"Aunt Fenella inherited Mona's estate. I didn't inherit anything."

The man frowned. "I suppose I just assumed that she was sharing her fortune with you. I sort of assumed that was why you moved to the island."

"I moved to the island because my sister and I came to visit Aunt Fenella and I fell in love with the island while I was here."

"So you quit your job and moved halfway across the world? That's very brave."

"I'd already decided to make some big changes to my life before my vacation here. I was coming out of a long-term relationship and wanting to change jobs, so when Aunt Fenella suggested that I move here, I didn't take much convincing."

"I have to ask. Are you staying in her flat on the promenade?"

Margaret nodded. "It's a wonderful apartment, er, flat."

"You can call it an apartment," the man replied with a laugh. "The building is called Promenade View Apartments, after all."

"Yeah, why is it called that?" Margaret asked, looking from the waiter to Ted and back again.

They both shrugged.

"You'd have to ask Maxwell Martin. He named the building when he converted what was a luxury hotel into luxury flats," the waiter said. "But if you get a chance to talk to Maxwell Martin, there are better things to ask him."

"Oh?" Margaret asked.

He nodded. "Everyone on the island wants to know why he and Mona were together for decades but never married, for a start."

Ah, but I know the answer to that, Margaret thought.

"I don't really believe in ghosts," the man continued. "But a friend of mine does. She keeps trying to talk to different spirits every week. Maybe I'll see if she can try to chat with Maxwell."

"Good luck," Margaret said. *He's been hanging around what used to be the ballroom in Promenade View since he passed away. Or so Mona claims. And she's a ghost, so she should know.*

"But I can't stand here talking about Mona and Max all day," the waiter said. "I'll go and get your drinks."

As he walked away, Margaret sighed. "Life on a small island," she said softly.

Ted nodded. "When I was on secondment across, I forgot just how small the island can feel sometimes."

"I really love it here, but it is uncomfortably odd feeling as if everyone on the island knows who I am."

"Mona made certain that everyone talked about her. She seemed to thrive on the attention, even as she got older. It was only natural that people would be interested in whoever inherited her estate."

"Then they should be interested in Aunt Fenella, not me."

Ted chuckled. "They were interested in Fenella, especially when she wasn't just Mona's niece, but she also kept stumbling over dead bodies everywhere she went."

"I suppose I can understand why people would talk about that, but none of that was Aunt Fenella's fault."

"No, of course not. And I understand from Daniel that things are going much better on their honeymoon."

Margaret nodded. "I talked to Aunt Fenella last night. She said they've been gone almost two months and haven't found a single dead body yet."

"The 'yet' is worrying," Ted said with a laugh.

"I really hope they don't find any at all during their year away."

"That makes two of us. Maybe if they can just relax and enjoy their travels, Daniel will want to come back after a year."

"Do you think he might not want to come back?"

Ted shrugged. "If I were married to a very rich woman who wanted to travel the world with me, I don't know that I'd want to go back to police work, no matter how satisfying I find the job."

"Maybe you should be looking for a very rich woman."

Ted picked up her hand. "I'm quite happy with the woman I've already found," he said.

Margaret felt herself blushing. "I'm glad to hear that," she said.

"Here we are," the waiter said loudly. "Your drinks." He put the glasses on the table and then looked around the mostly empty dining room. "I understand you have a sister," he said.

"Yes, Megan," Margaret replied.

"She's the one who got involved with the man who was murdered a few months ago."

Margaret made a face. "It wasn't quite like that."

"You came to visit the island together. I take it she didn't fall in love with it the way that you did."

"She did, actually, but she isn't ready to move across the Atlantic, at least not yet. She's on sabbatical from work this year, but she recently met a new man, so she wants to stay in the US until she sees where that relationship is going."

"Well, if it doesn't work out, I'm single," the man said with an exaggerated wink.

Margaret smiled at the man, who had to be sixty-something. There was no way he was an appropriate suitor for her sister, who was younger than Margaret.

"Are you ready to order?"

Margaret looked at Ted, who shrugged.

"You go first," Margaret said. "I'll figure out what I want while you're ordering."

She quickly read through the menu and chose something almost at random. After they'd both ordered, the waiter walked away.

"Hello," she said, grinning at Ted.

He smiled back at her. "Hi. How are you?"

"I'm fine, but I'd be better if I got to see more of you."

"This time it wasn't my fault."

She nodded. "Work has been crazy. I'm sorry I've been putting in so many hours, but I think I'm done with all of the late nights for a while."

"I hope so. I've missed you."

"I've missed you, too."

"Can you tell me what you've been working on that's taken so much time?"

"We've been working on updating some of the manufacturing protocols within the company. That's meant I've needed to be there to see what's done at different times of the day. I can go into more detail, but I suspect you'd find it all a bit dull."

"I think most of the work most people do every day is fairly dull."

Margaret laughed. "Except for your job. I'm sure it's never boring."

Ted shook his head. "It's very quiet at the moment. I've been catching up on paperwork, which is even more boring than you can imagine. It isn't as if crime has stopped on the island, but there hasn't been anything major since the body at Atkins Farm last month. On Monday, I actually got asked to help find a missing kitten."

"Did you find him or her?"

"It was him, and I didn't find him."

"Oh no."

"He's fine. He wandered home on his own after a few hours."

"That's good to hear."

"I have been talking to a friend about something interesting," Ted said.

"Here we are," the waiter said, putting a plate of food in front of Margaret. He set Ted's plate down. "Is there anything else right now?"

Margaret glanced at her plate and then looked at the waiter. "It looks wonderful. I don't think we need anything else."

He nodded. "Just shout if you need me."

"What do you think he'd do if I actually shouted?" Ted asked as the waiter walked away.

"Please don't."

Ted laughed. "I've nothing to shout about, at least not yet. This is exactly what I ordered, and it looks wonderful."

The pair chatted about the food and cooking methods while they ate. The waiter brought them dessert menus while they were finishing their final bites.

"Get the chocolate cake," he said as he handed Margaret a menu. "It's American-style chocolate cake with layers of chocolate buttercream between the cake layers. It's topped with hot fudge and whipped cream."

"That sounds amazing," Margaret said.

"Maybe we could split one," Ted suggested.

Margaret nodded. "That's a great idea. And after we eat it, we can take a long walk on the promenade to burn off a few of the calories."

"As long as it isn't raining," Ted told her.

"It was a lovely sunny day when we came inside."

"But this is the Isle of Man. You never know."

"So, one chocolate cake with two forks?" the waiter asked.

Margaret nodded.

He was back a few minutes later with a large slice of cake.

"We're never going to finish this," Margaret said as she picked up her fork.

"I think we might," Ted said with a grin.

"I ate too much," Margaret said a short while later as she and Ted left the restaurant.

"We both ate too much, but that cake was too good. We had to eat it all."

"It was really good."

"And now we can take a long walk to make up for it."

Margaret looked up at the clear skies. "It's the perfect evening for a long walk."

Ted took her hand, and they walked across the street to the wide promenade by the water.

"I don't think I'll ever get tired of living by the sea," Margaret said after a few minutes.

"It isn't just the views. I'm convinced the sea air is good for my health."

Margaret nodded. "I feel happier and healthier than I have in years, in spite of the number of extra desserts I've been having since I moved here."

"Life is better with pudding, or dessert, if you prefer."

"I will learn to speak British English eventually."

"It doesn't really matter if you do or not. I can understand you."

"I should hope so," Margaret said with a laugh.

"Hello, Margaret," a loud voice called.

Margaret stopped and looked around and then waved at the woman who was crossing the street toward them.

"Elaine, hello," she said when the woman reached them.

"Hello," Elaine replied. "How are you tonight?"

"We're fine," Ted said. "Are you taking a walk on your own?"

Elaine nodded. "Shelly and Tim are going to be meeting me in a short while for dinner. I thought I'd take a walk first, though, because I'll probably want pudding."

"We did it the other way around," Margaret told her next-door neighbor. "We already had our pudding."

Ted grinned at her. "Well done," he mouthed silently.

"I won't walk far," Elaine said. "But it is a lovely evening."

"It's my first summer on the island. So far, it's been pretty perfect," Margaret said.

"I've had an offer on my house," Elaine told them. "I'm probably going to take it, just to get rid of the house. I can't even consider buying anything over here until I get rid of the house in Bolsover, after all."

Margaret knew that Elaine had grown up on the island, but she'd moved across for university and had moved back to the island only a few months earlier after a lifetime of working as an accountant. She still owned her small house in Bolsover, near Chesterfield, and Margaret knew she was eager to sell it.

"Good luck," Ted said. "I hope it all goes smoothly."

Elaine shrugged. "I can't complain if it all falls through. Shelly is letting me stay in her flat for as long as I like."

Shelly Quirk had bought the apartment next door to Mona's just six months before Mona's death. The sudden loss of her husband had made Shelly decide to change everything in her life. She'd sold the house she'd shared with the man for most of their married life. Additionally, she'd taken early retirement from her career as a primary school teacher. Once she'd moved into Promenade View, she and Mona had very quickly become friends. Mona had helped Shelly recover from her bereavement, encouraging the sixty-something woman to embrace life.

After Mona passed away, Shelly had been one of the first people to welcome Fenella to the island. Fenella had been delighted to make a new friend, and she'd also been happy when Shelly began dating Tim Blake, an architect who also performed with a local band. Fenella had insisted on paying for Shelly's dream wedding when the pair got married, an event that had brought Elaine back to the island for a long-overdue visit. When Elaine decided to move back, Shelly was quick to offer her a place to stay. She and Tim were planning to get rid of either his house or Shelly's apartment, but they had yet to make a decision as to where they wanted to live now that they were married.

With Elaine staying in the apartment, Shelly and Tim usually stayed at his house, but now the couple were talking about selling both properties and buying something together that they could make uniquely theirs. They weren't in any hurry, though. Both Shelly and Tim were still enjoying getting to know each other better and settling into married life together.

"So how are you?" Ted asked Elaine as the trio walked along the promenade together.

"I'm good, thanks."

"And how is Ernie?" Margaret asked.

"He's also good," Elaine said. "We're still trying to work out where we're going, but we enjoy each other's company, regardless."

The pair had met not long after Elaine's move back to the island. Ernie had an apartment on the third floor of their building. Just last month, Elaine had been worried that Ernie had gone missing, but she'd eventually learned that he'd simply gone across to revisit his former hometown in Wales. Ernie was a widower, and Margaret knew he was hesitant to get involved with anyone else out of respect for his former wife.

"I'm glad you're working on it," Margaret said. "He seems like a nice guy."

"He is a nice guy, but he's also a bit dull," Elaine said. "I'm not certain he's interesting enough for me to stay with him long-term."

"He was a teacher, wasn't he?" Ted asked. "He must have lots of interesting stories from his teaching days."

"He has a lot of stories, anyway," Elaine said.

Margaret laughed. "Not interesting ones?"

"Sometimes they can be." Elaine shrugged. "We'll see. It isn't as if there are dozens of men knocking on my door, eager to take me out. Ernie is a nice person, and we have fun together. Maybe that is as good as it gets at my age."

They walked in silence for a few minutes before Ted spoke again.

"Here comes trouble," he muttered.

Margaret looked around and then frowned when she spotted the woman walking toward them.

"Good evening," Heather Bryant called as she got closer. "I was hoping I might bump into you tonight."

Heather was an investigative reporter for the island's only newspaper, the *Isle of Man Times*. Margaret thought she was rude, nosy, and annoying.

"Me?" Elaine asked. "I'm flattered."

Heather looked surprised for a moment and then laughed. "I wasn't necessarily talking to you, but I'm happy to see you. I understand you've been seeing Ernie Stone, a relative newcomer to the island."

Elaine narrowed her eyes. "You haven't been here much longer than Ernie," she said.

Heather laughed again. "No, of course not, but I've already come to love the island. It's so unique and interesting. I'm fascinated by its history and by the wonderful people I've met here."

"Uh huh," Elaine said skeptically.

Heather sighed. "No one believes me when I talk about how much I love it here. I've only been here for a few months, but I fully intend to make the island my home for the long term."

"I'm sure Dan Ross must love that," Ted whispered in Margaret's ear.

Dan had been the island's only investigative reporter for decades before Heather moved to the island. Since her arrival, his byline had all but disappeared from the paper's front page. Heather seemed to cover all of the island's most interesting news, leaving Dan to write articles about things like missing pets, women's guild meetings, and the opening of new branches of the island's bank.

"Good for you," Elaine said. "I'm not planning on leaving again."

Heather nodded. "But maybe you'd feel differently about the island if you'd moved here to get away from a police investigation."

"What does that mean?" Elaine demanded.

Heather opened her eyes wide. "You didn't know? I just assumed, since you're friendly with Ernie, that you knew."

Margaret put her hand on Elaine's arm and squeezed gently. Elaine took a slow, deep breath.

"I don't know anything about a police investigation involving Ernie. I don't think you do, either. I think you're just trying to cause trouble," Elaine said after a second breath.

Heather frowned. "Now why would I do that? The next time you're in a very public place with Ernie, maybe you should ask him what really happened to his wife."

"She died," Elaine said flatly.

"Yes, but how?" Heather asked. "Have you ever asked him?"

Elaine shook her head. "It isn't any of my business."

"It will be if you marry him, write a new will, and then die under mysterious circumstances," Heather said.

"Actually, in that case, it will no longer be my business, because I'll be dead," Elaine told her with a slightly smug grin.

Heather frowned. "You know what I meant. I apologize for trying to help you. I just feel as if women should stick together. If we hear something unpleasant about someone, we should share that with everyone who knows that someone."

"What exactly did you hear about Ernie?" Ted asked, his voice suddenly very much that of a senior police inspector.

"I'm not going to repeat it. It might have just been speculation or rumors. I just thought it would be helpful to give Elaine a heads-up. I never should have said anything," Heather said, frowning.

"Maybe we should talk about something else," Margaret suggested.

"The weather is lovely," Elaine said flatly.

"Inspector Hart, do you have any comment on the current downturn in the number of arrests being made by the Isle of Man Constabulary each day?" Heather asked.

Ted grinned at her. "The weather is nice. Crime rates are down. We can't arrest people if they aren't committing crimes."

"So you're maintaining that crime rates have fallen in commeasure with the fall in arrests?"

"We have an entire department that deals with your questions," Ted said. "I'm just a hard-working inspector."

"Except you aren't working very hard at the moment, are you? From what I've seen, no one in the constabulary is working very hard at the moment," Heather said.

Ted muttered something under his breath before he smiled again. "I'd invite you down to the station to see just how hard I'm actually working every day, but I doubt you want to watch me do paperwork for hours."

Heather smiled. "I'd be happy to do that, actually. It would make for an interesting story. It could be a sort of 'day in the life of' kind of feature. And who knows, maybe while I'm there, someone will get brutally murdered and I'll be allowed to tag along on the investigation."

Ted shook his head. "That isn't how investigations work. And I'm not interested in being part of a story."

"I need something to fill the pages of the paper," Heather said. "If someone doesn't rob a bank or kill someone soon, I'm going to have to start making things up just to sell papers."

"I hope the paper isn't going to start putting fiction on the front page," Margaret said. "But I can't see anyone on the island complaining about a decrease in crime here."

Heather shrugged. "It doesn't have to be crime. A house could burn down. A car could drive up a tree or into the sea. Just something that makes headlines, that's all I need."

"Or maybe you could write about happy things," Elaine suggested. "Students graduating from university and coming back to the island, maybe. Or new restaurants with amazing chefs. People would enjoy reading about those things."

Heather made a face. "There are other reporters at the paper who cover those topics. I'm an investigative journalist. I need something to investigate."

"I'm a police inspector, and I'm quite happy that I don't have anything to investigate at the moment."

"Because you won't lose your job if you don't create headlines."

"I can't believe you'll lose your job, either," Margaret said. "Surely your boss doesn't want you making up lies just to sell papers."

Heather gave her a wicked smile. "I wouldn't be too sure about that."

"It's my night off," Ted said. "Even if something does happen, you won't hear about it from me."

"What about you?" Heather asked Margaret.

"What about me? I'm not a police inspector. I can tell you all about the work I do as a chemical engineer, if you want."

Heather frowned. "I was thinking more about doing an article about your aunt."

"Aunt Fenella?"

"Yes, her. I'd love to hear her entire life story."

Margaret shrugged. "I'm sorry, but I'm not really comfortable talking for her. She'll be on her honeymoon for another ten months or so. Maybe she'll give you an interview when she gets back."

"That's far too many months into the future. I need headlines now. And what I really want from Fenella is to hear all about finding all those dead bodies. She's never really talked about it, not publicly, anyway. I think the island's residents have a right to know more about her experiences."

"Why?" Margaret demanded.

Heather blinked at her. "Why what?"

"Why would the island's population have any right to hear about Aunt Fenella's experiences? Finding someone dead is a horrible experience. I'm certain my aunt doesn't want to talk about it. I wouldn't, if I were her."

"Of course, you've found your own dead body or two," Heather said. "Maybe you'd feel better about the experiences if you talked about them."

"If I decide I want to talk about them, I'll find a therapist," Margaret said. "I certainly won't share them with the world."

"It would be interesting to compare your experiences to your aunt's. She tripped over her first dead body the day after she arrived on the island. How long had you been on the island before you stumbled over that poor dead man in the alley behind Promenade View Apartments?"

"No comment," Margaret said flatly.

"And that alley was where Fenella found her first body, too, wasn't it? How interesting. Of course, Fenella found several more bodies. How many have you found?"

"No comment," Margaret replied.

"I'll have to check my notes. Does anyone else think it's odd that there hasn't been a single dead body found since Fenella left the island, though?"

"Not at all," Margaret said quickly.

Heather shrugged. "I find it odd. I know that old skeleton turned up last month, but I'm not counting that as a dead body. The last one that was found was that poor girl who was murdered up at the Point of Ayre. You were there when she was found, weren't you?" she asked Margaret.

"You know I was," Margaret said with a sigh.

"Interesting," Heather said. "Of course, Fenella was there, too."

"So was I," Elaine said.

Heather looked at her. "You were? Did you see the body?"

Elaine frowned and then shook her head. "I was in the house, staying warm and out of the wind."

"What happened when you heard a body had been found?" Heather asked.

"I felt quite unwell," Elaine replied.

Heather pulled out a notebook. "Tell me more. Tell me exactly how you felt when you were told that there was a dead person just outside."

Margaret caught Elaine's eye and slowly shook her head.

"No comment," Elaine said. "It was a terrible tragedy, and no one should be gossiping about it."

"It isn't gossip," Heather said. "It's news."

"It was news when it happened. That was months ago. Now it's gossip," Elaine countered. "And it's in poor taste. A young woman lost her life. Show some respect."

Heather inhaled slowly. "How is your new job?" she asked Margaret.

Margaret frowned. "It's good, thanks."

"I've heard all sorts of stories about Park's and about its owner."

"I'm sure you have. I don't care to hear them," Margaret said.

"One person I talked to suggested that Arthur Park hired you only because he wants to sell the business."

"That doesn't make any sense at all," Margaret said.

"Of course it does. What would happen if you went into work tomorrow and Arthur told you he was closing down the company?"

"I'd start looking for another job."

"Would you, though? Or would you ring your Aunt Fenella and ask her to buy the company? No doubt Arthur would sell it to her for a hugely inflated price, but she'd pay it in order to let you keep your job."

Margaret stared at her for a moment and then shrugged. "If you say so," she said.

Heather shook her head. "I'm just trying to warn you, that's all."

"At least if you do have to start making up stories, you have an overactive imagination," Elaine said tartly.

Heather laughed. "I can't argue with that."

"I think it's time to head for home," Ted said.

Margaret nodded. "I'm ready to sit down and relax."

The foursome turned around and began a slow stroll back toward Promenade View.

Heather sighed. "I can't convince any of you to answer a few questions, can I?"

"I'll answer a few," Elaine said.

"Excellent! What happened at The Seaview when you found the dead woman in the hotel room where Shelly's wedding guests were supposed to be staying?" Heather asked.

"Not that question," Elaine said. "Try again."

"Is there any truth to the rumor that you've moved back to the island to avoid answering questions about one of your largest accounts? An account that is currently being investigated by the inland revenue?"

Elaine laughed. "You do have a very vivid imagination. To the best of my knowledge, none of my former accounts are currently being investigated by the inland revenue, but if they were, it wouldn't be because of anything I did."

"May I quote you on that?" Heather asked.

Elaine raised an eyebrow. "No," she said.

Heather sighed. "If any of you change your mind and want to talk, you know where to find me," she said before she walked to her car, which was parked on the promenade.

Margaret, Ted, and Elaine watched as she got into the car and drove away.

"She's nothing but trouble," Elaine said.

Ted nodded. "She's ambitious and she's ruthless. I don't think she'd go so far as to make up a headline, but I'm certain she'd be happy to stretch the truth to make her headlines more spectacular."

"Let's hope the island's crime rates continue to fall, then," Margaret said. "Maybe she'll get so bored that she'll go back across to wherever she came from."

"Where did she come from?" Elaine asked.

Ted shrugged. "I've no idea."

"Do you really think she's going to stay on the island long term?" Margaret asked.

"I think she'd be gone tomorrow if she got an offer from a newspaper across," Ted said. "But I think she'll maintain the fiction that she wants to be here until that happens."

"Let's talk about something more pleasant," Margaret suggested.

"Which is just about anything," Elaine said with a laugh. "You don't really think there was anything suspicious about Ernie's wife's death, do you?"

Ted shook his head. "When he was missing last month, I took a little look at him. Aside from one speeding ticket about twenty years ago, his record is clean."

"And he just went back across to visit the place he used to live," Margaret added. "He wouldn't have done that if he'd run away to the island to hide."

Elaine nodded. "I don't suppose I can ask him about it, can I?"

"You could try..." Margaret was cut off by a loud ringing noise.

"That's my mobile. It's probably Shelly and Tim wondering where I am," Elaine said as she dug through her purse. "Ah ha!" she said as her hand emerged holding her phone.

"Hello?"

There was a short silence before Elaine spoke again.

"I wasn't expecting that. Ring me later."

She pushed the button to end the call and then dropped her phone back into her bag.

"What's wrong?" Margaret asked.

"Shelly and Tim are going to be late," Elaine said. "They just walked out of his house and discovered that his car has been stolen."

2

"Tim's car has been stolen?" Margaret repeated.

Elaine shrugged. "That's what Shelly said. Tim was ringing the police while she rang me to let me know that they were going to be late."

"How awful for them. How does that even happen?" Margaret asked. She looked at Ted, who shrugged.

"I can ring the station and try to find out more. Give me a minute," he said. As he pulled his cell phone out of his pocket, he took a few steps away from the two women.

"It's a good thing Heather isn't still with us," Elaine said. "I'm certain she'd love to hear about the stolen car."

"Is it possible that Tim simply forgot where he parked?" Margaret asked. She shook her head. "I just hate the idea of someone stealing cars on the island."

"Don't we all? I'm very glad we have a parking garage under our building. Our cars should be safe there, shouldn't they?"

"I would expect so. You need to have a keycard to get in or out of the garage. There are security cameras, too, which should help keep car thieves away."

Elaine nodded. "I feel as if I should be watching the promenade, looking for Tim's car."

"How long ago did he leave it?"

"Shelly said it could have been stolen hours ago. Whoever took it has probably already put it on a ferry to the UK. That's why I was thinking it might get driven down the promenade. Someone might be heading straight for the ferry with it."

Margaret looked over at the Sea Terminal. One of the island's large ferries was just pulling away from the dock.

"If the car was stolen an hour or more ago, the thief could have gotten it on that ferry," she said. "It wouldn't have been reported stolen by the time they loaded the ship."

"At least if it is on that ship, they can stop it at the other end," Elaine said. "The thief would have been smarter to wait and steal it after Tim and Shelly went to bed for the night. Then he or she could have driven it onto the overnight ferry. The thief could have driven away in Liverpool before Tim even noticed that the car was missing."

"That's a scary thought."

"And there are cameras on the car decks," Ted said as he rejoined them. "If someone did steal a car and manage to get it across, we'd have several pictures of that person. You also have to show identification in order to sail. I don't think it would take us long to track down the thief, even if he or she managed to get to Liverpool with the car."

"That's good to hear," Margaret said. "Were you able to learn anything about Tim's car?"

"The first constable on the scene only just arrived. He's taking Tim's statement now. An alert has been issued for the car. I'll check for updates in the morning."

Margaret nodded.

"Maybe I should just go and get myself something to eat," Elaine said.

"We'd join you if we hadn't already eaten," Margaret told her.

Elaine shrugged. "I've eaten nearly all of my meals on my own since I left school a great many years ago. While it's nice to have company, I'm quite capable of dining alone."

"Maybe you should give Tim and Shelly a few more minutes,"

Margaret suggested. "Surely it won't take them long to report the car stolen."

"Probably not," Ted said. "It's a fairly simple report to take."

They strolled slowly back down the promenade, chatting about nothing much for five minutes. Margaret jumped when Elaine's cell began to ring again.

"It's Shelly," she said before she answered the call. "Hello?"

Margaret and Ted exchanged glances as Elaine listened for a short while. She nodded several times, but never spoke. "I'm on the promenade. I'll see you in five minutes, then," she said eventually before ending the call and putting her phone away.

"They've finished with the police already?" Margaret asked.

"She said they couldn't do much more than say that the car was gone. The constable who arrived first took their statement and said that an inspector would follow up as needed," Elaine replied. "Luckily, Shelly's car was parked next to Tim's, so they're on their way here now to collect me. We're going to go somewhere and get dinner as planned."

"That's good," Margaret said.

The trio walked to the edge of the road and took seats on a bench. Just a few minutes later, Shelly's car pulled up in front of them. Shelly waved from the passenger seat and then rolled down the window.

"Hi, Margaret. Hi, Ted. Would you two care to join us for dinner?" she asked.

Margaret shook her head. "We already ate, but thank you anyway."

"Sorry about the car," Ted said.

Shelly shrugged. "We have confidence in the island's policemen and women."

Ted laughed. "That's good to hear."

Elaine climbed into the back of the car and fastened her seatbelt.

"We'll probably be at the pub later," Ted told Shelly.

"Maybe we'll see you there," Shelly replied.

Margaret waved as the car pulled away. Then she smiled at Ted. "What now?"

"We could walk the promenade a second time, or we could go and get a drink at the pub."

"Hmm, let me think about that," Margaret said with a laugh. "We should walk again, but I think I'd rather go to the pub."

"Yeah, me too."

While there were many pubs on the island, Margaret knew exactly which pub Ted meant. They were only a short walk away from the Tale and Tail, which was right on the promenade. Once a mansion owned by one of the island's wealthiest families, the company that had purchased the property years earlier had turned most of the building into a luxury hotel. They had left the large library at the front of the property largely untouched.

Shelves full of books still lined the walls on both levels. A small bar had been added to the center of the large ground floor space. There was a spiral staircase that led to an upper level where chairs and couches were scattered around low tables. An elevator allowed guests to return to the ground floor without having to navigate the spiral stairs after they'd enjoyed a drink or two.

The new owners had also added a number of cat beds to the space. A dozen or so rescued cats and kittens now called the pub home. Guests could read in the pub or even borrow books. They could also cuddle a kitten or a cat while they enjoyed a book and a drink. Many of the cats ended up getting adopted by the pub's guests, but once they'd been given a home at the pub, they were welcome to stay there for the rest of their lives.

It didn't take long for the pair to walk to the Tale and Tail. Ted pulled open the door and then followed Margaret inside. She smiled brightly at the bartender as they crossed to the bar.

"Good evening," he said. "Your usual?"

Both Margaret and Ted nodded. The man filled their glasses and then took Ted's credit card. A minute later, the pair headed for the stairs. The upper level was all but empty. An older woman was sitting at a table near the stairs, lost in a book. On the other side of the room, a young couple were having what looked like an intense conversation. Margaret and Ted chose a couch as far from everyone else as possible and settled in.

"Hello," Margaret said a moment later as a large black cat approached them.

He stopped and stared at her for a moment and then seemed to shake his head. As he turned and walked away, Margaret frowned.

"I didn't mean to scare him off," she said.

Ted shrugged. "Maybe he's just in a bad mood."

As Margaret took a sip of her wine, two small orange kittens came racing toward them.

"Should I talk to them?" Margaret asked Ted.

He laughed as the pair jumped onto the couch and began to climb all over him. "I don't think they'll mind either way," he said.

A minute later, the pair had calmed down and settled, one on each of Margaret's and Ted's laps.

"This is just about perfect," Margaret said as she sat back and rubbed the kitten's head.

"It is."

"Are you worried about Tim's car?"

He shrugged. "I won't be the inspector assigned to the case, if that's what you mean. We have a team that deals with theft at all levels."

"Do you think you'll be able to get the car back?"

"I'd like to think so. It's a Saturday night. Most cars taken on Saturday nights are taken by kids looking for some excitement. They often end up crashing the stolen car into a tree or driving it into someone's front garden, but the cars nearly always turn up."

"I'd hate to think that someone is going to drive Tim's car into a tree."

"Maybe whoever took it will be careful with it."

Margaret frowned. "I can't see a car thief being careful with a stolen car."

"He or she will be very careful if the plan is to sell the car, especially if it was stolen to order."

"Stolen to order? Does that happen on the island?"

"Not usually, but it does happen across. The problem for thieves over here is getting the car off the island."

Margaret nodded. "You said something about being able to monitor cars on the ferry."

"Stolen cars are reported to the ferry company as soon as the car is reported missing. Once that happens, if someone tries to get that car onto the ferry, he or she will be stopped. Cars are also checked as they get off the ferry, so if the car is reported stolen while the ferry is at sea, it will get stopped when the thief tries to leave the ferry."

"And you can't exactly take a car on a plane."

"I think you can, if you have the right plane, but you can't take a car on a commercial flight, anyway."

"So if you steal a car on the island, you're stuck with it."

"More or less. There was a pair a few years ago who set up a system to steal cars from one of the hire car companies. One of the guys who worked for the company was behind it. He'd hire out the car and then steal it. He rented a storage unit and hid the cars he'd taken in the unit."

"What was he going to do with them?"

"The plan was to put them into containers and then get them on the ferry that way, but containers are subject to random inspection. He had an accomplice at the ferry company, but that guy kept wanting more money, so the cars just sat in the storage unit while the two of them fought about getting the cars off the island."

"And then they were caught?"

"They were. More worrying is the thought that someone might have set up a chop shop here on the island."

"Where they strip the cars for parts and sell those instead of trying to get rid of the entire car?"

Ted nodded. "Someone tried it a few years ago. They managed to steal about a dozen cars over a few months, but then they got greedy and started taking cars almost every day. It didn't take long for us to track them down after that."

"It's a small island. I'm surprised they got away with it at all."

"They'd hired out one of the big warehouses at an industrial estate. They could drive the cars in, strip them for parts, and then ship all of the parts across. It was a very efficient operation, actually, run by a guy who was smart enough to get away with it for longer than he should have."

"Where did he go wrong?"

"As I said, he got greedy, or rather some of the men working for him got greedy. They started bringing in more cars than the shop could handle, which meant leaving a few parked outside the warehouse. They covered them, but that probably only made them look more suspicious. We'd already been watching the warehouse because a neighbor had rung the station to suggest that there might be something illegal happening there, so we would have caught him eventually, anyway, but once they started leaving stolen cars outside the building, it was very easy to start making arrests."

"Maybe someone on the island learned from those mistakes."

"I hope not. If Tim's car doesn't turn up in the next day or two, I might suggest that someone take a look at all of the island's large warehouses, just to be on the safe side."

"I could fall asleep," Margaret said a few minutes later as she stroked the kitten in her lap. "Half a glass of wine and I'm ready for bed."

Ted slid an arm around her. "I know what you mean. Maybe we should go back to your place and go to bed," he whispered in her ear.

Margaret laughed. "That wasn't at all what I was suggesting."

"I know, and I didn't expect you to say yes, either, but – ah, here's Shelly."

Ted waved at the woman who'd just reached the top of the stairs. She waved back and then walked toward them. When Mona had encouraged Shelly to embrace life following her husband's death, one of the things that Shelly had chosen to do was to begin dressing in bright colors. Today she was wearing a bright pink shirt that was covered in white polka dots. Her pants were lime green. The combination was a bit surprising, but it looked just right on Shelly.

"Tim is getting us drinks," she said as she sank down into the chair opposite Margaret.

"Where's Elaine?" Margaret asked.

"Ernie rang her while we were having dinner. He invited her to meet him at the pub next to our building for a drink. Of course she said yes."

Margaret laughed. "Elaine needs to introduce Ernie to the Tale and Tail."

"Indeed. I don't know if he knows that it exists. He was a teacher, though, so I'm certain he'll love it in here."

"I'm surprised Elaine has never mentioned it to him before."

"They usually meet for lunch or for afternoon walks on the promenade. I believe this is the first time Ernie has invited Elaine out in the evening."

"Does that mean things are getting more serious?"

Shelly shrugged. "Elaine seems uncertain how she feels about the man, but it does seem as if they're courting. I'm doing my best to stay out of it."

"That's probably wise," Margaret said.

Tim appeared at the top of the stairs a moment later. He was carrying two glasses, and he handed one of them to Shelly as he joined them.

"I'm sorry about your car," Ted said as Tim sat down in the chair next to Shelly's.

"Yeah, I can't imagine what happened to it," Tim said. "It isn't as if it's anything special."

"What is it?" Ted asked.

Tim named the make and model, both of which were unfamiliar to Margaret.

"It's just a little two-door coupe," Shelly said. "And a ten-year-old coupe at that."

Tim nodded. "I bought it secondhand about five years ago. I wasn't planning on keeping it for long, but I needed a car in a hurry after my previous car died. It's been a good little car for me, though. I'm going to miss it if it doesn't get found."

"It was probably just some kids," Ted said. "Older cars aren't usually in high demand. Car thieves tend to be a lot more interested in newer models."

"Which is another reason why I was happy to keep driving my car," Tim said. "Last year I was going across for work a lot and I usually took the car with me on the ferry. I never worried about where I parked it in the UK because I didn't think anyone would want to steal something so old and a little beat up."

"It's more than a little beat up," Shelly murmured.

Tim laughed. "I'm nowhere near as careful with it as I should be. I've never hit another car, but I might have bumped into a few pillars in various parking garages around the island and in the UK. None of the dents are very big, though."

Shelly shook her head. "Define big."

"Seriously, though, do you really think it was just kids?" Tim asked Ted.

He nodded. "That's the most likely explanation. The ferry company will have been notified, so they'll be watching for it in case someone had the bright idea to steal it and take it across, but it's been a long time since someone actually tried to do that."

"Wasn't Herman Merman the last guy to try it?" Tim asked.

Ted laughed. "I'm not certain he was the last one to try, but I do remember his efforts."

"The entire island remembers his efforts," Shelly said, laughing.

"Okay, tell me the story," Margaret said.

The other three exchanged glances.

Ted grinned. "I'll tell it, because I was part of it."

"You were? I didn't know that," Shelly said.

Ted nodded. "I was just a constable in those days, dreaming of one day becoming an inspector and getting to investigate serious crimes. Mostly, I directed traffic around accidents and took preliminary statements whenever anything interesting happened. Then the inspectors would come and take over."

"And now that's your job," Shelly said.

"And I try hard to be nicer to the constables than some inspectors were to me."

"But you were going to tell me about Herman Merman," Margaret said. "Was that really his name?"

Ted nodded. "Herman's parents thought it would be fun if his name rhymed. They named their daughter Ermine."

"Like the small furry animal?" Margaret asked.

"Exactly like that. She had it changed by deed poll as soon as she turned eighteen," Shelly said.

"To what?" Margaret had to ask.

"To Joan. She still lives on the island. She's Joan Christian now," Shelly told her.

"I suppose that's a good deal better than Ermine Merman," Margaret said.

Shelly laughed. "I'd think so, anyway."

"But what about Herman? Was he happy with his name?" Margaret asked.

Shelly shrugged and looked at Ted.

"I've no idea," Ted said. "He never said anything to me about his name. He might have hated it, but when I met him we had other things to discuss."

"Like the stolen car he was driving," Tim suggested.

Ted nodded as both Shelly and Tim began to laugh.

"What is so funny?" Margaret demanded.

Ted grinned. "Herman was only about nineteen. He'd left school with very few qualifications and was mostly just hanging around various pubs doing not very much with his life."

"He wasn't stupid," Shelly said. "But he was lazy."

"And then he found himself a girlfriend," Ted continued. "Betty Quayle had also left school with only a few qualifications. She was more ambitious than Herman, though."

"She was clever, but not smart, if that makes sense," Shelly said. "I'd taught both of them in primary school. Betty was always scheming, but her plans always had major flaws."

"So when she and Herman decided to move to the UK, they never should have let Betty do the planning," Tim said. "Except Herman wasn't capable of doing it, either."

"What happened?" Margaret asked.

"They didn't have any money, and they knew they'd need a car to get around once they got across, so Betty decided that the easiest thing to do would be to steal themselves a car," Ted said. "According to Herman, they spent some time looking around the island, trying to find the best car to steal."

"They might have been better off stealing something less nice," Shelly said.

Ted nodded. "But Betty set her sights on a brand-new car," he told

Margaret. "And not just any car. She wanted a fancy sports car." He told her the make and model.

"Wow. I don't know a lot about cars, but I do know that those are expensive," Margaret said.

"So maybe not the best car to steal, especially if you've never stolen a car before," Tim said.

"I can't wait to see where this is going," Margaret said.

"Betty came up with a plan," Ted said. "She and Herman went to the car dealership and asked to take the fancy sports car for a test drive."

"And he said no way," Margaret guessed.

"Oh, no, he let Herman take the car for a drive. He went with him, though. Betty stayed behind at the dealership. When they got back, Betty was sobbing in the waiting room. This was enough to fluster the car salesman, which gave Herman time to press the key into some clay to copy the key. Once Betty calmed down, they left with their little bit of clay. Betty had a friend who was able to use the imprint to make a key."

"This must have been years ago, then," Margaret said.

"It was," Ted replied. "Probably twenty years ago, when I was just starting out in the police."

"So what happened next?" Margaret asked.

"They waited a few days and then, late at night, went back to the dealership," Ted said. "There, they cut the padlock off the gate, opened the gate, and then used their key to open the car. Then they drove away with it."

"So far so good," Margaret said. "Or bad, really. You know what I mean."

Ted nodded. "They drove it to a friend's house. That friend had a garage, so they tucked the car into the garage and then they went to bed."

"Surely they should have tried to get the car on the very next ferry," Margaret said.

"That would have been a lot smarter than what they did," Ted told her.

"What did they do?" Margaret asked as Tim and Shelly both

chuckled.

"They, um, tried to modify the car," Ted said. "We got the call the next morning about the theft. The dealership had cameras, but this was twenty years ago. The images were blurry at best. And Herman and Betty had worn hoods and ski masks, so they couldn't be clearly identified. We were given their names, though, because of the recent test drive."

"So you were watching them," Margaret suggested.

"We were keeping an eye on them, yes," Ted agreed. "I was working nights, and I was told to drive past the building where they lived at least twice a night. I took it upon myself to drive past it even more frequently. While we were watching them, they were busy working on the car."

"What did they do?" Margaret asked.

"They painted it," Shelly said, laughing. "They painted it green."

Margaret frowned. "What color was it originally?"

"Black," Ted said.

"And they thought that a coat of paint would be an adequate disguise?" Margaret wondered.

"They seemed to think so," Ted said.

"Except they didn't buy proper paint," Shelly said. "They just bought interior paint, the kind you'd use to paint the walls of your house."

"Can you use that to paint a car?" Margaret asked.

Ted shook his head. "You can, but you won't get very good results," he told her. "In their case, they did a terrible job painting it and then panicked because the entire island was talking about the theft, so they booked ferry tickets for the next day. Herman added a second coat of paint before they left for the Sea Terminal."

"And it was raining," Shelly said.

Tim nodded. "Hard."

Ted grinned. "We'd been alerted that the couple had purchased ferry tickets for themselves and a car. Since we knew neither of them owned a car, I was sent down to the Sea Terminal to intercept them before they boarded the ferry."

"You can imagine the pictures in the local paper," Tim said.

Margaret nodded. "I take it the paint ran," she said.

"That's one way of putting it," Ted said. "It was really amazing. The two of them pulled up at the ferry dock in a car that was bleeding color and pretended that everything was perfectly normal."

"And then you arrested them," Margaret said.

"And then I stopped them and questioned them," Ted said. "And while I was doing that, a team from the constabulary moved in to surround the car. I'm standing there, trying not to laugh as the car slowly drips green paint everywhere. Herman is sitting in the car insisting that he just bought it but doesn't have any paperwork yet. Betty started to cry as soon as I appeared, sobbing about how they just wanted to start over somewhere new and that I was ruining everything."

"How could you?" Margaret teased.

Ted laughed. "And then the inspector in charge of the investigation moved in. When he approached the car, Betty jumped out and ran away. She actually ran onto the ferry and hid. It took ten men over an hour to find her."

"Where was she hiding?" Margaret asked.

"In one of the men's restrooms," Ted said.

"The men's restroom?"

Ted nodded. "She didn't think anyone would look for her there."

"The way I heard it, she was right," Tim said. "I heard that she was only found because one of the constables who was part of the search team needed the loo."

"I can neither confirm nor deny that statement," Ted said. "It wasn't me who found her."

"What about Herman? Did he try to get away too?" Margaret asked.

"No, he was very cooperative. He just kept saying that Betty had told him that it was okay for them to take the car. When she was finally arrested, she told us that the entire thing had been Herman's idea."

"I think I would have believed Herman," Margaret said.

Ted shrugged. "They both went to a prison across for a while. Herman got a longer sentence, but he ended up getting out sooner because he behaved himself while he was inside. Betty got herself into even more trouble while she was in prison. Actually, the last I knew, she was still there."

"Wow, it's been twenty years," Margaret said.

"I'm going to have to check and see if she's still there," Ted said. "Now that we're talking about her, I'm curious."

"Maybe she got out and came back to the island," Shelly said. "And maybe she stole Tim's car."

Everyone laughed.

"What happened to Herman, then?" Margaret asked.

"He went to prison for a few years and then moved back to the island," Ted told her. "Then he went back to holding down barstools rather than jobs. The last I knew, he was still drinking heavily and working lightly."

Tim nodded. "He's a regular at the Stoat and Groat in Ramsey. The band plays there once in a while. He seems to be a harmless enough guy."

"As long as he doesn't get mixed up with another woman like Betty," Margaret said.

Ted nodded. "She was nothing but trouble for him."

"So Herman was the last person who tried to drive a stolen car onto the ferry," Margaret said.

"As far as I can remember, anyway," Ted said. "His story is particularly memorable."

"Let's hope no one is busy painting my car right now," Tim said. "I quite like the car just the way it is."

The foursome chatted about the various cars they had all owned over the years while they finished their drinks. Then Margaret and Ted said reluctant goodbyes to their kitten friends, and they all walked out of the building together.

"We're staying in my flat tonight," Shelly said as they turned toward Promenade View. "Tim is going to borrow my car to get to work tomorrow, and I didn't want to be stuck at his house with nowhere to go."

"Tomorrow is Sunday," Margaret said.

Tim sighed. "I only have to go in for an hour or two," he said. "The owner wants a few minor modifications made to one of the plans I drew up last month. It should only take an hour, but it might take two if the owner comes to watch."

"Maybe you'll be able to find Tim's car by the end of tomorrow," Shelly said. "I'd rather he not need to take my car to work on Monday."

"You can always drive me to work and then collect me at the end of the day," Tim said. "We'll work it out."

Shelly nodded. "I can survive without a car for a few days. If your car is still missing after that, we might need to think about finding a replacement, though."

Tim frowned. "But I love that car."

They walked into the apartment building and made their way to the elevators. A minute later, the elevator doors opened on the top floor.

"It was good to see you tonight," Margaret said as they reached her door.

"It was good to see you, too," Shelly replied, giving Margaret a quick hug.

She and Tim continued down the corridor to the next door while Margaret used her keycard to open the door to her apartment. As she and Ted stepped inside, she waved at Shelly before closing the door.

"I can't stay long," Ted said with a yawn. "I'm falling asleep on my feet."

"You don't have to stay at all," Margaret replied as he pulled her close.

The kiss made her forget all about time. When he lifted his head, she smiled at him.

"Or you could stay for a short while," she suggested.

He chuckled. "We should have gone back to my place. You could have stayed for the night. I know you feel weird about having me stay here."

"It's not my apartment," Margaret replied. *And then there's Mona,* she thought.

He shrugged. "I understand. Maybe we should go away for a weekend, just the two of us."

"I'd like that."

As they settled on one of the couches facing the floor to ceiling windows that showcased the sea, Margaret remembered something.

"Earlier, you said something about talking to a friend," she said.

Ted laughed. "And then the food arrived, and I forgot all about it."

"It can't have been all that interesting," Margaret teased.

"Actually, I think it's very interesting, but you might not agree."

"Try me."

"You know I met a lot of police officers from jurisdictions around the world while I was on secondment."

Margaret nodded.

"We've all kept in touch on social media and through email. One of them recently suggested that we talk about cold cases amongst ourselves."

"That does sound as if it could be interesting."

Ted grinned. "I've just been sent the details of a very interesting cold case. I thought you might enjoy hearing all about it."

A bright flash of light made Margaret blink. When she opened her eyes, Mona was sitting on the chair next to her, holding a small pink notebook.

"Tell me everything," Mona demanded.

3

Mona had passed away years earlier, but she had yet to actually leave the luxury apartment that Maxwell Martin had had built just for her. When Margaret had first visited the island, she'd been unable to see or hear Mona, but once Margaret had actually moved there, Mona had become visible to her. Now, after a few months of living together, Margaret still wasn't sure how she felt about sharing her apartment with a ghost.

"Is it too late to start this conversation now?" Ted asked.

For a moment, Margaret was tempted to say yes, just to annoy Mona. Instead, she shook her head. "I don't have to be up early tomorrow. Come into the kitchen. I'll make some coffee and we can have a few cookies while we talk."

"Decaf, right?"

Margaret laughed. "That's all I would ever drink this late at night."

She set the coffee pot brewing and got down a box of chocolate-covered cookies. After piling a dozen or so onto a plate, she put the plate on the counter in front of Ted. By that time, the coffee was ready. After pouring out two cups, she walked over and joined Ted at the counter.

"Should I take notes?" she asked as Mona slid onto the stool on Ted's other side.

He shrugged. "You can if you want, but I'm not expecting you to solve the case or anything. I just thought you might find it interesting."

"And you're allowed to share all of the details with me?"

Ted chuckled. "I'm not breaking any rules. The officer in Ohio isn't breaking any rules, either. He's only sharing what's already been covered in the press. From what he's said so far, it doesn't seem as if he's withholding anything, though. I got the impression that the papers know as much as he does about the case."

"That doesn't sound good."

"Harper Glen is a small town. The man who owns the newspaper also owns the local bar. From what Brady said, he often knows more about what's happening in town than the police do."

"Brady?"

"Brady Watters is the local police officer in charge of the case. I can't remember now if he's the local sheriff or exactly what title he has. I met him on a training course. We weren't too bothered about what titles people had in their jurisdictions back home. I just called him Brady."

Margaret nodded. "So tell me about Brady's case."

Ted pulled a notebook out of his pocket. He flipped through a few pages and then cleared his throat. "It all started on a lovely summer day," he said.

"When?" Mona demanded.

Margaret frowned. "Recently?" she asked.

"Ten years ago, almost exactly. It was actually July 2008."

"And it was a lovely day? And the weather matters?"

"Yes, because the murder happened outdoors."

"It was murder, then," Margaret said sadly.

Ted nodded. "Murder at Barker Stadium," he said in a dramatic voice.

"Barker Stadium?" Margaret repeated, making a note of the name.

"According to Brady, calling it a stadium is a bit of a stretch. It's really just a field behind the high school with a few bleachers on either side. But apparently the state provides funding for sports stadiums but not athletic fields, so every high school in Ohio has its own 'stadium.'" Ted put air quotes around the last word.

"Who was Barker? Or doesn't it matter?"

"It doesn't matter, but I did ask," Ted said with a grin. "Bart Barker owns a used car lot. He sells a lot of cars to high school students, or more likely to their parents. According to Brady, Bart likes to be seen as supporting the community, so he pays to put his name on places where he might find potential customers. The local community college has a Barker Field, and the senior center has a Barker Community Room."

"Interesting, but probably not relevant. Not unless Bart Barker is a suspect."

"According to Brady, he's not."

"Was there a game that night?" Margaret asked after making another note.

"There was. It was actually a doubleheader. First the local middle school baseball team took on a team from a nearby town, and then the local high school team took on their rivals from just down the road. I have all the details about both of the games if you're interested, but I don't think they're relevant."

"We can skip that for now, then."

"What does matter is that after the second game, after nearly everyone had gone, someone noticed that there was a man still sitting in the bleachers. Not only was he still sitting there, but he wasn't moving."

"Do you have any pictures of the scene? I'd love to be able to see exactly what you're talking about."

Ted grinned. "As it happens, I can pull some up on my phone. Alternatively, grab your laptop. All of the pictures are on the town's newspaper's website."

Margaret got her laptop from the desk and carried it back to the counter. While it was firing up, she grabbed a cookie. Ted read out an address for her and she typed it into her web browser.

"Just hit the archive link," Ted said, "and then search for 'Barker Stadium Murder.'"

A moment later, Margaret and Mona were staring at a black and white photo under the headline "Man Dead at Barker Stadium."

"It just looks as if he's sleeping," Mona said.

Margaret nodded before she remembered that Ted couldn't see or hear Mona. "It looks as if he's simply fallen asleep," she said.

"And that's why the photo exists, actually. The reporter who was there to cover the game was on his way out when people started talking about the man on the bleachers. The reporter turned around and snapped the picture, thinking it would go well with his article about what had been a fairly dull doubleheader."

"Oh?"

Ted shrugged. "I don't know much about baseball, but the first game was scoreless and there was only a single score in the second game. I'm told each game took about two hours. That's a long time to sit around watching no one score."

"Who won the game that had a score?" Margaret had to ask.

"The Harper Glen team."

"I suppose that's good." Margaret went back to looking at the picture. "What happened next?" she asked.

"Someone shouted at the man to try to wake him, but he didn't wake up. Then a man went over and gave him a shake. If you scroll down, you'll see what happened when he did that."

Margaret scrolled down and frowned at the next picture. The man who'd appeared to be sleeping now looked awkwardly stuck between the rows of bleachers.

"When he fell over, someone rang 911," Ted said.

Margaret scrolled down a bit further and found another picture of the body. This one had been taken from much closer and focused on the man's face. It was immediately obvious that he was dead.

"I can't believe the reporter kept taking pictures," Margaret said with a frown. "This one is quite horrible."

"That one was never printed in the paper," Ted told her. "Apparently, every photo ever taken gets included in the archives, but some photos are deemed not appropriate for the paper."

"It must have been a difficult photo for his family and friends to see."

"I would imagine so."

"He looks young," Mona said. "And he was very handsome."

"What do you know about the victim, then?" Margaret asked Ted.

"Let me just tell you that the body remained where it was until the police arrived. The first uniformed officer on the scene took one look and called for backup. Brady arrived about twenty minutes later. By that time, everyone who'd been at the game had left, aside from the man who'd tried to wake the victim and the reporter from the local paper."

"Everyone else left?"

Ted nodded. "According to Brady, that didn't surprise him. It didn't take him long to get a complete list of who had been at the game, so he was able to question everyone who'd been there the next day."

"They should have stayed, though."

"I agree, but Brady didn't seem bothered that they'd gone. To be fair, there were only a handful of people still there when the body was found. There had been more like fifty or sixty people at the game."

"Does that mean that there are fifty or sixty suspects?"

"No, but there are quite a few."

"Tell me about the victim, then."

"The victim was a man called Sean Payne. He was in his early forties when he died."

"And was one of his children on the team that was playing that night?"

"No, he and his wife, Susie, didn't have any children."

Margaret looked up from her notes. "Did he just love baseball or was he there for some other reason?"

"He was there with a woman called Nina Hicks. Nina's son was on the high school team."

"What do you know about Nina?"

"She was also in her early forties. Her husband was Ronald, and their son is Ronald, Junior."

"And why was Sean at the game with Nina?" Mona asked.

"Why was Sean at the game with Nina?" Margaret repeated.

"According to Brady, Sean and Nina were having an affair," Ted said.

Margaret frowned. "They were having an affair?"

Ted nodded.

"Was it common knowledge? So much so that they went out to very public places together?"

"From what Brady said, yes. It was common knowledge in Harper Glen, and the pair were not the least bit discreet."

"So where were Susie and Ronald, the other spouses, on the night of the game? Was it night? It looks like night in the pictures, but maybe that's just because they're black and white."

"It was night. The first game started at six and finished not much before eight. The second started at half eight and finished after ten. As for where the spouses were, that's part of the problem with the case. Neither has an alibi."

"But surely, if they'd been at the game they would have been spotted."

"Maybe, but maybe not. Sean was sitting at the top of the row of bleachers. You can see in the photos that he was leaning back against some boards. He was stabbed between the gap in those boards."

Margaret shuddered. "How did someone reach that high up?"

"First of all, it isn't as high as it looks. There are only a few rows of seats. Brady reckoned that someone over six feet tall could have reached up and stabbed Sean from the ground. Regardless, there were several large wooden blocks under the bleachers. They were used for equipment storage. Any one of them could have been pulled out and stood on by someone wanting to reach Sean."

"Are there pictures of that?" Margaret asked. She scrolled through a dozen more photos. They showed her everything she wanted to see.

"I wouldn't have tried standing on one of those boxes," Mona said.

Margaret shrugged. "The boxes don't look very stable," she said.

"Brady pulled them all out and tested each of them. They were all capable of holding his weight, and he's over six feet tall and over two hundred pounds, or so he told us."

"Were they tested for evidence that they'd been used that night?" Margaret asked.

"Brady did a visual inspection of them all, but he found footprints and marks on all of them. Several of the people who'd been at the game told him that they'd seen kids pulling them out and standing on them during the games that night."

"So someone walked up, pulled out a box, climbed on the box, stabbed Sean, and then walked away?" Margaret asked.

"That's one possible explanation."

"What else could have happened?"

"Brady determined that someone sitting next to Sean could have stabbed him from behind. It would have been awkward, but it would have been possible."

"So Nina might have killed him."

"Or the man sitting on his other side."

"Who was he?"

"A man called Greg Owens. He and Sean were friendly rivals in that they both owned pizza shops in the town. According to Brady, the town is just about big enough to support two pizza shops. From what he knows, both Sean and Greg were making comfortable livings from their businesses."

"So how did someone manage to stab the man without anyone seeing anything?"

"According to Brady, it wouldn't have been all that difficult. The field was lit with bright floodlights. The lighting around the bleachers was switched off during the game. Apparently, where Sean was sitting was in almost total darkness. The area behind the bleachers was completely dark. Brady reckons it wouldn't have been difficult for someone to come up behind the bleachers and kill Sean without being seen."

"Someone with the skills of a ninja, maybe," Mona said.

"Surely it would have been difficult to manage in the dark," Margaret said.

"The local toy shop sold night vision goggles," Ted replied. "Brady said that every high school kid in town had a pair and that quite a few of the town's adults had them as well. They weren't anywhere near as sophisticated as the ones you can get today, they were basically just toys, but they probably would have given our killer enough vision to do what he or she wanted to do."

"That makes the murder sound planned."

"Brady reckons it was. Apparently, Sean always sat at the top of the bleachers because he wanted to be able to rest his back against the boards at the top."

"That makes sense. The killer still had to get to the stadium, though."

"Nearly everyone who was at the game simply walked to the stadium," Ted told her. "Most of the people there lived within a mile of the high school. Nina had driven, but she had to bring cakes and cookies for the bake sale."

"The bake sale?"

Ted chuckled. "There was a bake sale in between the two games. The parents of the various team members did one every game night. The money raised was used to support the team."

Margaret shook her head. "We're doing this all wrong. I'm just getting confused. Let's start at the beginning. When did Sean arrive at the stadium? Was he alone? Had he walked?"

"I should be better at this, shouldn't I?" Ted asked with a chuckle. He took a sip of coffee and a deep breath. "Our story begins around five o'clock on the evening of Saturday, the twelfth of July 2008. Actually, I'll go back a bit further. Sean spent the day with his wife, Susie. They went grocery shopping and then went to a movie together."

"What did they see?" Margaret asked.

Ted grinned. "I wondered that, too. They saw the latest Indiana Jones film."

"I thought that one was a bit of a mess."

"I don't think I've seen it."

"Sorry, where were you? They went to a movie, and then what?"

"They went to a movie and then went home and had an early dinner together. Then Sean told Susie that he was going to the high school for the doubleheader. Susie told the local papers that she knew exactly what that meant – that Sean was going to see Nina. She admitted that they argued before Sean left."

"I'd do more than argue," Margaret muttered.

"According to Susie, she was trying to do something about the situation, but she loved Sean and didn't want to lose him. She said she just kept hoping that Nina was just a passing infatuation. Apparently, Nina wasn't the first woman Sean had become involved with during their marriage."

Margaret sighed. "I'm sort of speechless, really. I can't imagine why she stayed with him."

"In her interview with the local paper, she sounded as if she wasn't certain why she stayed with him, either. She did say that they'd been married for a long time and that she couldn't imagine her life without him. She also said they still enjoyed each other's company a great deal. Apparently, they'd had a really nice day together that Saturday, right up until Sean left to go and see his other woman."

Margaret made a few notes. "So what time did he leave home?" she asked.

"According to Susie, they had dinner at five and he left not long after. He left on foot, carrying a small backpack with some drinks and snacks for the game. Brady was unable to find anyone else who saw him leave or spotted him on the walk from his house to the stadium, but he doesn't believe it matters, really. He knows that Sean was at the stadium, in his seat, before the first pitch of the first game."

"And that was at six?"

"Exactly at six. Apparently, there was a small ceremony where a local celebrity threw the first pitch. That evening, the celebrity in question was a grocery shop clerk who'd just won 'clerk of the week' or some such thing. The woman in question threw the first ball and then left. She's not a suspect."

"Sean was in his seat at six. What about Nina and Greg?"

"Nina and Greg were both in their seats before the first pitch, too. And they both stayed in their seats until the final inning of the first game. At that point, Greg needed to use the loo and Nina needed to start setting up for the bake sale. This is based on their statements and also on the statements of the many witnesses."

"So Sean was left on his own. Are we certain he was still alive at that point?"

"He was definitely still alive at that point. He had a conversation with one of the women who was sitting nearby."

"Is the conversation relevant to the murder?"

"Brady didn't think so. The woman asked Sean if he could donate a dozen pizzas for a high school band party. Sean told her to email him the request, and he'd consider it. He told her that he needed to check his donation budget, because he'd been giving away a lot of pizzas lately, but that he hated to say no."

"Too bad Greg wasn't there to offer to help," Mona said.

Margaret glanced at her. "I wonder why the woman didn't make her request while Greg was there," she said. "Maybe he would have jumped in with an offer to help when Sean hesitated."

Ted shrugged. "If you think it's relevant to the murder, I can have Brady go back and ask the woman why she waited to ask until Greg left his seat."

"It probably isn't relevant to anything. I'm just curious," Margaret said.

"Sean stayed in his seat after the game, even though most people got up and walked around," Ted continued. "There was half an hour between games and nearly everyone at the stadium went to the bake sale."

"I would have."

Ted laughed. "Me too."

"So what happened next?"

"The second game started around half eight. Nina went back to her seat, carrying a few brownies that she hadn't managed to sell. Apparently, Sean was happy to have them, and he gave her a ten-dollar bill in exchange."

"That seems a lot for a few brownies."

"Sean had a reputation in town for being generous. Nina said she didn't ask for any money, but she wasn't surprised when he gave her some."

"Did he eat the brownies?"

"He ate two of them and gave the third to Greg, who had also returned to his seat."

"Greg didn't do it," Mona said. "No one could kill a man who'd just given him a brownie."

Margaret laughed. Ted gave her a strange look.

"Sorry, I just thought that Greg must be innocent, then, because he couldn't kill someone who'd just given him a brownie," Margaret said, blushing.

"I don't think I'm going to cross him off the list of suspects just because of a brownie," Ted said.

"Fair enough. They might not have been very good brownies," Margaret replied.

Ted chuckled. "Anyway, the men ate the brownies, and they all watched the game. By all accounts it was a pretty boring game. Nina said later that Sean fell asleep early in the second inning. He woke up when the team finally scored in the fourth. Apparently, he and Nina shared a fairly passionate kiss to celebrate the run."

"So when you said they were open about the affair, you meant it."

"Indeed. Several witnesses commented on the kiss. Apparently, when the team scored, several bright lights flashed around the stadium, which gave everyone an opportunity to see Nina and Sean, um, celebrating."

"So Sean was definitely still alive at that point."

"He was. And then, according to Nina, he went back to sleep. Greg said he wasn't paying much attention to Sean, but that it didn't surprise him that Sean had fallen asleep. He said he was struggling to stay awake himself and he had a son on the team."

"Did they all stay in their seats until the end of the game?"

"Greg went to use the loo again at the bottom of the fifth. He did go back to his seat after that, but after another inning he decided to watch the rest of the game while standing on the sidelines. He told the papers that he didn't think he'd be able to stay awake otherwise."

"What about Nina?"

"She stayed where she was until the game finished. She told the papers that when it was over, she thought it would be funny to leave Sean asleep on the bleachers. She'd expected him to wake up when the lights came on, but he hadn't, so she decided to sneak away and leave him."

"Was she gone by the time anyone realized that Sean was dead?"

"She was. So was Greg. As I said earlier, nearly everyone had left before someone tried to wake Sean."

Margaret looked up from her notebook. "So who are the main suspects? Greg and Nina seem to have had the best opportunity."

"Brady reckons everyone in town had plenty of opportunity. As for means, the knife was a hunting utility knife that was available in more than one shop in the area. Brady said just about every house in town probably had one, including his."

"So everyone in town had the means and the opportunity. That has to mean that so did any number of random strangers."

Ted nodded. "That's one of the complications of the case. There were dozens of people at the game who were supporting the opposing teams. They tended to stay on the opposite side of the field, where there were bleachers for the visitors, but many of them came across to buy things from the bake sale. Brady's problem is coming up with a possible motive for any of them."

"Let's talk about people who definitely had motives first."

"That would be his wife and his lover's husband," Mona said.

"Susie had an obvious motive," Ted said. "Although she insisted that she didn't. She told the paper that she was hurt that Sean was cheating, but that he'd done it before and that she knew they'd get through it and be stronger eventually."

"Which is what you would say if you'd just murdered your cheating husband," Margaret said.

Ted shrugged. "It's in her favor that there was only a small life insurance policy on Sean."

"But she did admit that they'd had a fight just before he died."

"She did."

"What about Nina's husband?"

"Ronald was also at the game. Remember, their son was playing. He sat about as far away from his wife and Sean as was possible without sitting on the opposite side of the field."

"And presumably he could have waited until after dark and then gone behind the stands and stabbed Sean."

"Definitely. He admitted that he didn't stay in his seat for the entire game. He didn't even arrive until after the first game. He said he had no interest in watching the middle school kids play."

"What did he say about the state of his marriage?"

"He told the paper that his marriage was personal and between him and Nina and that it wasn't anyone else's business."

"True, but unsatisfying."

Ted chuckled. "Brady said that he didn't get much more out of the man in his interviews with him, but I never told you that."

"So we don't really know if he was upset that his wife was having an affair or not."

"Brady reckons he wasn't happy about it, but that he wasn't prepared to end the marriage because of it."

"Are they still married?"

"I don't know. So far Brady has only shared information from ten years ago. He's promised to provide updates once we've all had time to read through what he's sent. We're supposed to have a group discussion about the case on Monday afternoon."

"During work hours?"

Ted nodded. "It will be during work hours for me. It will be early morning for Brady. Everyone will be joining from wherever they are in the world."

"Let's get back to the suspects," Mona said. "What about Nina?"

"I assume Nina is a suspect," Margaret said.

"She is. She told the papers that she and Sean were very close friends, who'd come to really care for one another in the months before his death. When asked about the state of her marriage, she said her marriage had nothing to do with her friendship with Sean."

"Maybe they were just friends."

Ted shook his head. "They weren't shy about showing their affection for one another. Everyone in town knew they were having an affair."

"How long had the affair been going on?"

"From what Brady could determine, the affair had started only a few months before Sean's death. Before that, he'd been involved with a woman called Ruth Myers."

Margaret sighed. "And was Ruth at the game?"

Ted grinned. "She was. Her son was also on the high school team."

"Is she also a suspect, then?"

"She is, although she told the paper that she and Sean had had some fun together and then ended things by mutual agreement."

"I feel as if there's more to the story."

"Ruth's closest friend gave the paper a sensational interview about Ruth's affair with Sean. She claimed that Ruth had been expecting Sean to leave Susie for her and that she'd been devastated when Sean ended things."

"What a horrible friend."

Ted nodded. "I'd bet an entire pound that they are no longer friends."

"Okay, so we have Susie, Nina, Ronald, Greg, and Ruth on the list of suspects so far. All of their motives were personal, aside from Greg. Is that right?"

"I believe so," Ted replied. "There was one other suspect on Brady's short list. A man called Rick Butler was also at the game. His son was on the middle school team, but he stayed to watch the high school game."

"Let me guess, Sean slept with his wife, too."

Ted shook his head. "Rick and his wife got divorced when their son was only a toddler. As far as I know, she and Sean were only acquaintances."

"So why is Rick a suspect?"

"Rick used to work for Sean. Sean had let him go just a few weeks earlier."

"Why?"

"According to Susie, Rick was unreliable, often coming in late or leaving early. Rick insisted that none of that was true, and that Sean was just trying to ruin his life."

"Why would Sean want to ruin his life?"

"The two men had known each other since they'd been in high school together. Rick had gone away to college and then came back to Harper Glen to start his own business. He bought a small printing company, and for many years he was very successful. Eventually, though, one of the big chains opened a store nearby. He was unable to compete and ended up bankrupt. That's when he took the job with Sean."

"How long before Sean's death did all of this happen?"

"He started working for Sean about a year before Sean died. Susie told the paper that the two men fought a lot. Apparently, Rick seemed to think that because he'd owned his own business, he knew more than Sean did. Susie said Sean had wanted to get rid of Rick for ages, but that he felt sorry for the man so he'd kept him on for as long as he could."

"And Rick tells a different story?"

"Rick claimed that Sean was a terrible manager and that the only reason the pizza place even stayed in business was because of him. He said he didn't want Sean dead, because he was looking forward to watching the business fail now that Sean had fired him."

"But Sean had been running the business for years before he'd hired Rick."

Ted nodded. "I didn't say Rick was right or even that he made sense. I'm just telling you what he told the paper."

"Is that everyone? It seems like a long list. Susie, Nina, Ronald, Greg, Ruth, and Rick. Did I miss anyone?"

"Just anyone and everyone who lived in the town," Ted said. "Which is probably why the case remains unsolved."

4

"So what do you think happened?" Margaret asked Ted.

He shook his head. "You have the newspaper website now. Why don't you read the articles yourself before we talk about the possibilities? I've given you the highlights, but there is a lot more in the paper than the things I've told you."

Margaret nodded. "I'm not going to do that tonight."

Ted laughed. "I wasn't expecting you to. It's late. I need to go home and get some sleep. I'm supposed to have tomorrow off. I'd love to spend the day with you."

"I'd like that. What would you like to do?"

"We went to Peel Castle not that long ago. What about Castle Rushen?"

"Oh, yes, please. I think I could visit Castle Rushen every day for a month and still miss things."

Ted nodded. "And then we can have lunch at the restaurant across from the castle."

"The same place we ate last time?"

"If that's okay with you."

"It's fine with me. The food was excellent."

Ted chuckled. "It's very good there. If I'm honest, I think I suggested the castle as an excuse to eat at that restaurant."

"Well, I'm looking forward to both things."

She walked him to the door and then kissed him goodnight.

"I'll be here around half nine. That should give us plenty of time to get to the castle before they open at ten," Ted said after the embrace.

"Perfect."

Margaret watched him walk down the corridor. After he'd boarded the elevator and the doors had slid shut, she closed her door and made certain it was locked properly. When she turned back around, Mona was still sitting in the same place, looking through her notebook.

"Are you really going to bed?" she asked as Margaret walked toward her.

"Absolutely. I'm exhausted."

"But there are pages and pages of articles about the murder on here," Mona said as she stared at Margaret's computer.

"You're welcome to read them all while I get some sleep. We can talk about what you've found in the morning."

"We can talk about what I find after you've read the articles. I'll read them now. You can read them over breakfast."

"Or maybe tomorrow night. There isn't any rush. I do have other things to do."

Mona sighed. "Ted is inviting you to help him with an investigation. You need to show him that you can help solve cases so he'll share more with you in the future."

"I will read the newspaper articles, but not tonight. I don't expect Ted to have more cases to share with me, though. This was just a random conversation between him and some friends."

"Some police inspector friends. I'd be willing to bet that all of Ted's friends have unsolved cases they'd like to talk over with the group. This could be the first in dozens or even hundreds of cases that Ted is going to consider."

"Or it could go nowhere." Margaret yawned. "For me, for right now, it's going nowhere, anyway. I'm going to bed."

She went into her room and shut the door before Mona could reply. As soon as she'd done so, she realized that she'd left lights on in the living room and kitchen. Sighing, she walked back out and began to switch off the lights, ignoring Mona as she went. Mona was focused on the laptop screen, anyway.

"Should I leave a light on for you?" Margaret asked as she walked back toward her bedroom door. It seemed odd to leave lights on, but it also felt rude to turn them off and leave Mona in the dark.

Mona looked up and nodded. "Just one, please. I'll switch it off when I leave."

Margaret opened her mouth to ask how that worked, but shut it again, leaving the question unasked. Mona rarely answered questions about the afterlife and when she did answer, it was impossible to know if she was telling the truth or not. It was simpler not to ask.

"Good night," she said in her doorway.

"Good night," Mona replied, not looking away from the computer.

Margaret went into her room and shut the door. Then she got ready for bed. As soon as her head touched the pillow, her brain began to replay everything that Ted had said about Sean Payne's murder. Margaret rolled over and squeezed her eyes shut.

"Go to sleep," she muttered as she flipped her pillow over. Half an hour later, she finally fell into a restless sleep.

"I overslept," she told Katie the next morning. "And I left you with Mona and shut my door so you couldn't wake me. I am sorry."

Katie stared at her for a moment and then seemed to shrug. Then she shifted her gaze to her empty food bowl.

Margaret was quick to fill it. "I am sorry," she said again as Katie began to eat daintily.

Katie was Fenella's cat. One of the reasons why Fenella had been so willing to let Margaret stay in her apartment while she was on her honeymoon was so there would be someone there to look after Katie. Most mornings, Katie woke Margaret up by tapping on her nose at exactly seven o'clock. While Katie often slept in Fenella's room, she sometimes slept with Margaret. Typically, Margaret left both bedroom doors open so Katie could move around as much or as little as she wanted during the night.

"I was annoyed with Mona," Margaret tried to explain to the small animal. "And I'd left a light on for her, which would have disturbed me. And I wasn't thinking. I am really sorry."

When Margaret had woken up just after eight, she'd found Katie tapping on her bedroom door. It seemed unlikely that the soft sound had woken her, but Katie's sad face had been more than enough to make Margaret feel guilty.

"I'll do better from now on. I promise," Margaret said. She refilled Katie's water bowl and then dropped a few treats onto the top of what was left of Katie's breakfast.

"Meroow," Katie said appreciatively.

"And now I need to get a shower and get dressed before Ted gets here."

As she walked back through the living room, Margaret noticed that her laptop was closed and the light that she'd left on was now off. Shaking her head, she went back into her bedroom and got ready for the day. She was just finishing the last of her oatmeal when someone knocked on the door.

"Good morning," she greeted Ted.

"Good morning. How are you today?" he asked after their kiss.

"I overslept, and before I went to bed, I shut my bedroom door, which meant that Katie couldn't wake me."

"Oh dear. Was she very angry with you?"

"She was a little angry because she was very hungry."

"I doubt having breakfast an hour later will hurt her."

Margaret shrugged. "I never shut my bedroom door. I'm annoyed with myself for doing so last night."

"You weren't thinking clearly because you were thinking about my murder investigation."

"You aren't wrong. Even though I was exhausted, when I got into bed my brain refused to stop thinking about Sean and his untimely death."

Ted hugged her. "I'm sorry. I shouldn't talk about cases with you."

"I'm glad you talk about cases with me, but maybe next time we can talk several hours before bedtime."

"Deal. Are you ready to go?"

Margaret nodded and then slid on a pair of shoes. She grabbed her purse and then looked at Katie. "Be a good girl," she said. "I've filled up the automatic feeder with your lunch. I'll be back in time for your dinner."

Katie nodded and then curled up on the floor near the window. Margaret turned to Ted.

"Let's go."

"Did you have a chance to read any of the articles about the murder?" Ted asked as they rode the elevator to the ground floor.

"Sorry, no. Would you rather skip the castle so I can read the articles?"

Ted laughed. "Not even a little bit. Poor Sean has been dead for ten years. Another day here or there isn't going to change anything."

They walked outside. Ted was parked nearby. He held Margaret's door for her, shutting it carefully after she'd gotten into the passenger seat. Then he walked around and climbed behind the wheel.

"Castle Rushen, here we come," he said as he started the engine.

"Is there any news on Tim's car?" Margaret asked as they headed south.

Ted frowned. "There isn't, which is worrying. I really expected it to turn up by now. I was afraid it might turn up wrapped around a tree, but I was certain it was just taken for a joyride."

"What happens now?"

"Someone will probably visit the Sea Terminal today and remind everyone there of the importance of checking all vehicles against the watch list. There might even be an extra inspection of the various containers that are being loaded onto the ferries today. There isn't a lot more we can do, although I'm sure the inspector in charge of the case will be doing his best."

"Meanwhile, the thief could have already taken the car apart and started selling the bits and pieces."

"I doubt he or she is moving that quickly, but it's possible. More likely, whoever took it has hidden it somewhere, in a garage or a shed or something similar. He or she might not know for certain what to do next."

They talked about car thieves and stolen cars for the rest of the journey to Castletown. There, Ted found a parking space near the castle. As they walked from the car to the castle, they passed the Old Grammar School. Margaret stopped to read the sign on the door.

"I can't believe this was built in 1200 AD," she said as she patted the wall. "It's so small. It's hard to imagine it as a church or as a school."

"Have you ever been inside?" Ted asked.

Margaret nodded. "Aunt Fenella brought me and Megan here once when it happened to be open. I assume you've been inside multiple times."

He grinned. "It was part of the school trip sequence that we did in primary school. I believe we visited Castletown in year three and year five, spending time at the castle as well as the Old Grammar School. In years four and six, we visited Peel Castle."

"How exciting for you. We didn't have anything this interesting to visit."

"The Old Grammar School wasn't the least bit interesting to me when I was a child. I felt as if anything older than me was too old to be interesting."

"My goodness. Your poor mother."

Ted laughed. "I was a trial for her. Luckily, she loved me anyway. She still does, actually. And she wants to meet you."

Margaret frowned. "She does? You've told her about me?"

"Of course I've told her about you. I talk to her every week."

"Okay, I've just realized that we've never really talked about your family. You've met my sister and my parents, but I don't even know if you have siblings. Tell me everything."

"I will, as we walk around the castle. Otherwise, we'll stand here for ages and then get too hungry to enjoy Castle Rushen."

"Didn't you say that your father worked in construction?" Margaret asked after they'd paid their admission and were making their way across the castle's courtyard.

He nodded. "I'll tell you all about my entire family after the movie. You do want to see the movie, don't you?"

Margaret nodded. "I remember it being really good."

"It's a nice introduction to the island's history and the castle," the man from Manx National Heritage said. "Go right in and take seats. The movie will be starting in five minutes."

The couple sat at the back of the small room. They were the only ones there. A few minutes later, the door slid shut and the room went dark. The movie started after a moment.

"It was better than I'd remembered," Margaret said as they exited the small room.

"It was good," Ted said. "And now we start to climb."

Margaret nodded and then began to make her way up the narrow, winding, stone staircase. She stopped when she reached the first landing.

"These must have been horrible prison cells," she said, nodding at the small, dark, damp spaces on either side of the landing.

"I can't imagine staying in one of these. I can't even imagine staying in the nicer parts of the castle, though."

"I know what you mean. Even the furnished rooms feel cold and dark."

"What do you want to know about my family?" Ted asked as they began to climb again.

"Start with the basics. I'll probably have questions."

"My father's name is Todd. He spent his entire working life doing construction work for one of the island's builders. He didn't mind the work, but I think he always regretted not going to university. He's a smart man who could have done a lot more with his life if he'd had the opportunity. As it was, his father passed away when he was a teenager. Dad was the oldest of six, so he ended up having to do what he could to help his mother. All five of his siblings went to university. My father made sure of that."

"Good for him. He should have considered going later."

"He did think about it, but he made good money in construction, and by the time his siblings were all out of the house, he'd met my mother. Mum is Elizabeth, but everyone calls her Beth. She was only seventeen when she met my dad. He was ten years older. They got married a few days after her eighteenth birthday."

"Ten years is a big gap."

Ted shrugged. "According to my mother, she was madly in love. She'd been planning to go to uni, but she decided she'd rather get married and have babies. She said she knew someone would marry my father while she was away if she tried going to uni."

"Are they still together?"

"No, they aren't. They were together for nearly thirty years before they both just decided that they wanted out. It was a friendly divorce, at least as much as those things can be. I was in my mid-twenties and my sister is two years older, so there weren't any children to worry about. They split all of their assets exactly in half or so I'm told."

"And it was a mutual decision?"

"That's what Tracy and I were told, anyway."

"Tracy is your sister?"

"Yeah, didn't I say that? Tracy is my sister. She's two years older and she lives in London."

"Married? Children? What does she do?"

"She's been married and divorced twice. After the second one, she said she wasn't going to make the mistake of getting married again. She's been living with her boyfriend, Howard, for a few years now, but she's adamant that she'll never marry him. For what it's worth, I don't think Howard wants to get married, either."

"I suppose that's fair enough."

Ted nodded. "She doesn't have any children. She never really wanted them, and I can't imagine her having any now. My mother bought her a dozen different dolls when she was little. Tracy had no interest in playing with any of them."

"Motherhood is very demanding. Not everyone wants to deal with everything that goes into it."

"I love my sister dearly, but I don't think she'd make a very good mother."

"She'd probably surprise you, if she ever did decide to have a child, but it sounds as if she knows that isn't something she wants."

"You asked what she does. She works for an international import and export business. She travels a great deal, which she loves, and she makes really good money, which she also loves."

Margaret laughed. "Good for her."

"We don't see each other as often as I'd like, because of her job and her travels, but we talk or text at least once a week. She usually rings me in the middle of the night because she never pays attention to time zones. I tend to text her silly things that I see online."

"Now I want to meet her."

"She wants to meet you, too. She's thinking of coming to the island for a visit before the end of the year. She tries to come back at least every few years, but it's complicated by the fact that both Mum and Dad live across."

Margaret frowned. "We never finished talking about them."

"Let's focus on one thing at a time," Ted suggested as they walked out onto the castle's roof.

He held her hand as they walked across the roof and then climbed even more stairs. A room at the top of the castle held an interesting exhibit. Margaret read as much of the information as she could, only stopping when she knew she'd never remember another word. Then they headed back down into the castle.

"We were talking about the divorce," Ted said as they walked into the first of the castle's furnished rooms. "It was friendly. Mum told me that she and Dad had simply grown apart over time."

"She was only seventeen when they met. It's hardly surprising that she changed over the years."

"I'd be divorced, too, if I'd married the girl I was seeing when I was seventeen."

"Oh?"

He laughed. "Her name was Lola. She was eighteen, and I thought going out with an older woman made me much cooler than I was."

"Were you very much in love?"

"Mostly, I was swamped by hormones and teenaged awkwardness. We were together for two years, from the time I was seventeen until I went away to uni. When I left for uni, we both swore that we'd stay together forever. She rang me two days later to tell me that she'd met someone else."

"How awful for you."

"On the contrary. I was relieved. I hadn't met anyone else, but I'd already noticed that there were a lot of pretty young women at uni with me. If she hadn't ended it when she did, I suspect I would have ended it not long after."

"But maybe if you'd stayed on the island, you would have stayed together."

Ted shrugged. "Maybe, but Lola has been married and divorced six times. I doubt, if we had married, that it would have lasted."

"Six times?"

"The last time I bumped into her, she just laughed and said she likes weddings, but not marriages."

"It would be a lot easier for everyone if she just threw herself a big party every few years."

"That's very true."

They walked into the throne room and stopped.

"It isn't very grand, really," Ted said.

"It's grand for the island. And it's grand for the time in which it was built. The entire castle is huge and solidly built. Compare that to the houses where most people lived at the time."

"Except most if not all of the houses built at that time aren't still around."

"Exactly. But you were telling me about your parents. You were in your mid-twenties when they got divorced?"

"I was. Mum was only forty-seven, which isn't terribly old. Once the divorce was final, she decided to move across. Actually, she might have decided to move across before she even filed for divorce, but she didn't say anything about moving until the divorce was final."

"Where did she go?"

"First to Liverpool, then to Manchester. She'd stayed at home with Tracy and me for years, but eventually she'd started working for one of the local banks. It was bought out by a UK bank, so when she went across, she was able to transfer to their offices in Liverpool. She moved to Manchester when she was offered a better job there with a different bank."

"And is she still in Manchester?" Margaret asked when Ted got distracted by the portraits on the wall.

"He looks like a troublemaker," Ted replied, pointing to one of the portraits.

Margaret laughed. "You should know if he was or not. Didn't you study Manx history in school?"

"I did, but I don't remember any of it. But where were we? Mum stayed in Manchester for a few years and then she met her second husband."

"Oh, she remarried, then?"

"She did. Nigel was a customer at the bank. A very important customer, actually. He's very wealthy, but Mum didn't know that when she first met him. At least, that's what she says now," Ted said with a wink.

"Do you like him?"

"I do, actually. He's surprisingly down to earth, considering he inherited a fortune when he was in his twenties. He and his first wife had three children before she died of cancer. He never thought he'd get married again, and then he met Mum."

"That sounds very romantic."

"It is, rather. I believe it took him some time to persuade my mother to let him take her out. They got engaged about six months after their first dinner together. Mum insisted on a prenuptial agreement and made certain that Nigel's children will get the bulk of his estate when he dies. I'm told they all think she's wonderful."

"She sounds wonderful."

"She's just my mum."

Margaret grinned. "I'm looking forward to meeting her now."

"She doesn't come back to the island very often. When I was across, I got to see her fairly regularly, which was nice. We're going to have to go across to Manchester to see her one day."

"I'd like that. I think I'd like that. The idea makes me kind of queasy, but meeting someone's parents is scary, even at our age."

Ted nodded. "I was nervous about meeting your parents, but they're wonderful."

"What about your dad? How did he deal with the divorce?"

"The same way he deals with everything. He just carried on. I said to Tracy, once it was all over, that I suspect that Dad is much happier on his own than he ever was when he was married and had children underfoot. I think he fell in love with Mum and married her because that was what you did in those days. Mum wanted children, whatever Dad thought, although Mum once said something about wanting more than just two but not being able to persuade my father to have any more."

"It's a tough decision."

"One we will need to talk about eventually."

"I hope so," Margaret said.

Ted took her hand and squeezed it gently. "But not today. Today we're talking about my father and how much happier I think he is now that he lives alone."

"And you said he's not still on the island?"

"Weirdly, no."

"Weirdly?"

Ted shrugged. "He loves the island. I never imagined that he'd leave, but about five years ago a friend of his moved to Cornwall. Dad went to visit a month later and fell in love with it. Before he came back to the island, he bought himself a little cottage. Then he came back, packed his things, and left."

"Cornwall? That seems far away."

"I try to visit at least once a year. I usually fly into London and rent a car from there. Dad comes back to the island at least as often. I'm expecting him to come over for a fortnight or more later this summer, actually."

"He's retired now?"

"He retired early. Construction work is hard on the body. He'd been in the job for forty years by that time and he'd built up a solid pension. He's happier now than I've ever seen him."

"And he's single?"

"He has a girlfriend in Cornwall, although it seems silly to call a woman in her sixties a girlfriend."

"We do need better terms for such things."

"She's a widow who lives in a cottage near my father's. They go out for meals and spend time together, but neither is interested in getting more serious than that. Dad told me that he likes having someone to spend time with now and again, but that he mostly prefers his own company."

"What's her name?"

"She's called Ella. She and her husband never had children, so she sends Tracy and me cards for our birthdays every year. She told me once that she's quite happy with that level of parenting but isn't interested in doing much more."

Margaret laughed. "Now I'm looking forward to meeting her."

"It might be a while before you get to meet her. She doesn't usually come to the island with Dad when he visits."

"Imagine trying to cook for an entire castle full of people in there," Margaret said as they reached the medieval kitchens.

"I can't imagine cooking for more than a handful of people in my very modern kitchen," Ted replied. "And when I say a handful, I think the most I've ever cooked for is four, and that nearly killed me."

Margaret laughed. "I've cooked for as many as twenty people, but that was in my parents' house. I couldn't possibly cook for that many in Aunt Fenella's apartment."

"Twenty people? What did you make?"

They were still talking about food and cooking as they walked along the castle walls before finally exiting the historical site.

"Lunch?" Ted asked as they walked back toward the car.

"After all this talk about food, yes, please."

The little restaurant was just as good as they'd both remembered. They enjoyed their meals and dessert as well.

"And now what?" Ted asked as they got back into his car.

"You could take me home and I could start reading those newspaper articles," Margaret suggested.

"Or we could head down to the beach in Port Erin. It's a lovely day for a walk on the beach."

"That sounds much nicer than reading about murder."

The beach was full of happy families, older couples, and groups of teens. Margaret and Ted walked hand in hand from one end of the sandy stretch of beach to the other.

"Ice cream?" Ted asked.

"We had dessert after lunch."

"We did, but there isn't anything better than soft ice cream on a hot day."

"It's soft ice cream? I haven't had soft ice cream in years."

"Maybe you should get some today, then."

Margaret laughed. "Okay, let's get some soft serve."

Ted got a large cone filled with vanilla ice cream. Margaret opted for a small.

"It's still huge," she said as the man in the truck handed her a cone.

"But it's all whipped up, so it's barely anything at all," Ted told her, taking a big bite from the top of his twist.

They walked back along the sand, heading toward the car, eating their ice cream.

"This is really delicious, but I don't think I'll want any dinner," Margaret said.

"We can get sandwiches or something later," Ted suggested.

"I might be able to manage a sandwich."

When they got back to the car, Margaret wiped her hands and her face before throwing away the napkin that had been wrapped around her ice cream cone. Ted did the same.

"Home? Your place or mine?" he asked as they got into the car.

"If we go to my place, I'm going to feel as if I have to read the newspaper articles."

Ted laughed. "Then we'll go to my place and watch telly instead."

"I'm too full of ice cream to argue."

At Ted's apartment, they curled up and watched an old movie until it was time for Katie's dinner. Because it was still a beautiful night, they walked back to Promenade View. After Katie had been fed, they went to a nearby café for sandwiches before taking another stroll on the promenade.

"Work tomorrow," Margaret said as Ted walked her home.

"For both of us. If it's still as quiet as it's been, I might end up helping with the hunt for Tim's car."

"I really hope it turns up. I hate the thought that someone is stealing cars on the island."

At her door, Ted kissed her.

"I'll ring you tomorrow," he said after the embrace. "If it stays quiet, we can have dinner together."

"That sounds good. I probably still won't have read through the newspaper articles, though. Not unless you want to have a late dinner."

"Let's see how it goes. For now, get some sleep. You've another busy work week ahead."

Margaret nodded. "I can't believe how strange it feels to be working full time again. I was only out of work for months, not years, but I'm definitely out of practice at it."

They kissed again before Margaret let herself into her apartment. Mona was sitting on the couch, waving a string at Katie, who was batting at it enthusiastically. As Margaret shut the door, the piece of string seemed to vanish in a tiny puff of smoke. Katie rushed over to get some attention from Margaret.

"You've been out all day," Mona said.

Margaret nodded. "Ted and I had a lovely day together."

"I don't suppose you read the articles while you were at Ted's flat?"

"No, I didn't. I'll read them tomorrow. If I have time."

Mona nodded. "For what it's worth, I didn't find much in them that Ted hadn't mentioned. There were one or two things that I found odd, though. We'll talk about it once you've had a chance to read them."

Before Margaret could reply, Mona seemed to shrink rapidly, getting smaller and smaller until she disappeared with a popping noise.

"She's just trying to make me want to read the articles sooner rather than later," Margaret said to Katie. "But I want sleep more than anything else. The articles will wait."

Katie didn't reply. Margaret checked that Katie's water bowl was full and then got herself ready for bed. This time she remembered to leave the door open. Before she switched off the light, she checked that her backup alarm was set. Katie was always very reliable, but Margaret didn't want to turn up late for work with "my cat overslept" as her excuse. The alarm was set for quarter past seven. After switching off the light, Margaret got into bed. She was asleep within minutes.

5

"Good morning," Margaret said the next morning. Katie stared at her for a moment and then jumped down and ran to the kitchen. Margaret could hear her shouting at her empty food bowl a moment later.

"You didn't shout yesterday, did you? I can't believe I would have slept through all of that." Margaret filled her bowl and then refilled her water. "And now I need a shower."

An hour later, she was ready to leave for work.

"Your automatic feeder is full and ready to measure out your lunch every day for the rest of the week," she told Katie. "Mrs. Jacobson should be back soon, but for now, it seems to be working."

Katie yawned and then wandered toward the windows.

Mrs. Jacobson lived across the hall. She loved animals, but she'd moved in with her daughter, who was allergic to cats. Since Margaret had started working, Mrs. Jacobson had been coming over every working day to give Katie her lunch and spoil her for a bit. At the beginning of the month, though, Mrs. Jacobson had gone on vacation. She was going to be gone for six weeks, which meant that Margaret had needed to find another option.

She'd found the automatic feeder in the ground floor storage room that belonged to the apartment. Mona had suggested that she look for it there, telling her that Aunt Fenella had bought it but never actually used it. So far, it seemed to be working perfectly, but Margaret was certain that Katie missed Mrs. Jacobson's visits, even though she was still getting fed on schedule.

"At least I know you're not starving all day," Margaret muttered as she checked that the feeder was fully loaded. She grabbed her purse and headed for the door. "Be a good kitten," she told Katie. "I'll see you later."

Katie lifted her head and replied with a soft "mewww" that made Margaret smile.

The drive to work didn't take long. Margaret parked and walked inside Park's Cleaning Supplies. Joney Caine was already sitting behind the reception desk.

"Good morning," Margaret said brightly.

"Good morning," Joney replied. She'd been the office manager at the small company since its earliest days thirty-seven years earlier. Her short grey bob was perfectly in place, and today her glasses were green and matched her dress almost exactly.

"How are you today?" Margaret asked.

"A bit worried, actually," Joney replied. "I was just reading the local paper. Did you know a car was stolen in Douglas over the weekend?"

Margaret frowned as she looked at the paper on the desk in front of Joney.

"'Car Thief Steals Car in Broad Daylight,'" she read. "I did hear about that. I know the car's owner."

Joney sighed. "What has the island come to if it isn't safe to park your car in town on a sunny Saturday afternoon?"

"I'm sure it's safe enough. It isn't as if dozens of cars were taken. It was only one."

"Only one so far. That's how it starts. Once the thief gets away with one, though, he or she will want more and more."

"The police are working on finding the car and the thief."

Joney beamed. "Is your handsome boyfriend on the hunt?"

"It isn't actually his case, but he did say he might try to help out if he can."

"From what the article says, it wasn't a new car."

Margaret shook her head. "It was about ten years old."

"Who steals a ten-year-old car?" Arthur Park walked through the door behind the reception desk. Arthur was sixty, with a full head of grey hair and bright blue eyes.

"That door isn't soundproof," Joney said with a laugh.

Margaret grinned. "I keep forgetting that."

"I hope I'm not interrupting a private conversation," Arthur said.

"Not at all," Margaret assured him.

"We were just talking about the stolen car," Joney said. "But you heard that much."

"And I'll ask the same question again. Who steals a ten-year-old car? It can't be worth very much," Arthur replied.

"Unless it was stolen to order," Joney said. "I watched a documentary about that the other night. There are garages in the UK where you can request any car you want. Some of them are legitimate, run by people who hunt down people who own the car you want and try to persuade them to sell it to you. Others are owned by unscrupulous people who simply steal the car that is wanted."

"But surely most people want new cars or maybe fancy sports cars. This was just an ordinary coupe, or so it said in the paper, anyway," Arthur said.

Margaret nodded. "Tim said it wasn't anything special."

"According to the documentary that I saw, people decide they want certain cars for all sorts of reasons. Maybe they want to replace a car that they've loved for a long time with an identical model that's in better condition, for example."

"Whatever it is, it's worrying," Arthur said. "When these things happen, I worry that a criminal gang from across has decided to make the island home."

"Oh, I hope not," Joney said as the building's front door opened.

"Good morning," Rachel Bass said, smiling at each of them in turn. Rachel was a pretty blonde in her forties. She was the company's business manager. "What do you hope not?" she asked Joney.

"We were just talking about the car that was stolen on Saturday," Joney told her.

"A car was stolen on Saturday? On the island?" Rachel asked.

Joney held up the newspaper. "Read it for yourself."

As Rachel reached for the paper, Arthur laughed. "There isn't much to read in there. I think Heather struggled to write an entire front-page article with the information she had."

"Do you know more than the papers?" Rachel asked Margaret. "I mean, you're involved with a police inspector."

"I might know more than the papers, not because I'm involved with Ted, but because I know the man whose car was stolen," Margaret said.

Rachel chuckled. "It's such a small island. Does Heather identify the owner of the car?"

Joney shook her head. "She just says that a car was reported stolen on Saturday afternoon. Then she talks about that time that the guy at the car hire place tried to steal a few cars and failed miserably."

Arthur grinned. "He was a terrible thief, although he wasn't working alone."

"And his accomplice was just as bad," Rachel said.

"Which is a good thing as far as the police are concerned," Margaret said.

Everyone nodded.

"It is a good thing. Most criminals aren't terribly smart. The ones that get caught definitely aren't very smart," Joney said.

"And the ones who don't get caught get elected," Arthur murmured.

"So what else can you tell us about the missing car?" Rachel asked Margaret.

She shrugged. "It was parked on the street outside my friend's house. When he went out to go somewhere, it was gone."

"Was it a very expensive new car?" was Rachel's next question.

"It was a ten-year-old coupe," Margaret told her. "Or so I'm told. I'm not entirely certain what a coupe is, though."

"It's just a small car with only two doors," Arthur said. "Although car manufacturers seem to want to play around with the definition all the time."

"They just want to do whatever they think will sell more cars," Joney said.

"I suppose we can't really blame them for that," Rachel said.

"Usually, when cars are stolen, they turn up really quickly," Joney said. "It isn't as if you can drive them very far on the island."

"It's usually kids," Rachel said. "They get bored and decide it would be fun to take a car and go for a drive. Most of them end up abandoned with a few extra dents and dings."

"Or they get wrapped around a tree or stuck in a hedge," Arthur said.

"Which could still happen to the missing coupe," Joney said. "Although if it hasn't turned up yet, it probably wasn't taken by kids going joyriding."

"Unless they drove up to the Point of Ayre or into the Curraghs or something. It's a small island, but there are still places where someone could leave a car for days or weeks before it would be found," Rachel said.

"Surely someone from the police will be out checking all of those places," Joney said, looking at Margaret.

She shrugged. "I assume so. It isn't Ted's case, and even if it was, he doesn't really talk about cases with me."

"I just hope the car turns up safe and sound," Arthur said. "Maybe the owner just forgot where he parked it."

"I think it would have been spotted by now if that were the case," Joney said.

Arthur shrugged. "You never know."

"Anyone want to go for lunch today?" Joney asked.

"I do," Rachel said quickly.

"Me too," Margaret said.

"I wish I could," Arthur told them. "But I'm meeting some friends for lunch today. We've been trying to arrange something for weeks. I don't dare cancel, even if I'd rather be with you three."

"Go have fun with your friends. We'll talk about women stuff so you won't miss anything," Joney told him.

Arthur laughed. "I guarantee your conversation will be more interesting than mine. We'll talk about sports, and I'm not terribly interested in most sports."

Margaret grinned. "Before this turns into a long conversation, I need to get to work."

"Lunch at midday?" Joney asked.

"That sounds good," Margaret replied.

Midday was British for noon, and Margaret had already decided that she quite liked the term. As she walked to her office, she wondered why the word wasn't used in the US where midnight was common. Still puzzling over the differences in the common language, she put her purse in a drawer and then fired up her computer.

"You looked a bit dazed," Joney said to her when she walked back into the lobby just before noon.

"I've been crunching numbers and staring at reports all morning," Margaret explained. "My brain is fried."

"We'll make you laugh all through lunch," Joney said.

"That sounds wonderful."

"What sounds wonderful?" Rachel asked as she joined them.

"We need to make Margaret laugh. Her brain is fried."

"Let me guess – lots of numbers, not enough coffee," Rachel said.

Margaret nodded. "I didn't eat enough breakfast. Tomorrow I'll have some fruit and yogurt to go with my oatmeal."

Joney switched on the answering machine before the three women left the building. She stopped to lock the door. A small sign next to the door told visitors to use the door at the back if the front door wasn't open.

"Which way?" Rachel asked as they reached the sidewalk in front of the building.

There were two cafés within easy walking distance of the company, one to the left and the other to the right. Margaret thought the food was excellent at both of them.

"We could flip a coin," she suggested after a moment.

Joney laughed. "Let's start doing left on Mondays and Wednesdays and right on Tuesdays and Thursdays. On Fridays we should make an effort to go somewhere else."

"So that would make today a left," Rachel said.

The three women turned and began the short stroll to the café.

"So how is going out with a police inspector?" Joney asked. "And if that's a rude question, just tell me that it's fine, and I'll change the subject."

Margaret laughed. "It isn't a rude question. I'm happy to answer it, although I can't say all that much. We've only been dating for a few months. So far, it's been interesting, I'll say that much."

"Interesting? Tell me more," Rachel said. "I go out with different men all the time and very few of them are interesting."

They all laughed as they walked into the café. It was mostly empty, so they chose a table in a corner. The waiter was quick to take their drink order. As he walked away, Margaret spoke again.

"Ted can't tell me anything about the cases he's working on, but we do talk about them sometimes. We talk about the things that have already been released to the press at least," she said.

"It must be fascinating, having a front row seat into a murder investigation," Joney said.

"Except I barely see him when he's investigating a murder."

"I never thought about that. Does he work a lot of extra hours when he's working a difficult case?" Joney asked.

Margaret nodded. "And even when he isn't working, if it's murder, he's always on call."

"Okay, maybe I don't want a police inspector boyfriend," Rachel said. "I'm not certain I'd trust him enough. What if he told me he was investigating a murder, but he was really cheating?"

"You'd know if he was investigating a murder," Margaret told her. "It would be all over the local news."

"I suppose that's true, but I don't think I want a man whose job is that important. I went out with a doctor once. That was bad enough. We were having a very romantic dinner when his phone went off and he had to rush to Noble's because one of his patients had been brought into A & E. I realized at that point that I was too selfish to get involved with a doctor," Rachel told them.

"I hope the patient was okay," Joney said.

Rachel shrugged. "I have no idea."

"Ted can't talk to me about the cases he's investigating, but the other night he was telling me about a cold case that one of his colleagues is investigating," Margaret said just before the waiter reappeared.

"Tell us more about this cold case," Joney said as the waiter walked away, having delivered their drinks and taken their order.

"Oh, yes, please," Rachel said. "We'll talk through the possibilities and unmask the killer, no problem."

They all laughed.

"The case is a murder that took place in Ohio in the US," Margaret said. "And it happened ten years ago."

"Ten years is a long time for someone to get away with murder," Joney said.

Margaret nodded. "The problem is that just about anyone in the small town could have done it."

Rachel rummaged around in her purse before pulling out a small notebook. Then she started digging in the bag again. "I know I have a pen in here somewhere," she muttered.

"I'll lend you a pen," Joney said. "But if I do, then I get partial custody of your notes. I don't have a notebook with me, but I want to have access to notes on the case as we try to solve it."

"You could take notes on your phone," Rachel suggested.

Joney shook her head. She opened her purse and pulled out a pen. "You take notes. Once you're done, I'll take pictures of your notes with my phone. That's a lot easier than trying to type while Margaret is talking."

Rachel nodded. "Thank you," she said as she took the pen. "I'll try to write more neatly than normal."

"I can read Arthur's writing. Yours can't be worse than his."

Both women laughed.

"Okay, I'm ready," Rachel told Margaret.

"I haven't had a chance to read the newspaper articles myself, but Ted told me the key facts about the case," she replied. "Let me give you the address for the website. You can go and read the newspaper articles for yourselves later."

Rachel carefully wrote down the website address that Margaret gave her.

"Something to do when I get home tonight," Joney said. "There isn't anything good on telly tonight."

Rachel nodded. "Even if there was, this is a real live murder investigation."

"Go on, then, who died? How did he or she die? Who are the suspects? Tell us everything," Joney said to Margaret.

"It was July. The murder happened at a high school baseball game."

"High school? Please don't tell me that the victim was a high school student," Rachel said.

Margaret shook her head. "The victim was a man named Sean Payne. He was around forty."

"Married? Children? If he was at a high school baseball game, he must have had a child on the team. How horrible for his child," Joney said.

"He was married, but he and his wife didn't have any children."

"So why was he at a high school baseball game? Is that a small-town American thing to do?" Rachel asked.

"It's not anything I've ever done," Margaret told her. "According to Ted, Sean was there because the woman he was having an affair with had a child on the team."

"The wife killed him," Rachel said, putting down the pen. "Case solved. That wasn't difficult. Next time, make it harder."

Margaret grinned. "You sound very certain."

"I am certain. What kind of a person meets his other woman in a very public place that way?" Rachel asked. "I assume it was a very public place."

"It was," Margaret agreed. "Ted said that neither Sean nor Nina seemed to care who knew about the affair."

"Nina was the other woman?" Joney asked.

As Margaret nodded, Rachel picked up the pen and wrote down Nina's name. "What is her surname?" she asked, pausing with the pen in her hand.

"Hicks," Margaret replied.

"And her son was on the high school baseball team," Joney said thoughtfully. "And she didn't mind that he knew that she was sleeping with someone other than her husband, his father."

"Apparently," Margaret said. "I haven't read the newspaper interviews with the various people involved yet, but I assume she was asked about her marriage and her relationship with Sean."

"Here we are," the waiter said, putting a plate down in front of Rachel. He quickly passed out the rest of the food. "Does anyone need anything else right now?" he asked when he was done.

"No, thank you," Joney said.

He nodded and walked away.

"Okay, start at the very beginning," Rachel said after she'd eaten her first bite. "You said it happened at a baseball game. Where were they playing? And how did he get killed without anyone noticing?"

"There are pictures on the newspaper's website," Margaret told them. "There is a small stadium behind the high school. It's more of a playing field with a few bleachers than a proper stadium, but it's called Barker Stadium."

"So Sean was sitting in the bleachers?" Joney asked.

"He was sitting on the top bench. There were a few wooden slats along the back for people sitting at the top to lean against," Margaret told them. "The bleachers were only four or five rows high. A tall person could have reached up and stabbed Ted from behind easily enough."

"So the killer had to be tall. How tall was his wife? What was her name? Did you tell us that?" Rachel asked.

"I'm not very good at this, am I?" Margaret asked with a laugh. "I'm bouncing all over the place with the story. Sean's wife was Susie, and I've no idea how tall she is. It doesn't really matter, though, because there were large wooden boxes being stored under the bleachers. The police reckon that anyone could have pulled one out and climbed on it in order to reach Sean."

Rachel shivered. "I can't imagine climbing on a box and stabbing someone."

"Even if it was your husband and he was cheating?" Joney asked teasingly.

Rachel grinned. "Maybe then."

"There must be suspects other than the wife, though. Otherwise the case would have been solved ten years ago," Joney said.

Margaret nodded. "There's a long list of suspects. Let me tell you what happened first, though."

"Is everything okay?" the waiter asked, looking at their plates that had barely been touched.

"It's good," Margaret assured him, taking a big bite of her sandwich.

"We're just talking too much to eat," Joney said. "We'll try to eat more and talk less."

"We can eat. Margaret can talk," Rachel said, laughing.

The waiter nodded and walked away, a slightly bemused look on his face.

"You can eat after you tell us everything," Rachel said.

"Let's see how fast I can get through this, then," Margaret said. "Sean and his wife spent the day together. After they got home, they had dinner before Sean said he was going to the game. According to Ted, Susie admitted that she and Sean got into a fight when he told her that he was going to the game. She knew he was going to see Nina, and she wasn't happy about it."

"Does anyone blame her? I'd be furious," Rachel said.

Joney shook her head. "I'd be gone. No one would get away with treating me in that way."

"It wasn't the first time he'd cheated," Margaret said.

"Why do women stay with men who cheat?" Rachel asked.

"I don't know," Margaret said. "I'm really hoping there's a lot more information in Susie's newspaper interview than what Ted told me."

"Okay, we're getting sidetracked. Sean wanted to go to the game. Susie wanted him to stay home. He really should have listened to his wife," Joney said.

Margaret nodded. "They lived close enough to the school for him to simply walk to the stadium. It's a small town. A lot of people lived close enough to the stadium to walk there."

"And after dark, anyone could have walked there unseen," Joney guessed.

"Pretty much," Margaret said. "And it was dark by the time the high school game ended. There was a middle school game first."

"So when did everyone realize that Sean was dead?" Rachel asked.

"When he didn't move off the bleachers after the game. He was still alive when the home team scored the only run that was scored in the entire game, because he and Nina shared a kiss after the score. He died at some point after that kiss and before the end of the game."

"And Nina didn't notice that he'd gone very quiet?" Joney asked.

"Apparently, he'd already fallen asleep once, during the first part of the game. She told the paper that she just assumed he'd fallen asleep again. When the game finished, she thought it would be funny to sneak away and leave him sleeping."

"Or she killed him and wanted to get away before anyone realized he was dead," Joney suggested.

"Also a possibility," Margaret said.

"She probably wanted him to leave Susie for her," Rachel said. "Maybe she wanted Sean to marry her."

"She would have had to get a divorce first," Margaret said.

"She was married?" Joney asked. "Was her husband at the game?"

"She was married and yes, Ronald was at the game," Margaret said.

"Forget about the wife killing him," Rachel said. "Ronald is now at the top of my list of suspects."

"What did he think of the fact that his wife was having an affair?" Joney asked.

Margaret shrugged. "Apparently, he refused to talk about his marriage with the paper."

"I suppose I can't blame him for that," Joney said. "He's at the top of my list, too."

"So far, the list is Ronald Hicks first and then Susie Payne. I can't imagine anyone else had as strong a motive as those two," Rachel said.

Margaret took a couple of bites of her sandwich before she replied. "I'd add Nina to the list," she said. "Maybe she did want to marry Sean. Or maybe she was hoping that her husband would get the blame and she could be rid of both of them."

"Oh, that's very clever," Joney said. "Maybe she tried to frame Ronald but got it wrong."

"Is there anyone else on the list?" Rachel asked after adding Nina's name.

"There are three others," Margaret said.

Joney frowned. "That's a lot of suspects. No wonder the case was never solved. But surely no one else had as strong a motive as the people we've already discussed."

"Greg Owens owned a rival pizza shop. Did I tell you that Sean owned a pizza shop? According to the paper, the pair were friendly rivals," Margaret said.

"I suspect they hated one another but behaved nicely in public," Joney said. "Was the town big enough to support two pizza places?"

"Apparently, they'd both been in business for years, so it must have been," Margaret said. "Which isn't to say that Greg didn't decide he'd prefer to be the only pizza place in town."

"It's an interesting motive. I think Sean's wife and Nina's husband had stronger motives, but Greg definitely goes on the list. Maybe his business was struggling, but no one knew it," Rachel said before making a note.

"Who else?" Joney asked.

"Pudding?" the waiter asked as he began to clear away the now empty plates.

"I need cake," Rachel said. "I need something sweet to counteract all the horribleness of murder."

"Murder?" the waiter echoed, frowning.

"We're just talking about a murder investigation," Joney said. She glanced at the other two women and then looked back at the waiter. "From a book," she added.

The waiter nodded. "I'll bring you pudding menus," he said before he walked away.

"Maybe you shouldn't have said anything about murder," Joney said to Rachel.

She shrugged. "Murders happen every day. Talking about them doesn't make them happen more often. Besides, we're trying to find a killer."

The waiter handed them each a dessert menu without saying a word. They ordered quickly and then waited until he'd walked away to resume their conversation.

"Did you say there are two more suspects?" Rachel asked.

Margaret nodded. "Ruth Myers was the woman who'd been involved with Sean before he started seeing Nina."

"Was she at the game?" Joney asked.

"She was. She also had a son on the team."

"It really is a small town," Rachel muttered as she made another note.

"How did their affair start and how did it end?" Joney asked.

"I'm not sure about the first thing, but apparently she told the paper that they'd had some fun together and then decided to end things amicably."

"Yeah, right," Rachel said.

"One of her friends told the paper that Ruth had been devastated when the relationship ended. The friend alleged that Ruth wanted to marry Sean."

"Except he already had a wife," Joney said.

"So much for that friendship," Rachel said.

Margaret nodded. "Ted doesn't know yet where any of the suspects are now, but the detective in Ohio who is in charge of the case is supposed to be providing that information to him shortly. I really want to know if Ruth ever forgave that friend."

"I doubt it has anything to do with the murder, but I want to know, too," Joney said.

"If the friend suddenly turned up dead, it might be relevant to her murder," Rachel said.

"Chocolate cake," the waiter said, putting a plate down in front of Joney. He quickly distributed the rest of the desserts before rushing away.

"We've been coming here for years," Joney said. "And one of us makes one odd remark and we're suddenly unpopular."

"He'll forget all about what I said by the next time we eat here," Rachel said. "But who is the last suspect? I can't believe there are more suspects."

"The last suspect is Rick Butler. He worked for Sean for about a year before Sean let him go. He was at the game because he had a child on the middle school team. After they finished, he stayed for the high school game."

"Sean let him go?" Joney asked. "Was there bad blood between the men?"

"Apparently," Margaret said. "Sean told people that Rick had been unreliable, but Rick denied the accusation. The two men had known one another since high school as well. There could be any number of reasons why Rick disliked Sean."

"So either Sean was killed because of his personal life, or he was killed because of something to do with the pizza place," Joney said. "Which seems more likely?"

"The man was cheating on his wife, and he didn't care who knew it," Rachel said. "It sounds as if his personal life was a car crash. His murder must have been because of something personal."

"I'll disagree, just to play devil's advocate," Joney said. "I think the police need to take a closer look at Sean's business."

"I forgot to mention that Susie also worked for Sean," Margaret added.

"So maybe she had a personal and a professional motive," Joney said. "Maybe she didn't care that he was cheating, but she hated how he talked to her at work."

"I think we need to read the newspaper articles for ourselves," Rachel said. "And I'm so eager to get started that I want to take the afternoon off."

Margaret and Joney both laughed.

"I'm eager, too, but I'll get to it after work," Joney said.

Margaret nodded. "I might not even get around to it tonight. If Ted is free, I'd rather spend time with him."

"If I had a handsome police inspector to snuggle up with, I'd do that tonight, too," Rachel said. "As it is, I don't, so I'll be reading the newspaper articles from Harper Glen, Ohio."

"We'll talk about the case again once we've all read the articles," Joney said. "Between us, we should be able to work out what happened to Sean, even if we can't prove it."

6

The trio were still chatting about Sean as they walked back to the office. Once they arrived, Joney made photocopies of the pages in Rachel's notebook.

"I'm going to want to make notes on the notes," she explained. "We'll talk again tomorrow."

"Great," Margaret said before heading to her office. She spent an exhausting afternoon doing the same things she'd done all morning.

"Hurray for five o'clock," she said eventually.

Joney grinned at her as she walked back into the lobby.

"I had some spare time this afternoon, so I started looking at the newspaper website. There's so much more to the story than you told us," she said.

"Is there? I haven't looked yet," Margaret replied.

"I found the interview with Susie fascinating," Joney said.

"So did I," Rachel said as she joined them. "I felt sorry for her, but I still think she killed him."

Joney shrugged. "I'm reserving judgment until I've read all the interviews. I took a quick look around the site, and it seems as if the paper interviewed absolutely everyone connected to the case in any way."

"Ted said that the detective in charge of the investigation told him that the paper knows almost as much about the case as the police do," Margaret said.

"That's sad for the police, but good for us," Rachel said.

"We'll have it solved in no time," Joney said.

Margaret grinned. "I hope you're right."

As she drove home, she found herself looking forward to starting to read through the website herself. Having friends to talk about the case with made it more interesting for her. "Not that I don't consider Mona a friend," she muttered as she parked Fenella's sensible car in its spot.

After checking her mailbox, she made her way up to the top floor and let herself into her apartment. For a moment, she just stood and stared at the amazing view of the sea below her.

"I can't quite believe this is my life now," she told Katie, who'd come running to greet her.

"Meeooww," Katie said.

There were three messages on the answering machine. Margaret pressed play and then sat down to listen.

"Hi, Margaret. You're probably at work. The time difference is confusing me. I was just checking in to see how you are. Things are wonderful here. Daniel and I are having an amazing time seeing the world. I'll call you back another day. You know how to reach me if you need anything. Love you!"

Margaret smiled. "Aunt Fenella is having fun, then," she said to Katie. "I hope you don't miss her too much."

Katie jumped up into Margaret's lap and curled up in a ball. She began to purr as soon as Margaret started to stroke her back.

"Does that mean that you're happy enough just to have someone to spoil you now and again?" Margaret asked with a chuckle.

The answering machine beeped as the second message began.

"Ah, yes, Ms. Woods, this is Orson Butterfield. I'm trying to reach you with regards to your Aunt Mona's estate. Please ring me back at…"

Margaret shook her head before deleting the message. "I do wonder what his scam is, but not enough to call him back."

Katie lifted her head long enough to nod before putting it down again. The machine beeped again.

"Ah, Margaret, it's Ted. I'm sorry, but I'm not going to be able to get away for dinner tonight. I've been lent to the car theft team for a day or two. We have a lot of things to do to try to find Tim's missing car."

Frowning, Margaret deleted the final message. "I guess I'm on my own tonight," she said.

Katie made a loud sound.

"Aside from you, of course," Margaret said quickly.

"I'm here, too," Mona's voice seemed to come from every direction. A moment later, the room filled with smoke. As the smoke cleared, Margaret spotted Mona sitting on the couch next to her.

Margaret waved a hand to clear the smoke faster. "I'm not sure if that's better or worse than the clouds," she said.

Mona shrugged. "The clouds were fun, but they did have a bad habit of wanting to stay around. The mist clears quite quickly."

"How are you?"

Mona stared at her for a moment. "Still dead," she said eventually.

Margaret laughed. "Yes, of course. I just meant in general."

"I'm fine. I've been considering your cold case. We should talk about the suspects. You've nothing else to do tonight besides read the newspaper articles."

"That's very sadly true, but before I do that, I want to make myself something nice for dinner."

"Or you could order pizza and get started immediately."

Margaret laughed. "Let's compromise. I'll throw a frozen pizza in the oven and then start reading. We can talk about the first suspect or two while I'm eating, assuming I have time to read enough about them while the pizza is cooking."

"I suppose that will have to do. I'm going to pop over and have a short chat with Queen Victoria while you're making your pizza. She visited the island, you know, which means her ghost can visit as well."

"She visited the island?"

"Almost. She was a bit seasick and never actually left her royal yacht, but Albert came ashore. She was near enough that she can now visit the island, anyway."

"I'm not going to bother arguing," Margaret said.

Mona grinned. "It would be pointless," she said before she disappeared. Margaret waited for the smoke or the fireworks or something, but it seemed that this time Mona had simply vanished.

"I need to go and get some dinner," Margaret said to Katie.

Katie simply wiggled into a more comfortable position. Margaret sighed and then looked out the window at the water. As she watched the waves, she felt herself relaxing after the difficult day at work. She was starting to drift off to sleep when the phone at her elbow rang.

"Hello?"

"Hello, Big Sister." Megan's voice came down the line.

"How many times have I told you not to call me that?" Margaret replied, her tone teasing. "I don't like to think of myself as big in any way."

"Isn't that better than hello, old sister?"

Margaret laughed. "I'm older, not old. And what's wrong with just hello, sister? I'm quite happy that I'm your sister. No modifier needed."

"Hmm. I'll think about that."

"How are you? I hope nothing is wrong?"

"No, nothing is wrong. Not at all. I just miss my big, er, older, er, my sister."

"I miss my little, younger sister, too."

"I should have moved when you did. I know I'm only on a sabbatical. I will have to go back to work eventually, but I should have spent as much of my year as I could on the Isle of Man."

"Does that mean that you and your new boyfriend are no longer together?"

"Oh, no. We're still together. He's wonderful, really. I want you to meet him."

"There has to be a but in there somewhere."

Megan laughed. "You know me too well. I guess I'm just feeling restless or something. Carter is terrific. We have a lot of fun together."

"But?"

"But nothing," Megan said firmly. "We're very happy together."

"Does that mean you're willing to tell me all about him? The only thing I know about him is his first name, and that's only because you just said it now."

"He's Carter Blake. What else do you want to know?"

"Everything. How old is he? What does he do? How did you meet? Start there. I'm sure there will be more."

Megan sighed dramatically. "He's forty, or nearly. He's an investment strategist, and no, I don't know what that means. I do know that he's quite wealthy and that his family has loads of money."

"Oh?"

"You sound as if you don't approve."

"It was a single syllable."

"But it was a disapproving syllable."

"I don't disapprove. Very wealthy people worry me, though."

Megan laughed. "I can't imagine why. Carter has been spoiling me rotten since I found out who he actually is."

"What does that mean?"

"It means, when we met, I thought he was just some guy who was hanging out at the coffee shop near my apartment. Since I wasn't working, I was spending a lot more time in the coffee shop. Carter seemed to be there nearly every time I went in."

"Does he strategize from the coffee shop, or did he have some time off?"

"He works from the coffee shop sometimes. He can work from anywhere. He was in town, visiting some friends, but they have small children, so he used to come to the coffee shop to get some work done every day."

"And have you met those friends?"

"I have. They're lovely. Carter went to college with the guy. They were fraternity brothers. Carter likes to travel a lot. Apparently, he has a lot of fraternity brothers with whom he stays as he moves around the country."

"Surely, if he's so wealthy, he could afford to stay in hotels."

"He could, but he said staying with friends is a lot more fun. He stays in hotels a lot, too, because he doesn't have a home right now."

"That's worrying."

Megan laughed. "That's what I said, but it's all fine. He had an apartment in New York City, but he got tired of big city life, so he decided to travel across the country, looking for a new place to live. He was planning to buy a house as soon as he found somewhere that felt like home to him. So far, he hasn't found that place."

"So where is he staying now?"

There was a short silence on the other end of the line.

"He's staying with you," Margaret said flatly.

"For the moment, yes. I can't seem to find anyone to sublet my apartment. You know I've been trying. Since I'm stuck here until that happens, I couldn't see any harm in letting Carter stay with me for a week or two."

"And what happens after a week or two?"

"He's looking for an apartment of his own. He wants to stay in the area, at least for now, but he doesn't want to buy a house here."

"I don't trust him."

"Because you haven't met him yet. You'll love him when you meet him. He's handsome and clever and he treats me like a princess."

"So when can I meet him?"

"When are you next coming back to the US?"

"I don't have any immediate travel plans. I just started a new job, remember?"

Megan sighed. "So we'll have to come and see you, then. I don't think we'll manage it during the summer, but maybe in the fall."

"I didn't realize your summer was that busy."

"My summer isn't busy at all. Carter is busy, though. He's traveling back and forth to New York City every few days for work and to see his family. He said things will be quieter after August, though."

"So you can come and visit in September?"

"Maybe. Or maybe October."

"You'll have to get a hotel. I'm not sharing a room with you and Carter."

Megan laughed. "I'm sure Carter will happily pay for a hotel room. There are tons of hotels on the promenade. We'll be able to stay nice and close to you."

"Now I really miss you."

"I miss you, too. How are things on the island? How is Ted? How is work?"

"Work is tiring, but good. I love what I'm doing, but today was a long day full of numbers and graphs and charts. I should finish the report tomorrow morning, though. Then I can get back to doing other, more interesting, things."

"And Ted?"

"Ted is fine. He's working tonight. He works a lot."

"Are you sure you want to get involved with a police inspector?"

"Sometimes I do wonder, but Ted is really terrific, aside from the working too much thing."

"If he's working tonight, does that mean he's working on another murder investigation? Please tell me you aren't a suspect in this one."

Margaret chuckled. "There haven't been any murders recently. Ted is working on finding a stolen car, actually."

"Ah, car theft is less scary than murder."

"Indeed."

"But less interesting, too."

"Apparently, there's been a downturn in crime on the island. Heather Bryant was complaining about it to Ted the other night."

"She must be the only person in the world who hates it when people commit fewer crimes."

"I suspect some of her investigative reporter colleagues feel the same way, but I still find Heather incredibly annoying."

"Was this before or after the car was stolen?"

"Before."

"Did anyone check to see where she was when the car was taken? Maybe she was simply trying to create some headlines for herself."

Margaret laughed. "I almost hope that's true."

"Anything else going on over there that I should know about?"

"I don't think so. Aunt Fenella called today while I was at work. She left a message to say that she and Daniel are having a wonderful time."

"Good for them. Maybe I should marry Carter and join Aunt Fenella and Daniel on their luxury trip around the world."

"First of all, I don't think anyone wants you on their honeymoon – not even Aunt Fenella, who loves you. Secondly, surely Carter has to work, even if you are on sabbatical."

"He could take some time off. I'm sure he would if I asked nicely."

"Thirdly, does he want to marry you? And do you want to marry him?"

"He's made a few remarks that suggest that he's thinking about a long-term relationship for us, but that could just be talk, I suppose. I won't make any wedding plans until he produces a ring. Which suggests that I do want to marry him, and I'm not actually saying that. I'm not sure how I feel, really. I suppose I'll wait and see what happens if he ever does come up with a ring."

"Have you met any of his family?"

"Not yet. They have an estate on Long Island and a summer home in Cape Cod. His parents have been married for over forty years, and his father's parents have been together for over sixty years."

"So when are you going to meet them?"

"I'll meet them eventually. Carter keeps talking about having me fly to New York with him one of these days. But he's going for work, not fun. Besides, I think he said his parents were going abroad for the summer. There isn't any rush. We're just having fun at the moment."

"I'm glad you're having fun. I won't trust him until after I've met him, though."

Megan laughed. "I expected as much from you. Mom and Dad haven't met him yet, either. We keep trying to arrange something but everyone is too busy."

"But you've met his fraternity brother friend?"

"I have. He's a nice guy with a lovely wife and three adorable, but incredibly noisy, children. Once I spent a few hours at their house, I knew exactly why Carter wanted to find somewhere else to stay."

"That's fair enough, but I'm not happy that he's staying with you."

"Like I said, it's only temporary. He's looking for an apartment, but he wants somewhere perfect, or close to perfect."

"Maybe he should lower his standards."

"Maybe. He's fine staying here for now, though. He's away for work so much that I'd barely see him if he wasn't staying here."

"You know I worry about you."

"I know you do. I worry about you, too. You're living in a foreign country, after all."

"Yes, but I'm living alone and dating a police inspector."

Megan laughed. "Okay, that probably makes you safer than I am, but Carter is terrific. You'll see."

"I hope you're right."

"Look, the last guy I fell for was married and only interested in me because he thought I was going to inherit Aunt Fenella's money one day. Carter doesn't even know I have an Aunt Fenella. When I told him that my sister lived on the Isle of Man, he'd never even heard of it."

"Maybe he's just a good actor."

"You wait until you meet him. You'll be sorry you said anything negative about him."

"What else is going on with you?"

"Not much. I was talking to Matthew the other day. He said he might decide to pop over and see you one day."

"I'd love to see him."

Matthew was their cousin. He was ten years younger than Margaret and he was studying to be a dentist like his father, Jacob. Jacob was two years younger than Joseph, who was Margaret's and Megan's father.

The pair chatted for a while longer, talking about a few of their relatives and mutual friends.

"I'd better go," Megan said eventually. "I need to get to the library to return some overdue books today."

"Overdue?"

"I'm kidding. I'm kidding. They're due today. I promise."

"And it's past time for my dinner. Katie was sleeping on my lap, and I didn't want to disturb her, but now she's going to have to go."

"I'll call you again soon," Megan promised. "Or you can call me anytime."

"Love you."

"Love you, too."

Margaret found herself blinking back tears as she put the phone down. When she'd first started talking about moving to the island,

Megan had insisted that she was going to move too, at least for the length of her sabbatical. Now, months later, Megan seemed disinclined to even visit, and Margaret missed her sister a great deal.

"Never mind. I can't tell her how to live her life," she muttered. "If I could, I'd tell her to get rid of Carter Blake. There's something fishy going on there."

Katie "meoowwed" loudly.

Margaret grinned. "I knew you'd agree with me."

Katie stood up and stretched and then jumped off of Margaret's lap and ran into the kitchen. As she began to complain loudly about her empty food bowl, Margaret stood up.

"I couldn't fill it while you were on my lap, could I?" Margaret asked as she walked into the kitchen. "Please stop shouting before the neighbors complain."

She filled Katie's bowl before turning on the oven. Then she pulled a pizza out of the freezer. After adding a few extra toppings, she slid it into the hot oven. While the pizza was baking, she tossed a small salad and ate it. Then she fired up her laptop and found her way back to the Ohio newspaper's website. A long list of links to articles about Sean's murder were given on the page with the pictures. Margaret clicked the first link and started to read.

She finished two articles before the pizza was ready. The first was the initial report from the scene, which gave very little information over several lengthy paragraphs. The second, from the following day, was slightly more informative, but didn't tell Margaret anything she hadn't already heard from Ted. As the oven timer buzzed, she clicked the link to the third article and then got to her feet.

The pizza was golden brown and looked delicious. Margaret slid it onto a paper plate before slicing it into pieces with the pizza cutter. She poured herself a glass of soda and grabbed some napkins before sitting back down in front of the laptop.

"Here we go," she muttered as she picked up a slice of pizza.

The headline of the article read "An Exclusive Conversation with Sean Payne's Devastated Widow." Margaret read the first few paragraphs and then got up to get a notebook and pen.

Half an hour later, the pizza was gone, and Margaret had a page of notes. A loud popping noise made her jump. A moment later, a large silver ball rolled into the room. Margaret stared at the ball as it shimmered and then slowly began to crack open. After a moment, it seemed to shatter. Hundreds of tiny fragments fell to the ground. Mona stared up at Margaret. She looked disheveled and angry.

"It was supposed to hover," Mona said as she slowly got to her feet. She ran a hand through her hair and then brushed bits of silver dust off of her dress. "It was supposed to hover through the air, not roll around like a pinball."

"Was it difficult to stay upright while the ball was rolling?" Margaret asked, biting the inside of her lip to keep herself from laughing.

Mona inhaled slowly and then sighed deeply. "It was impossible to remain upright. I shall be complaining to the angel supervision team about this one. I was sold this ball due to false advertising."

"Sold? Advertising?"

Mona waved a hand. "Semantics. The angel who gave me the ball assured me that it would hover, allowing me to stand inside it comfortably. It was also meant to split in the center to allow me to exit gracefully. Then it was to remain quietly in a corner until I was ready to depart again."

"So an angel lied to you."

"It certainly seems that way. Of course, the guilty party will claim that he was simply teasing. Many of the angels have playful spirits, but I'm not the least bit amused."

"I am," Margaret said.

Mona rolled her eyes. "What did you think of Susie?" she asked.

"I don't know what to think. She seemed very sad and a little bit lost, really. She said Sean was the love of her life, and that she couldn't imagine how she was going to live without him."

"I'm looking forward to finding out where she is now," Mona said.

Margaret nodded. "That will be interesting."

"They'd known each other for a long time."

"I can't imagine marrying a man that I'd met in kindergarten."

"She claims she never even looked at another man."

"Which is sweet, but also weird."

Mona chuckled. "I never looked at another man after I met Max."

Margaret frowned. "But you and he weren't even a proper couple."

"He gave me as much as he could. I was grateful to be a part of his life."

"And it sounds as if Susie was grateful to be Sean's wife, even though it seems as if he treated her quite badly."

Mona nodded. "She admits that he cheated on her multiple times."

"She also said that she wanted children, but Sean did not. I would have left him over that."

"And they worked together."

"And she said she was grateful to him for giving her a job because she didn't have any marketable skills."

"Except from what she said in her interview, she was more or less managing the pizza shop. It doesn't sound as if Sean was doing very much there at all."

"She does say that she was responsible for scheduling the staff, supervising the staff, supervising the kitchen, taking payments, taking orders, and a million other things. From what she said, Sean mostly sat in his office and watched sports on the television there."

Mona nodded. "She also said that it was very unusual for them both to have the same day off. I have to hope that Sean did more at the shop when Susie wasn't there than he did when she was there. Regardless, she said she'd rearranged the schedule specifically so that she and Sean would both have that particular Saturday off. She wanted them to spend the day together."

"And they did."

"And then he went to spend some time with his girlfriend."

Margaret sighed. "If I were her, I'd have packed my bags as soon as he walked out the door. Except I'd have left the first time he cheated."

"She said leaving never really crossed her mind. She loved him too much to give up on their relationship."

"Even though it doesn't seem as if he loved her very much at all."

"There is another possibility."

Margaret frowned. "She might have been lying throughout the entire interview. She had good reason to lie if she was the one who killed Sean."

"Exactly. Maybe she'd finally had enough and decided to get rid of him. Of course, once he was dead, she was going to insist that she'd been hopelessly devoted to him."

"This would be easier if we knew where she was now."

"I tried searching the newspaper's archives for any additional mention of her, but the only reference I found was in an article that was published recently. Apparently, the paper is going to publish a huge update on the case next week."

"Next week? I hope we don't have to wait that long to get an update from Brady. Did you search for everyone involved in the case?"

Mona shook her head. "I looked for Susie and Nina. I couldn't find any recent mention of either, but I also don't think the website's search function is very good. For each woman, it only pulled up one or two of the articles about the murder, even though they are both mentioned in just about every article."

Margaret frowned. "So there could be references to them in other articles, we just can't find them."

"The article next week should answer all of our questions, though."

"What did you think of Susie?" Margaret asked. "Did she seem like a devoted wife who was devastated by her husband's murder, or did she seem like a scheming murderer who'd had enough of her husband's cheating?"

"Yes."

Margaret raised an eyebrow. "That was an either/or question."

Mona nodded. "But the answer is yes. When I read her interview, I felt sorry for her. I still feel sorry for her, actually. Either she was devoted to a man who treated her badly, or she murdered him and will one day face the consequences of her actions. Either way, I feel sorry for her."

"Maybe she'd stopped being so devoted. Maybe she'd even fallen out of love. But maybe someone else killed her husband before she got to the point of wanting him dead."

"That would be the best-case scenario for Susie, anyway."

"The paper seemed to try to hint that she might have had affairs, too."

"I thought that, but they didn't come right out and say it, and Susie insisted that she'd never even looked at another man."

"The reporter who interviewed her asked her quite a lot of pointed questions about Rick Butler."

Mona nodded. "He even suggested that there was more to Rick's getting let go than just him turning up late now and again."

"But Susie insisted that she'd wanted the man fired for weeks or even months before Sean finally did it. She said he was rude to customers, came in late nearly every day, sometimes left early, and more."

"Which she would probably say if she had been having an affair with him."

Margaret sighed. "Maybe I should go and visit Ohio. I'd love to meet all of the suspects myself. Ted needs to ask Brady what he thinks of Susie. Can the things she said in her interview be believed?"

"I found myself wanting to believe her, but also hoping that she wasn't actually foolish enough to continue to stay with a man who could treat her so badly."

"According to this, the next interview was with Nina."

Mona nodded. "And it's an interesting one. I'll be back."

As she disappeared, the piles of shimmery silver dust that seemed to be everywhere also vanished. Margaret was relieved that she wasn't going to have to clean up after Mona's not-exactly-hovering ball, anyway.

She threw away her pizza plate and then got a few cookies out of the cupboard. Using the coffee machine that took pods, she made herself a cup of flavored coffee and then sat back down with her laptop. It took her only a few minutes to read the interview with Nina.

"She comes across as much nicer than I was expecting," Margaret said when she was done.

"I thought the same," Mona's voice said. "I didn't want to like her because she was sleeping with a married man while married herself, but she actually seemed like a decent person."

"She told the reporter that her marriage was between her and Ronald and wasn't the business of the paper or the people of Harper

Glen. She also said that she'd been told that Sean and his wife had an agreement that allowed him to see other people."

"She even went so far as to apologize to Susie for getting involved with Sean," Mona said as she appeared on the chair opposite Margaret.

"I can kind of see her point. She and Sean weren't discreet. Everyone in town knew they were involved. I can understand why she thought Susie was okay with it, really."

"She also says that she's sad that Sean was killed but that he was nothing more than a passing infatuation. They were having a bit of fun together, but they both knew it was nothing serious."

"But again, maybe she was just saying what she thought was the best thing to say, having murdered the man."

Mona nodded. "That's definitely possible, but I believed her more than I believed Susie."

"I did too, which I wasn't expecting. If I had to rank them, I'd rank Susie higher than Nina in terms of who killed Sean."

"I agree, although Nina was sitting next to him, which gave her more than ample opportunity to stick a knife in his back."

Margaret nodded. "According to the paper, the medical examiner determined that the knife could have been stuck into Sean from either side of him or from behind. I'm not sure how that's possible, but he's the expert."

"We know Nina was there. Susie claimed she was at home all night."

"Except then the reporter produced a statement from a neighbor who said he saw her going out just before sunset."

"To which Susie said she might have gone out for a walk – that she often did – but that it was so unimportant that she'd forgotten about it."

"Which is part of why I really doubted everything else she said."

Mona sighed. "You need to read the rest of the interviews. I'll be back in an hour."

7

Margaret read through the rest of the interviews and took notes while she ate her cookies and sipped her coffee. When she was done, she went back through her notes.

"It's a mess," she told Katie as she gave her a treat. "Anyone could have done it. Lots of people had motives. I think I'll stick to chemical engineering and leave murder investigations to the police."

"Nonsense," Mona said. As she appeared, a shower of confetti fell around her.

Margaret watched as the confetti pieces hit the ground. Each tiny piece seemed to explode into tiny fragments before disappearing.

"I liked that entrance," she told Mona.

Mona nodded. "The problem is the angel with the confetti doesn't like to share. It's a lovely effect, though."

"And it doesn't leave a mess behind."

"Never mind that. What did you think of the other suspects?"

"I think anyone could have done it. They all had motives, even if some of the motives were weaker than others."

"So let's talk about each of them in turn. What did you think of Ronald?"

"He refused to talk about his marriage or how he felt about Nina cheating. He did say that he didn't dislike Sean. I laughed when he said that he thought Sean's restaurant had better pizza than Greg's."

Mona nodded. "Was that something he said to try to make it seem less likely that he'd killed Sean?"

"Maybe. I thought he seemed like a likeable guy. He talked about going to the game to support his son, regardless of what his wife was doing. He even said he'd bought some cookies from the bake sale."

"Where does he go on your list?"

"At the bottom for now. Arguably, he had one of the stronger motives, but he didn't sound like a killer in his interview."

"I'd put him even with Susie and above Nina," Mona said. "He and Susie had the most reason to be angry with Sean."

Margaret shrugged. "He didn't seem angry. He seemed sad and confused. Of course, that was after the murder. I wonder what he was like before the murder."

"Maybe someone should ask Brady about that."

"I doubt he'd be able to remember much. It's been ten years, and I suspect the murder has overshadowed everything."

"It's still an interesting question."

"It is, but we're supposed to be working from the newspaper articles."

Mona nodded. "So tell me what you thought of Ruth Myers."

"That's a tough one. She came across as very vulnerable in some way. I didn't find her interview as interesting as the one with her closest friend."

"Indeed. I can't imagine she ever spoke to the woman again."

"Ruth seemed embarrassed that everyone seemed to know that she and Sean had had an affair. She claimed it was just a short-lived thing that didn't mean anything to either of them."

"And then her friend claimed otherwise."

"Yeah. According to the friend, Ruth fell madly in love with Sean as soon as the affair began. Allegedly, she was already planning a wedding and had told her son that he was going to be getting a stepfather."

"No one interviewed the son."

"The police might have, but he was only sixteen when Sean died. If the paper asked to speak to him, I suspect Ruth said no."

"I suppose I would in her place, especially if the friend was telling the truth."

"I'm not sure why the friend would lie, but I'm also not sure why the friend would say anything at all."

"It isn't something I would have done to a friend."

Margaret shook her head. "I have had friends who have made questionable life choices. Even if I haven't always agreed with their decisions, I've always done my best to support them. I'd never even consider going and giving an interview to a newspaper reporter about a friend's personal life."

"Did you believe the friend?"

Margaret thought for a moment. "It might just be the way the paper worded things, but I tended to believe the friend more than Ruth. I felt as if Ruth was saying what she wanted to believe was true, but that she wasn't being honest with herself or the reporter."

Mona nodded. "That's a very good way of putting it. Do you think she was upset enough with Sean to kill him?"

"If the friend was telling the truth, then she was heartbroken. I can see her wishing that Sean was dead, but I can't really see her killing him."

"I agree. She's at the bottom of my list based on what we've read so far. Of course, it's possible that she's not actually anything like the person she appears to be in the paper."

"Again, I wonder what she was like before the murder."

"Have Ted ask Brady about that."

"I might."

"What did you think of Rick Butler?"

"I disliked everything about him. Sean was murdered, but Rick still seemed to be blaming him for everything that was wrong in his life. It was clear that he was still angry that Sean had fired him."

"Do you think Sean was justified in getting rid of him?"

"Everything that Susie said about the man suggests that Sean was absolutely right to fire him. Even if Susie hadn't agreed, though, Rick came across as pretty awful. I can see him turning up for work late every day, and I can imagine he was rude to customers, too."

"He was obviously still angry that he'd been fired. Was he angry enough to kill Sean?"

"I think he might well have been angry enough to kill Sean. What I don't believe is that he actually did it. I don't think he's smart enough to have managed the murder the way it was done."

"He was at the game."

"His child played in the middle school game. He said he'd wanted to leave after that, but his son wanted to stay."

"If only his son had come and sat with his father. He could have given Rick an alibi."

"But no one wants to sit with their parents at a school sporting event," Margaret said.

"Rick did admit that he did some walking around during the high school game."

"Only after the reporter told him that several people had stated that he'd been in and out of his seat a dozen times."

"But he claimed he had back issues that made it difficult for him to sit still for a long time, especially on hard wooden bleachers with no back support."

Margaret shrugged. "Maybe he should have sat at the top like Sean."

"So where does he go on your list?"

"Near the bottom. Like I said, he was angry, maybe even angry enough to kill Sean, but he came across as loud and obnoxious. I feel like if he'd killed Sean, he would have gotten too excited, fallen off the box he was standing on, and then crashed to the ground shouting loudly."

Mona chuckled. "He does seem that sort of person. That just leaves Greg Owens. What did you think of Sean's business rival?"

"I'm not sure. He seemed quite bland and colorless, really. I did wonder if that was deliberate, to try to avoid suspicion, but I really didn't know what to think of him."

"He and Sean had been running competing businesses for many years."

"Indeed, and from all accounts, they were friendly rivals. Susie said something about how they helped each other now and again if either had supply issues."

"Yes, I was surprised to read that all of Greg's takeaway pizzas were put into Sean's boxes for a week in March when Greg ran out of boxes."

Margaret nodded. "I can't imagine how odd that must have been. If I were Greg, I would have felt as if I were advertising the competition."

"When he was asked, he said he hadn't had a choice, that he'd run out of boxes earlier than expected due to an upturn in business, and that he'd been nothing but grateful to Sean for the assistance."

"I don't suppose the police can look at the books for both businesses."

"What are you thinking?"

"I'm just wondering if Greg really did have an upturn in business or if maybe he was struggling and had put off reordering boxes due to the expense."

"That's an interesting point."

"I'd also like to know which business was more successful and by how much. Both Susie and Greg insisted that the town was large enough to support both restaurants and they both talked vaguely about making an adequate income. I'd really like some solid numbers for all of that."

"It would also be interesting to see any trends that might have developed over the years," Mona said thoughtfully. "For instance, was Sean's place slowly but surely getting more and more of the town's business?"

"Maybe Brady should ask everyone in town where they preferred to get their pizza ten years ago. We already know that Ronald preferred Sean's place, even though Sean was having an affair with his wife."

"Can you see Greg as the killer?"

"He seemed too boring to hate someone enough to kill them, but he had more opportunity than most. He was sitting right next to Sean. He could have simply waited until Sean was napping and then stuck the knife in his back."

"He seemed the sort who would stab someone in the back," Mona said.

Margaret nodded. "He's going near the top of my list. If we knew more about a possible motive, I might put him at the very top."

"Read me your list in order, then."

"Susie is at the top, although I think Greg and Rick are probably tied with her. I suppose Nina is next, and then Ruth and Ronald come last. But it's all very close. Mostly, they're all just jumbled up together."

"I have Susie and Ronald at the top of my list," Mona said. "Greg and Rick are next with Nina and Ruth at the bottom. I look forward to hearing where your work colleagues put everyone."

Margaret nodded. "But that's for tomorrow. For now, I want to forget all about Sean Payne, his complicated love life, and his murder."

"And I have other places to be," Mona said. "There's a party in the ballroom tonight. Max arranged it, which is worrying. I didn't think he knew anyone else to invite. We shall see."

She got up from her seat and then twirled very slowly. As she moved, her dress changed from a simple summer dress into a gorgeous evening gown. Her hair, which had been pulled back into a simple ponytail, twisted itself into an elaborate updo. Margaret blinked several times. When she looked at Mona again, Mona was wearing a diamond and emerald necklace with matching earrings.

"Have fun," Margaret said.

"Thank you," Mona replied. She walked out of the kitchen. Margaret followed her as she headed toward the door, walking effortlessly on five-inch stilettos. When she reached the door, Mona simply glided through it.

"I want to spin around and change into gorgeous clothes," Margaret said to Katie.

"Memoorww," Katie said.

Margaret laughed. "Yes, okay, I still want to spin around and change into Wonder Woman, too. But if I can't be Wonder Woman, I'd love to just spin my way into a gorgeous evening gown with matching shoes and jewelry."

She and Katie curled up and watched some television for an hour before Margaret went to get ready for bed. She was climbing under the duvet when her cell phone rang.

"Hello."

"I'm sorry I didn't ring earlier," Ted said. "And I'm sorry I had to work tonight."

"Did you find Tim's car?"

"No, but we have a few leads. We'll be chasing them tomorrow."

"During the day or in the evening?"

"Just during the day. I'm planning on spending the evening with you."

"Excellent."

Ted chuckled. "How was your day?"

"Work was fine. I spent the evening going through the newspaper interviews."

"Oh, good. We can talk about the case tomorrow night, then. Brady is going to provide me with updates on all of the suspects soon."

"Apparently the newspaper is going to do a follow-up report soon, too."

"Yeah, they're working with Brady on that. He wants to get the town talking about the case again. He's hoping that doing so might jog a few memories. Maybe someone will finally realize that they saw something significant that night."

"That would be good."

"It would be excellent. Did you come up with any questions for Brady about the case?"

"I was really curious about the people involved. I read their interviews and formed opinions about them, but I couldn't help but wonder what they were all like before the murder. I'll give you an example. In his interview, Greg seemed kind of boring. Is he really boring, or was he trying to seem dull so as not to attract any interest in the investigation?"

"That's a good question. I'll message it to Brady tonight. Maybe I'll have answers tomorrow night."

"That would be good."

They chatted for a few more minutes before they agreed that they both needed sleep.

"If I don't ring you, I'll be at your flat at six tomorrow," Ted said.

"I'll see you tomorrow."

"Love you."

"Love you, too."

Margaret hung up the phone and slid under the duvet. A moment later, she felt Katie jump onto the bed.

"Good night," she whispered.

"Merreoowww," Katie replied quietly.

Margaret shut her eyes and fell asleep almost immediately.

"Did you have time to read through all of the interviews last night?" Joney asked Margaret when she arrived at work the next day.

Margaret nodded. "I've no idea who killed Sean, though."

"Let's talk about it over lunch," Joney suggested.

"That sounds good."

In her office, Margaret sat down behind her desk and turned on her computer. By noon, she'd very nearly finished the difficult report she'd been working on for days.

"You look happier today," Joney said when Margaret joined her in the lobby.

"I'm nearly finished with the report. Then I can move on to other things."

"Good for you. I can't wait to hear your list of suspects."

"Hey, wait for me," Rachel said as she walked out through the door behind the reception desk. "And wait for lunch. Although we've already upset a waiter at one of our favorite places. Maybe we shouldn't talk about the murder at the other place."

"Of course we're going to talk about the murder," Joney said as she got up from behind the desk. "We need to come up with a way for the police to prove that Ronald did it."

"Ronald? He's at the bottom of my list of suspects," Rachel said.

"Then you need to turn your list upside down," Joney told her as they walked out of the building.

The walk to the café didn't take long. As soon as they were seated, a waiter took their drink order and told them about the daily specials. As he walked away, Rachel spoke again.

"What makes you think Ronald did it?" she demanded.

"Sean was sleeping with his wife," Joney replied.

"I thought he seemed quite sweet," Rachel said. "He seemed the type who wouldn't hurt a fly."

"So who is at the top of your list?" Joney asked.

Rachel shook her head. "Go down your list first. Then I'll do mine."

As Joney dug around in her purse, the waiter brought their drinks and took their order. As he walked away again, Joney pulled out a crumpled piece of paper.

"Here we are. My list," she announced. "Ronald, Rick, Greg, Susie, Ruth, and lastly Nina."

"I don't agree at all," Rachel said. "My list is Rick, Susie, Ruth, Greg, Nina, and then Ronald."

"It sounds as if you both disliked Rick," Margaret said.

"He was thoroughly disagreeable," Rachel said. "I can see him stabbing Sean to death and then finding a way to blame Sean for his own murder."

Joney nodded. "He'd claim that he was just standing on a box, trying to watch the game from behind the bleachers, when he fell forward and accidentally stabbed Sean with the knife he'd been holding for no reason whatsoever."

Margaret and Rachel both laughed.

"It isn't really funny, though," Rachel said. "I can see him doing just that."

"I didn't care for him either, but I'm not sure he would have managed to kill Sean without everyone in the area noticing," Margaret said.

Rachel shrugged. "Maybe he just got lucky. I find the idea that someone climbed up on a box and stabbed someone in a public place incredibly odd, even if it was dark, but someone did."

"Unless it was Nina or Greg who killed Sean," Margaret said.

Joney frowned. "I did wonder if I should move them both up the list a bit because they had more opportunity than anyone else."

"Maybe," Rachel said. "But I had them both quite low on the list based on what they said in their interviews."

"I had them higher than you did, but I still don't think either of them did it," Joney said.

The trio talked about the suspects while they enjoyed their lunch.

"No pudding for me today," Joney said after she'd eaten her last bite of lunch. "We've been going out far too often, and we always get pudding. My favorite trousers almost didn't button properly the other morning."

Rachel shrugged. "I want pudding, but I need to get back to the office. I have a meeting with one of our suppliers in twenty minutes."

"You're welcome to get pudding," Joney told Margaret. "I'll stay with you while Rachel rushes back."

"I don't need pudding," Margaret said, smiling as she used the British term. "Ted and I are supposed to be going out for dinner tonight. We'll probably get dessert, er, pudding, after dinner."

They waved to the waiter to get their checks.

"So why do you call it dessert?" Rachel asked as they walked back toward the office.

Margaret shrugged. "I've never even thought about the origin of the word. Why do you call it pudding?"

Rachel laughed. "I've no idea."

"Does the word pudding have any meaning in the US?" Joney asked.

"Oh, yes," Margaret replied. "It's a very specific type of dessert, made by mixing milk with, well, usually a box of powder from the grocery store. I don't know anyone who makes pudding from scratch, but I suppose you could."

"What's in the box of powder?"

Margaret thought for a minute. "I'm not sure. Sugar, flavorings, some sort of thickening agent. Pudding in the US is like a thick chocolate mousse. Or vanilla mousse, if you prefer vanilla pudding. Sort of like custard, I suppose."

"Interesting. If I ever travel to the US, I'll have to try it," Rachel said.

"The next time I talk to Megan, I'll have her buy a couple of boxes of pudding mix and send them to me," Margaret said. "You can make it at home and try it there."

"Oh, I'd like that," Joney said. "I'm intrigued."

Rachel nodded. "I want to try it, too."

Margaret made herself a note in her phone. "Knowing Megan, it will be weeks or even months before she gets around to it, but I will ask," she promised.

"There isn't any rush," Joney said as she unlocked the office door. "Do you eat it hot or cold?"

"I prefer it hot, or warm, really, but you can get mixes for either," Margaret replied.

"I love warm chocolate everything," Rachel said.

Joney nodded. "I want to try the kind that you eat warm, too, so there's really no rush. It sounds like the perfect pudding for a cool autumn evening."

"I won't tell Megan that you aren't in a rush, or she'll never get around to it," Margaret said with a laugh.

She walked back to her office and spent most of the afternoon finishing her report. Once that was done, she emailed a copy to Arthur. Then she spent some time in her small laboratory that was situated adjacent to the manufacturing facility at the back of the building. Stan waved to her as she left the lab a short while later.

"How are you?" he asked as she walked toward him.

"I'm good. How are you?"

Stan Mortimer was the company's head of production. He'd worked for Arthur for many years, working his way up from the production floor.

"I'm good. I haven't seen you back here in a while."

She nodded. "I ran a lot of tests in my lab, but then I had to write up a lot of reports about my results."

"That doesn't sound at all fun."

Margaret laughed. "Most of it wasn't too bad, but the last one nearly did me in. It's done now, though, which means I've finished all of my preliminary evaluations of everything. Hopefully now I'll be able to divide my time more evenly between lab work and paperwork."

"I'll look forward to seeing you back here more often, then."

She nodded. They chatted for a short while longer before Margaret noticed the time.

"I'm supposed to be having dinner with someone in less than an hour," she told Stan. "I'd better get home."

"Sorry to have kept you."

"Not at all. But you should be done for the day, too, shouldn't you?"

Stan glanced at the clock. "More or less. I just have to wait for the second shift supervisor to arrive."

The words were barely out of his mouth when the back door opened and the man Stan had been expecting walked in. Margaret waved and then said a quick goodbye to Stan. Back in her office, she shut her computer down for the night and then tidied everything else off her desk. Pens and pencils went into the top desk drawer. The sheets of paper she'd used for calculations and notes were dropped in the recycling box near the door. Satisfied that her office was neat and tidy, she locked the door behind herself and headed for the lobby.

"Are you going to see Ted tonight?" Joney asked as Margaret walked out from behind her desk.

"I hope so."

"I hope he has more to share about the case. I'm invested now."

"I don't know that he will, but I'll tell him that you and Rachel are on the case. I'm sure he'll feel much better about it once he knows that."

Joney laughed. "At least we can bring some different perspective to the investigation. It would be better if we saw things the same way, but I suppose Rachel can't be expected to see things properly."

"Hey," Rachel said as she joined them.

Joney grinned at her. "I heard you coming," she said. "The door isn't soundproof either way."

Rachel laughed. "Maybe you should go home and read through the newspaper articles again. Maybe you'd come around to see things my way."

"I can't see that happening, but I don't think I have anything better to do tonight, so I just might do that."

"Wouldn't it be amazing if we really did help solve the murder?" Rachel asked. "I mean, we read about murders all the time, in fiction and in the national and international news. I've never been involved in an actual case before."

"What about last month?" Joney asked. "You were involved in the case at Atkins Farm."

Rachel shook her head. "Not really. Maybe a little bit, but this feels different. Maybe it's because we got to read all of the interviews with everyone. I know they weren't proper police interviews, but I feel as if I know as much about the case as the police do."

"I hope not," Joney said. "They have to know where everyone is now, anyway."

"And we're going to find out, aren't we?" Rachel asked Margaret.

"I certainly hope so," she replied. "And I'd like that information sooner rather than later."

"You can say that again," Rachel said.

Joney nodded. "See what you can get out of Ted tonight."

"I might not even get to see him, but if I do, I'll see if he's had any updates."

Margaret and Rachel walked out of the building together.

"I always feel as if I'm leaving too early," she said to Rachel as they walked toward their cars. "Joney is almost always here when I get here and she's nearly always still here when I leave."

"But that's just Joney," Rachel told her. "She loves this company almost as much as she loves her husband. Sometimes I think she loves the company more, actually."

Margaret laughed. "She has been here a long time."

"She has, and she and Arthur are very close. She doesn't usually leave for the day until he's ready to go home. And he's often here until late, experimenting with formulas or talking to the guys back in production about something."

"I get the feeling he works very hard."

"He does, but he also sometimes just sits in his office and plays games on his computer. He always does what needs to be done to keep the company running profitably, but he's pretty laid back about it in his own way."

Margaret unlocked her car with the button on her keyfob. "I'll see you tomorrow, then."

"I hope you'll have something interesting to share about the case."

"I hope so, too, but I'm not optimistic."

"I'll be optimistic for both of us," Rachel said with a laugh.

Margaret drove home along the route that was becoming quite familiar. A short while later, she pulled her car into the parking garage under her building. Katie greeted her with a few shouts that Margaret chose to believe were happy sounds.

"I know you aren't just hungry. You're also happy to see me," she said to the small animal.

Katie was too busy staring at her empty food bowl to reply. Margaret sighed and then filled the bowl. After refreshing Katie's water, she went into her bedroom to change.

"Should I dress up for a fancy dinner or just throw on jeans and a T-shirt?" she asked her reflection as she brushed her hair.

"One should always assume that one's suitor will be treating one to the very finest fine dining experience," Mona said as she walked into the room.

"Should one?" Margaret asked, laughing.

Mona nodded. "There will be something appropriate in my wardrobe."

Margaret sighed. "I had a long day at work. I really want to put on jeans and a T-shirt."

"If you do, then Ted will be forced to take you somewhere casual."

"I think I can live with that. I don't really want anything fancy tonight, anyway. It's just a random Tuesday night."

Mona shrugged. "Every night can be a special occasion if you work at it."

"How was your party last night?" Margaret asked as she kicked off her work shoes.

"It was quite nice. I hadn't realized that Max has become acquainted with many of the building's ghosts. He invited all of them to join us in the ballroom. There was music and dancing. I believe everyone had an enjoyable time."

"You don't look happy."

Mona frowned. "Max is missing Bryan. He loves him very much, but he also cares about me. He's worried about leaving me behind if he goes on to the next stage so that he can be with Bryan."

"Do you want to go with him?"

"I'm not certain what I want to do. The entire subject makes me feel quite sad. I think it's best if I simply don't think about it at all."

Margaret opened her mouth to argue, but she was interrupted by a knock on the door.

"Hello," Ted said, pulling her close.

"I just got home," Margaret told him when he released her. "Just long enough ago to feed Katie and take off my shoes, but not long enough to change out of my work clothes."

"I'll talk to Katie while you change, then."

"Where are we going for dinner?"

"Where do you want to go? We can go somewhere nice, or we can get fish and chips and sit on the promenade. Or something in between."

"Fish and chips sound good. I'll put on jeans and a T-shirt."

Margaret walked into her room and shut her door. Mona was sitting on her bed.

"Are you okay?" she whispered.

Mona nodded slowly. "I will be. I just need a bit of time to think. I'll see you tomorrow."

"If Ted has any news about the case, I'll take notes."

Mona shook her head. "There won't be time for any news tonight," she said before she seemed to suddenly disappear into the floor.

Margaret stared at the spot where Mona had been standing. "It was like the ground opened up under her, but the floor looks perfectly fine," she said, sliding a toe along the floor close to where Mona had been. As she inched her toe forward, she put a hand on the chest of drawers next to her, ready to hold on tightly if the floor gave way. The spot where Mona had been standing didn't feel any different to the rest of the floor.

Shaking her head at her foolishness, Margaret quickly changed and then rejoined Ted in the living room.

"Ready to go?" he asked.

Margaret nodded. "I'm starving."

They were nearly at the door when Ted's cell phone rang. He pulled it out of his pocket and frowned at it.

"I need to take this," he said, tapping on the screen. He turned away from Margaret and took a few steps as he said "hello." When he turned back around, she knew it was bad news.

"I'm sorry," he said.

"What's happened?"

"A man in central Douglas just walked out of his house and discovered that his car was gone."

Margaret sighed. "Don't work too hard."

He smiled at her. "I never do," he said before he kissed her.

She watched him walk to the elevators before she shut her door.

8

"I could just eat something I already have," Margaret said as she leaned against the door. "That would make the most sense."

But now that Ted had put the idea of fish and chips into her head, that was the only thing that sounded good. After spending ten minutes looking through the refrigerator and all the cupboards looking for an acceptable alternative, she gave up and put on her sneakers. After grabbing her purse, she headed for the door.

"I won't be long. Be a good kitty while I'm gone," she told Katie.

Katie was lying in the sun. She picked up her head and gave Margaret a soft "mew" before putting her head back down and shutting her eyes.

"She's not going to miss me," Margaret muttered as she headed for the elevator.

There was a fish and chips shop quite close to her apartment, but Margaret preferred the food at one that was a bit farther away. As it was a lovely June evening, she decided to enjoy the walk to the shop she preferred. When she arrived, she discovered that she wasn't the only one wanting fish and chips that evening. There was a short line at the counter and nearly every table was full of customers enjoying their meals.

"I can always sit on the promenade," she muttered as she joined the back of the line. Once she had her fish and chips, she turned around and scanned the room, looking for an empty table. When she looked around a second time, she spotted someone waving at her.

"We have an extra chair," Shelly called as Margaret walked toward her. She, Tim, and Elaine were sitting together at a table for four.

"Hello," Margaret greeted them as she slid into the empty seat next to Elaine.

"Good evening," Shelly replied. "I think everyone on the island suddenly developed a craving for fish and chips."

Elaine nodded. "I come here at least once a week and it's never this busy."

"Thank you for letting me join you," Margaret said after a bite of crunchy batter and tender fish.

"You're more than welcome," Shelly said. "We would have invited you to join us if we'd known you didn't have plans for the evening."

"I did have plans for the evening, but then Ted had to work."

"I hope he's looking for my car," Tim said. Then he held up a hand. "I didn't mean that to sound as if I'm complaining. I know the police are doing everything they can to find my car. And I also know that Ted works on much more important things than the theft of an old car."

Margaret shook her head. "He is actually working on finding your car. Apparently, the crime rate is down at the moment, so he's been assigned to assist in the investigation."

"That's good news for two reasons," Shelly said. "It's great to hear that the crime rate is down, and it's also good news that Ted is on the case. If anyone is going to find Tim's car, it's Ted."

"It's odd that it hasn't turned up," Tim said. "I really thought it would end up abandoned somewhere. Kids usually either hit something because they aren't driving with care or run out of petrol. Either way, they usually just leave the cars where they crashed or the car died."

"Which suggests that the car wasn't taken by kids," Shelly said.

Tim shrugged. "Who else would want my old car? It can't be worth more than a few thousand pounds, if that."

"Maybe someone who doesn't even have a few thousand pounds," Elaine said.

"The street was full of cars. I'm pretty certain all of them were newer and in better condition than my car. If I were going to steal a car, I would have picked almost anything other than my car," Tim said.

Shelly laughed. "I've been telling you to get a new car since we met. I don't think yours would pass an MOT."

"Good thing the island doesn't have them, isn't it?" Tim asked with a wink.

"What's an MOT?" Margaret asked.

"It's an annual inspection of a car for safety and roadworthiness," Shelly explained. "It's required in the UK, but not here."

"Do they have such things in America?" Tim asked.

Margaret nodded. "Every state I've ever lived in has required an annual inspection. I'm not certain that every state does, though."

Tim shook his head. "I never realized that each state set its own rules for such things."

Margaret laughed. "Each state sets its own rules for lots of things. It's a complicated system that can be quite confusing when you cross state lines."

"Confusing how?" Shelly asked.

"Different states have different traffic laws," Margaret explained. "I believe they all allow right turns on red now, but it wasn't adopted in every state at the same time. Each state sets its own speed limits, cell phone use while driving laws, rules about car seats for children, and more. And that's just for driving. Years ago, different states had different legal drinking ages, too. People used to be able to drive across state lines and drink legally in a neighboring state even if they weren't legally able to drink in their home state."

"That's wild," Tim said.

"Legal age for marriage varies from state to state, too," Margaret added.

"This is fascinating," Shelly said.

Margaret shrugged. "Every state is different and some of them are very different indeed."

"The island must feel very different to you," Shelly said.

"It does, but I love it," Margaret replied.

"What do you miss from home?" Tim asked.

"Shopping malls."

Everyone laughed.

"We could use a big shopping mall," Shelly said. "I suspect just about everyone on the island complains about the shopping once in a while."

"I don't even like to shop, but I would like to see more shops on the island," Tim said.

Elaine nodded. "I'm already missing Meadowhall, and I only shopped there twice a year or so."

"Meadowhall?" Margaret repeated.

"It's a huge shopping mall in Sheffield," Elaine explained. "It's a short drive away from Bolsover, where I used to live."

"If you really need some retail therapy, the ferry company offers day trips to a couple of different shopping centers across," Shelly told Margaret.

"Day trips? Doesn't the ferry take three or four hours?" Margaret asked.

Shelly nodded. "You leave on the early ferry, around six or seven in the morning. Then they put you on a coach. You get most of the day to shop before you need to catch your coach back to the ferry terminal for the late ferry back to the island."

"That sounds like a very long day," Margaret said.

"It is a long day, but it makes a nice change. The biggest problem is that you can't buy all that much because you don't have anywhere to put all of your shopping," Shelly said.

Margaret made a face. "I'd hate to have to carry all of my bags around the mall for the entire day. I've been thinking that I need to do some clothes shopping, but maybe I'd better try to find what I want on the island."

"There are a few nice shops here," Shelly said. "Don't forget about Tynwald Mills. It's a bit of a drive, but the shops often have lovely things."

Margaret finished her last fry before wiping her hands on a napkin. "That was delicious," she said.

"It's our favorite place for fish and chips," Tim said. "I've never had a bad meal at any chippy on the island, but I think this one is the best."

Elaine shrugged. "It's good, but I think the chippy in Chesterfield is better."

"After all that lovely food, I'm glad we walked here," Shelly said as they stepped outside.

"I didn't have much choice," Tim said. "I can't drive anywhere at the moment."

Shelly patted his arm. "You know I'm happy to drive you where you need to go. You're also welcome to borrow my car if you need one."

He nodded. "And I don't go many places without you, aside from work."

"I didn't think you went anywhere without me," Shelly said with a grin.

Tim laughed. "Work and band practice. That's about it. And you sometimes come with me to band practice."

"Can you rent a car?" Margaret asked as they strolled along the promenade.

"I can. My insurance will cover one for a few days, at least," Tim said. "But Shelly and I had been talking about getting rid of one of our cars before mine was stolen. As I just said, we usually go everywhere together, aside from my work."

"And he can walk or bike to work," Shelly said.

Tim nodded. "It's a long walk, but I don't mind doing it if the weather is decent. It's a nice bike ride, but again, only when the weather is good."

"And the island's weather is often unpredictable," Margaret said as a cool breeze blew past them.

Shelly looked up at the sky. "It does look as if it might rain. Maybe we should walk a bit faster."

Elaine shook her head. "I'm not walking any faster. I'm not worried about a little rain."

"You said earlier that Ted had to work tonight. Does that mean he's making progress on finding out what happened to Tim's car?" Shelly asked.

Margaret shook her head. "Give me a second," she said. She pulled out her phone and pulled up the *Isle of Man Times* website. "Second car stolen in Douglas," the headline read. Margaret sighed and put her phone away.

"Ted got called into work because another car was stolen," she said.

"Another one?" Shelly asked. "Do you have any idea what happened?"

"Ted just said that someone walked out of his house and found that his car was gone. It's already headline news on the newspaper's website, though. Maybe they have more information."

Margaret pulled her phone back out and quickly read the article under the extra-large headline.

"So the car belonged to a man named Jeff Carlson," she told the others as she read. "It looks as if Heather had a long conversation with him after he was finished talking to the police."

"I hate feeling grateful to her, but I am, rather," Shelly said.

Margaret nodded. "I know what you mean. I have to admire how fast she worked, too. While I was eating fish and chips, she managed to hear about the theft, interview the victim, and get the story written and posted on the website."

"Dan Ross would still be trying to find his car keys," Shelly said.

Everyone laughed.

"Maybe she wasn't lucky," Elaine said. "Maybe she knew exactly what was going to happen before it happened."

"What do you mean?" Shelly asked.

"I mean, she was just complaining about how there hadn't been any good headline news stories on the island lately. An hour later, Tim's car was stolen. Maybe Heather had something to do with it," Elaine replied.

Margaret stared at her for a moment. "I know the woman is ruthlessly ambitious, but I don't think she'd do anything criminal for a story."

"She blocked the road up at the Point of Ayre illegally," Elaine replied.

"She did," Margaret agreed. "But that's a long way from actually stealing a car."

"Or two," Shelly said.

"I can see her doing it," Elaine said. "I can't see her killing anyone for a headline, but I can definitely see her stealing a car or two."

"What does the article say?" Shelly asked.

Margaret looked back down at her phone. "Apparently, Jeff had just gotten home from work. He parked his car on his driveway and then went inside to change clothes. When he came back out half an hour later, the car was gone."

"Someone stole it right off his drive?" Shelly asked. "That's very bold."

"Was the car locked?" Tim asked.

Margaret skimmed the rest of the article. "Jeff admits that he might not have locked the car, but he insists that he didn't leave the keys in it."

Shelly laughed. "Lots of people do, or rather, they did, not that long ago. People don't lock their doors, either. My former neighbor, before I sold my house, didn't even have a key for her front door. She'd lost it decades earlier. When she went out, she just left the door unlocked. She told me she usually locked it at night, when she didn't forget."

"I can't imagine that," Margaret said.

"The island felt a lot safer years ago," Tim said. "And for many people, it still feels safe."

"I appreciate that, but I still believe in taking sensible precautions. I'd never leave my car unlocked, let alone the door to my house," Margaret said.

"Does the article say anything else about the stolen car? What sort of car was it?" Tim asked.

Margaret looked at her phone again. She read out the make and model of the car. "It was seven years old," she added. "Jeff says he can't imagine why anyone would want it. Apparently, there were quite a few dents and scratches in the paintwork. He told Heather he wasn't always the most careful of drivers, especially in parking garages."

"So our car thief prefers old cars that need work," Tim said.

"Maybe the car thief is just bored and looking for projects," Elaine suggested. "Maybe the police should start looking for someone who just retired from a lifetime of working as an auto mechanic."

"That's an interesting idea," Shelly said. "A retired auto mechanic would probably be able to get inside a locked car and get it started."

"I believe most mechanics are given the keys when they work on cars," Tim said teasingly.

Shelly shrugged. "Let's just say a retired mechanic would be better able to steal a car than I would."

They all laughed.

"What else does Jeff have to say?" Tim asked.

Margaret read through the rest of the article. "Not much. He's shocked. He's upset. He can't believe his car was stolen. He'd always thought of the Isle of Man as a very safe place."

"All the usual stuff," Shelly said. "Is he from the island?"

"No. He moved here seven years ago with his wife and two daughters. Five years ago, they got divorced. His wife still lives in the house on the outskirts of Douglas that they bought when they first arrived. He bought his house when they separated."

"Where does he live?" Shelly asked.

Margaret read out the address. "Ted said it was in central Douglas."

Shelly nodded. "It's a nice area. It isn't terribly far from where I used to live. I assume he must live in one of the terraced houses on the south side of the street."

"Do terraced houses have their own driveways?" Margaret asked. She knew that terraced houses were what in the US were called row homes or townhouses.

"They don't usually – not the ones built when those were built, anyway – but a lot of the owners have paved over their front gardens to make parking spaces for their cars," Shelly told her. "From what I can remember, the front gardens there are just big enough for a small car. Finding street parking in that part of town is almost impossible."

Tim nodded. "When I was looking for a house, I looked at a house on that street. The owners hadn't paved over the garden, but the estate agent suggested that it was something I'd want to do as soon as I took possession. At least half of the houses in the row had already done so."

"He probably left the car unlocked," Elaine said.

"Mine was locked," Tim told her.

"It's a busy street. Someone must have seen something," Shelly said.

"I would imagine the police are going door to door now," Margaret said.

"I'd be willing to bet that several people saw something," Tim said. "But no one probably realized the significance of what they were seeing."

Shelly nodded. "Your car was taken from a busy street in broad daylight, too. There had to have been people around. No one pays any attention to people coming and going, though. As long as the thief acted as if he was the car's owner, no one probably noticed him."

"Surely the neighbors know who owns the car," Margaret said.

Shelly shrugged. "I suppose that depends on how well the neighbors know one another."

"Right after work, when I'm exhausted, I don't pay any attention to my neighbors or their cars," Tim said.

"But you only have street parking," Shelly said.

"Yeah, and once I've driven up and down the street a dozen times, trying to find a space, I'm just happy to find one and get out of the car."

Shelly nodded. "I'm the same when I park near your house. I just want to find a space. But I don't think I ever paid much attention to my neighbors' cars when I had the house, either. We all had parking in front of our homes. I used to wave when I saw someone getting into a car on a neighbor's drive, but I never paid much attention to who that person was."

"We should all be more observant," Elaine said. "But when you try to be more observant, people start to call you nosy."

Everyone laughed.

"Does the article say anything else?" Shelly asked.

"Heather reminds everyone to lock their cars. Then she speculates that someone might be stealing the cars when they need to get somewhere and then simply abandoning them when they're finished."

"Instead of ringing for a taxi, you mean?" Tim asked.

Margaret shrugged. "I suppose that's what she means. She says that she can imagine someone needing a car and simply helping themselves to the nearest one."

"No one would do that," Shelly said.

"If someone did, then surely he or she could return the car to wherever it had been taken from once the errand was completed," Elaine said.

"Heather suggests that the car thief, whom she's now calling the 'car borrower,' wouldn't want to continue driving the car any longer than necessary, so she reckons the borrower would simply leave the car in a random location somewhere on the island."

"Where it would be found fairly quickly, I assume," Shelly said.

"That's going to depend on where it was left," Tim said. "There are places on the island where you could leave a car and not expect it to be found for quite some time."

"Like the Point of Ayre," Elaine suggested. "It was lonely and empty up there."

"Except Aunt Fenella's cottage now has a tenant," Margaret said. "He'd report any cars that were left near the cottage, anyway."

"There are plenty of other places on the island that are fairly isolated," Tim said. "And we all know that there are certain very wealthy homeowners who rarely visit the island. I can think of two who have huge homes with massive parking areas around them and no one currently living in the houses."

Shelly nodded. "I hadn't thought of that, but I suppose a car could be left along the road that leads to the Hunter mansion, for instance. The road is so overgrown that you wouldn't even have to drive very far down it before the car would be impossible for anyone to spot from the main road."

"And the Hunter mansion wasn't one of the two I was thinking of," Tim said.

"And then there are abandoned businesses, too," Shelly said. "Your aunt owns an old, abandoned candle factory, for instance. Anyone could park a car there and leave it for years."

"The problem is, if someone stole the car because he or she needed it to get somewhere in a hurry, how could he or she later abandon it far away?" Margaret asked.

"Maybe the car thief rings for a taxi once he or she is done with the car," Elaine said with a wry smile.

"Maybe we should take a drive around the island, looking for my car in unusual places," Tim said.

"Ted said the police were already doing that," Margaret told him.

"And we should leave the investigation to them," Tim said.

"But if we get bored this weekend, maybe we could drive around for a bit," Shelly said. "We should make a list of places the car might be."

"I think it's more likely that the thief has a garage," Margaret said. "He or she might also have a way of getting the cars off the island."

"Good luck with that," Tim said. "It's hard enough to get a car you own off the island."

"Is it?" Margaret asked.

"It isn't actually that difficult," Shelly said. "It's just quite expensive."

Tim nodded. "The ferry company charges an arm and a leg to transport cars these days. The last time I needed to go across, I went as a foot passenger and then hired a car when I arrived in Liverpool."

"Which is probably another reason why car theft is so unusual on the island," Shelly said thoughtfully. "It isn't just the trouble of getting the cars off the island, it's all a big expense. I can't see there being much of a market on the island for stolen cars, either. Even if the car had been painted and given new number plates, you'd still run the risk of being seen by the previous owner every time you drove the car."

They were nearly back at Promenade View and the skies were getting increasingly dark.

"I was going to suggest getting ice cream and walking a bit farther, but I'm afraid we'd get caught in the rain if we tried it," Shelly said.

Margaret looked up at the sky. "I think you're right."

"We could get ice cream and go inside," Elaine suggested.

Margaret grinned. "I like that idea."

"It's a good one," Shelly said.

A new ice cream shop had just opened nearby. Margaret had only been there once, but she'd been impressed by the variety of flavors available. Now, she stood in front of the display case and slowly shook her head.

"They all sound good," she said.

"The salted caramel swirl is excellent," Shelly said. "I got that the first time I came here, and now I get it every time because it was so good."

"I like the everything chocolate," Tim said. "It's chocolate ice cream with chips and flakes and pieces of cake and more other chocolate things mixed in."

"I always have the mint ice cream," Elaine said. "It has chocolate chips and a chocolate swirl, too, but mostly it's just delicious ice cream."

"We can do an ice cream sample pack," the woman behind the counter said.

"What's that?" Margaret asked.

The woman held up a small plastic container that had six small compartments in it. "You can try up to six different flavors," she told her. "You get only a small scoop of each flavor, but you get to try a lot of them. It's something new that we're trying. If it's popular, we'll order more containers."

"I'll have that," Margaret said quickly. It didn't take her long to fill her six compartments. After the woman snapped a lid onto the container, Margaret paid her.

"I'll have that, too," Shelly said. "I want three of my scoops to be salted caramel, though." She filled the rest of the container with three different flavors.

When she was finished, Tim grinned. "I did think maybe my wife and I could share a sample pack," he said. "But clearly not."

After he ordered what he wanted in a sample pack for himself, Elaine asked for two scoops of mint.

"This is amazing," Margaret said after taking a bite or two. "I love it."

The woman behind the counter grinned. "I'll tell you a secret. My brother owns a company in the UK that makes dog treats."

She stopped when the store's telephone on the wall behind her rang. As she walked away, Margaret looked at Shelly.

"What do dog treats have to do with ice cream?" she asked.

Shelly looked down at her container full of ice cream. "I really hope nothing at all," she said.

Elaine shrugged. "There aren't any dog treats in my mint ice cream," she said smugly.

"There won't be any dog treats in any of our ice cream," Tim said. He took a large bite of one of his scoops of chocolate and grinned.

"Sorry about that," the woman said when she returned. "Where was I?"

"Your brother owns a company that makes dog treats," Margaret said.

The woman laughed. "What a terrible place for me to have stopped. The thing is, he ordered a bunch of containers for his company. He wanted six separate areas that could each be filled with a single treat. He thought what he ordered was going to be appropriate, but when the containers arrived, he realized that the sizing was all wrong."

"These containers?" Margaret asked, holding up her ice cream.

"Exactly. The sections are too big for single treats of the type that he makes, but not really large enough for the handful that most people would give their dog as a reward for something. The smallest order that could be placed was for five hundred containers, so he now had five hundred containers he couldn't really use. When he rang me, he said he kept staring at the containers, with their little round-bottomed sections, wondering what they could be used for. Then he'd realized that they were the perfect shape and size for a small scoop of ice cream."

"He's right," Shelly said.

The woman nodded. "When he sent me a picture, I told him I wasn't certain, but that he could send them to me, and I'd try them out. I told him that I'd pay him for them if I sold at least a hundred of them full of ice cream."

"And now you've sold three," Shelly said.

"Oh, I've sold a lot more than three," the woman laughed. "I was going to make a sign about them, but I don't think I'll bother. Just mentioning them to people seems to do the job."

"Only because you have so many wonderful flavors," Margaret said.

"I'm going to have to send my brother the money," the woman said. "And I suspect I'm going to have to order more containers soon, too."

"We'll be back for more," Shelly said.

"And I'll be back for the mint," Elaine told her.

When they got back outside, it was just starting to rain. They rushed to their building. Margaret had been working her way around the container, eating a single bite of each flavor at a time. As they rode up in the elevator, she shut her lid.

"Had enough?" Shelly asked.

"I want to keep eating, but I know I should stop," she replied. "I'm going to put the container in my freezer and eat the rest tomorrow."

"They are very small scoops," Shelly said as she spooned up another bite.

"They are," Margaret agreed.

"I think Elaine got more ice cream than we did," Tim said, looking at Elaine's empty bowl.

"I only had two scoops," Elaine said.

"But your scoops were huge," Tim replied.

"It isn't a competition," Shelly said. "Let's just all agree that we all got a lovely amount of delicious ice cream."

Tim laughed. "Who used to teach primary school, then?" he asked. "She hates when people argue," he told Margaret.

"We weren't arguing," Elaine said as the emerged from the elevator.

"And on that note, good night," Margaret said.

Everyone laughed.

"Good night," Shelly said as she, Tim, and Elaine continued past Margaret's door.

Margaret let herself into her apartment and then quickly put her leftover ice cream into the freezer.

"You're going to be a wonderful treat tomorrow night," she said as she patted the container before shutting the door.

"Are you talking to your ice cream now?" Mona's voice asked.

Margaret looked around and then sighed. "There's nothing wrong with talking to ice cream once in a while," she said.

A moment later, what looked like snow began to fall from the ceiling. Margaret reached out and watched, amazed, as an icy flake fell into her hand. It melted slowly. When Margaret looked up, Mona was descending with the snow. She was wearing a gorgeous winter coat with fur trim and a matching hat.

"It's fake fur," Mona said as her feet touched the ground. "I thought you'd want to know."

"Ghosts don't wear real fur? Is it real fur if it's ghost fur? I'm so confused," Margaret replied.

Mona shrugged and then snapped her fingers. The coat and hat disappeared. When Mona snapped again, the dusting of snow that seemed to cover every surface in the kitchen also vanished.

"Thanks for cleaning that up," Margaret said.

"Of course. But what's this I hear about another car being stolen?"

Margaret told her everything she knew about the second stolen car.

Mona sighed. "We never used to lock our cars," she said. "And very few people locked their doors. I can remember going to visit friends on the island and simply knocking and then opening the door and walking into the house. Everyone did it and no one thought twice about it."

"Yes, well, the world has changed."

Margaret sat down on the couch. "Are you feeling better today?" she asked Mona.

"Yes, of course. I refuse to let things bother me. Besides, we're about to get an update on the case. I can't wait to hear what Ted has to say."

9

Margaret sighed. "Ted is going to call soon?"

"Fairly soon. We can watch some telly while we wait."

Margaret thought about arguing but decided against it. If Mona didn't want to talk, she wasn't going to push her. The remote was sitting on the table next to her. She switched on the television and began looking for something to watch.

"This should be good," Mona said after a moment. "They repair damaged and broken items that have sentimental value to people. Sometimes the items have actual value, too, but not usually."

Margaret watched as a teddy bear was carefully unstuffed, washed, repaired, and then restuffed and stitched back together. An old grandfather clock was taken to pieces. Each piece was inspected and repaired before the clock was reassembled. And an old wooden table with a warped and cracked top was made good as new. When the show finished, Margaret turned off the TV.

"That was wonderful," she said. "I can't see a program like that doing well in the US."

"There weren't any car chases," Mona said.

Margaret laughed. "They could have added a car chase in between the teddy bear and the table."

They were still talking about the program when Margaret's phone rang. The screen told her it was Ted before she answered. She put the call into speaker mode for Mona's benefit.

"Hello."

"Hey. I miss you."

"I miss you, too."

Ted sighed. "It's too late for me to come over, and even if it wasn't, I'm still at work."

"Maybe we can see each other tomorrow night."

"I hope so."

"Can you tell me anything about the stolen car?"

"I can tell you that the owner gave Heather Bryant more information than he gave me," Ted said dryly. "If you read the local paper's website, you'll know as much as I know."

"I read it earlier."

"So did the entire island. I just hope it encourages people to start locking their cars."

"I can't believe people don't."

"Cars get stolen so rarely here. I think people just assume it's never going to happen to them."

"You should still lock your car."

"I agree. While cars aren't usually stolen, we do get reports of cars being entered and valuable contents being taken."

"And they do get stolen sometimes."

"Exactly. Jeff, tonight's victim, admitted that he probably didn't lock his car. He and his wife moved to the island to get away from living in Leeds city center. Apparently, he always locked his car there, but now that he was living on the island, he'd fallen out of the habit."

"I had fish and chips with Shelly, Tim, and Elaine. They were saying that Jeff lives on a busy street, so someone probably saw something."

Ted sighed. "We found two neighbors who saw the car being driven away. They both waved at the car thief, who apparently waved back."

Margaret laughed. "I don't suppose either of them could describe the person."

"They both said that they simply assumed it was Jeff driving, although one of them did say that he was surprised because the car actually stopped for the stop sign at the end of the road. Apparently, Jeff typically doesn't bother."

"So our thief is a careful driver."

"At least when he or she is driving a stolen car."

"And he or she looks enough like Jeff Carlson to pass for him when behind the wheel of Jeff's car."

"I think that covers about eighty percent of the island's adult population," Ted said. "The thief was wearing a baseball cap, which Jeff often does, or so I'm told. He or she was also wearing sunglasses. Jeff had several pairs and one of the neighbors said that he's never seen Jeff without them."

"Does that mean our thief stalked Jeff long enough to learn how to look like him, or was that going to be his or her disguise anyway and he or she just got lucky?"

"It's one of those."

Margaret laughed. "Did any of Tim's neighbors see Tim's car being driven away?"

"If they did, we haven't found them yet. We talked to everyone who was at home when Tim reported the car missing. We have a constable going back down the street tomorrow to talk to people a second time and to try to catch any neighbors that we might have missed."

"Tim sometimes wears a baseball cap, and I've seen him in sunglasses, too,"

"Yeah, I thought the same."

"Have you ever had a car thief who selected his or her victims based on their appearance?"

"Not that I know of, but it's a weird world full of strange people."

"That's very true."

"Speaking of strange people, I talked to Brady earlier today."

"Oh? Did he give you updates on all of the suspects?"

"Not yet. Tomorrow he's going to write up all of his notes on what everyone has been doing for the past ten years. He's promised to email them to me and to everyone else in the group by Saturday morning."

"And you'll be able to share what he tells you with me?"

"I can, because none of the information he's going to share will have come from police interviews. He's just going to tell us what he knows about everyone because they all live in the same small town together."

"I'm really eager to hear what happened after Sean's death."

"While we're waiting, I asked him your question about the suspects before the murder. Again, nothing he told me came from police interviews. He just told me what he knew about each of the people from life in Harper Glen."

"Let me get some paper so I can take notes."

Ted chuckled. "I don't have that much to tell you. It wasn't a long conversation."

"I still want to write it down. I told Joney and Rachel at work about the case and they both went to the newspaper website and read the articles. They're going to want to hear what you tell me."

Margaret left the phone on the table and walked over to the desk. She grabbed a small notebook and a pen and then rushed back to her seat.

"I hope I'm not keeping you from something important," she said.

"I'm taking a short break from watching CCTV footage of the area around where the car was stolen."

"CCTV footage? There are cameras in that area?"

"There are cameras all over the island, but the ones nearest to where Jeff lives don't seem to have captured the theft. Similarly, our thief seems to have managed to avoid being captured on any of the cameras near Tim's."

"So our thief knows where the cameras are located."

"Maybe, or maybe he or she just got lucky. The cameras are concentrated near businesses rather than in residential areas. It's possible that our thief simply made lucky choices when driving the stolen cars away from the locations from which they were stolen."

"Is it very boring, watching CCTV footage?"

"Boring and headache-inducing. The picture quality isn't great and the images flicker almost constantly. That's why we usually make constables do the job."

"You do?"

Ted chuckled. "I'm kidding. We do have constables help, but everyone takes a turn. It's tiring and hard on the eyes, so no one works for more than an hour or so at a time. Having said that, there are a lot of different directions our thief might have gone after he or she took Jeff's car. That means there are a lot of different cameras that might have captured the car's progress. That makes for a lot of hours of video screening."

"I'm sorry."

"I think I've done as much as I'll have to do, at least for tonight. Once we're finished talking, I have a few reports to write and file and then I'm heading home. If I'm lucky, the night shift will finish watching the footage while I'm sleeping."

"Good luck."

"Thanks, but let's talk about Sean quickly so I can get back to work."

"Sorry. I'm ready to take notes."

"So what I asked Brady was for him to tell me about each person the way he remembered them before the murder, starting with Sean."

"That's very good. What did he have to say about Sean, then?"

"He said that Sean was a nice guy who was well liked. Most of the town thought his pizza was better than Greg's, but Greg offered some pasta dishes that you couldn't get at Sean's restaurant, so it all balanced out."

"I don't suppose he can request financial records for both restaurants."

"I didn't ask, but I suspect the answer would be no."

"Okay, what else about Sean?"

"He had a reputation for being generous, but Brady also said that such a thing was more or less expected in a small town. Sean sent a couple of pizzas to the fire station every Friday, for instance. He also donated pizzas to the various high school sports teams when they had their team banquets every year."

"They had pizza for their team banquets? We used to get spaghetti, at least," Margaret said.

"From what Brady said, Greg used to offer to send pizza or pasta, but the teams voted every year for what they wanted. Sean's pizza always won."

"Which probably annoyed Greg no end. Imagine not ever being able to give away your food."

"Ah, but Greg gave away plenty," Ted told her. "From what Brady said, it sounded as if the kids preferred pizza from Sean's restaurant, but when the adults had meetings or events, they usually asked Greg to donate pasta."

"We can talk about Greg in a minute. What else did Brady say about Sean?"

"He said that everyone in town knew Susie, because she more or less ran the restaurant. I got the feeling that everyone in town felt sorry for her because they all knew that Sean was cheating on her. But then, Susie knew that, too."

"I wonder if anyone stopped eating at Sean's restaurant in protest of his behavior. That seems like something that might happen in a small town."

"If it did, Brady wasn't aware of it. He said that as far as anyone knew, Susie and Sean had some sort of agreement. He said that he ate at Sean's restaurant at least once a week and that Susie and Sean always seemed to be happy together there."

"Wow. I can't imagine working with my partner, but if I did and I knew he was cheating, you'd better believe I'd find a new job."

"She should have gone to work for Greg," Mona suggested.

Margaret nodded. "That's a great idea."

"What's a great idea?" Ted asked. "Susie finding another job?"

"Yeah," Margaret said, blushing.

Mona laughed softly.

"Anything else about Sean?"

"Not really, except Brady did say that he'd been surprised when he'd been told that Sean had gone to the high school baseball game. He knew that Sean was seeing Nina, but he didn't think that Sean was devoted enough to anyone to go and sit through a high school baseball game for them."

"Oh? That's interesting."

"Yeah. From what Brady said, Sean often went to sporting events at the schools, from the elementary school all the way through the high school, but he'd arrive either before the event began to pass out coupons and chat and then leave as soon as things started, or he'd arrive just shortly before the event was expected to finish, again with coupons and sometimes with gift certificates or something similar for the winners."

"But he didn't usually go and watch the games?"

"No, and especially not a middle school and a high school game."

"There was nothing in the newspaper articles that suggested that he'd passed out any coupons that evening."

"Because he didn't. There weren't any found on the body, either."

"What about Greg? Did he pass out any coupons at the game? Did he usually pass out coupons at games?"

"He usually brought a stack of coupons to his son's games and left them on a table. He did the same on the night of the murder. Brady said he reckoned that Greg is more of an introvert, who doesn't feel comfortable handing the flyers out."

"I can understand that."

"So that was Sean. We talked a bit about Susie. Brady didn't have much else to say, except that he thought she was a nice woman and that he'd never understood why she stayed with Sean when he was obviously cheating."

"But he thought they had an understanding?" Margaret said questioningly.

"Yes, because that was the only thing that made sense to him. I should add that Brady told me that there are a few couples in town that he knows have open marriages where both parties see other people. He'd never had an occasion to talk to Susie about the state of her marriage, so he made assumptions based on what he saw."

"Which was her husband cheating on her."

"And her not seeming to mind," Ted added. "Like I said, he was at the restaurant at least once a week. Sean used to do a special every Thursday for the local police and other first responders. Brady said that Sean would always let him have the special when he went in, even if it wasn't a Thursday."

"Did Brady think that Sean and Susie were in love?"

"He said he thought Susie cared more about Sean than vice versa, but that's probably because he knew that Sean was cheating, and he didn't think that Susie was."

"He didn't think that Susie was? Are you suggesting that she was?"

"No, I just worded that badly," Ted said with a laugh. "As far as Brady knows, Susie never cheated. She worked hard at the restaurant and seemed to get along fine with everyone, including her husband."

"Okay, what about the others? We talked a bit about Greg. What else did Brady say about him?"

"Not much. His wife passed away when their son was only a toddler. Greg worked hard to raise the boy and keep the restaurant afloat while dealing with his grief."

"How did she die?" Mona asked.

It took Margaret a moment to realize why Ted wasn't answering the question. "How did she die?" she asked.

"She lost control of her car on an icy road just a few days before Christmas," Ted said. "I asked Brady for the details, just in case there was something suspicious there, but from all accounts it was just a tragic accident."

"I'm still suspicious," Margaret said.

Ted chuckled. "That's fair enough. Let me tell you what Brady told me. Gina Owens was driving home from the nearest mall, which was more of a glorified strip plaza than a mall. That's word for word what Brady said."

Margaret nodded. "I know exactly what he meant."

"Right, well, it was about twenty minutes away from their home. It was late and it had been snowing off and on all day. The temperature was right around freezing, which meant the ice on the roads kept melting and then refreezing."

"Very dangerous."

"Indeed. According to the accident report, Gina was driving far too fast for the conditions, which was surprising, because she had the baby in the car. Brady reckoned she adored the baby. The car's boot was full of presents for his second Christmas."

"My goodness. How dreadful."

"When she drove around a corner, the car went into a skid. Marks left on the road suggest that she tried to brake, but that just made things worse. The car spun out of control several times before it hit a tree."

Margaret winced. "That poor woman."

"The front of the car was totally destroyed. Luckily, the baby was in the backseat, strapped into a car seat. He was crying but otherwise fine when the first car stopped at the scene just a minute or two later."

"How difficult for Greg."

"Brady said that he shut the restaurant for two days, but that was it. When anyone said anything, he just reminded them that he was now a single father with a son to support."

"People process grief in different ways. Maybe throwing himself back into work was his way of coping with his loss."

"Maybe. According to Brady, other than the sad loss of his wife, Greg is a fairly dull person. He works hard. He pays his bills and his employees. Brady didn't think he'd ever heard a single complaint about the man, but he also said that Sean was much more popular as a person."

"I can't wait to hear how he's been doing since Sean's death."

"Yes, that will be interesting."

"Okay, that's Greg. What about Nina? What was she like before her lover was murdered?"

"According to Brady, he was barely aware of her before the murder. Nina was a teacher at the high school. As far as he knew, she'd never cheated on Ronald before, but it's possible that she had, just with more discretion."

"I want to talk to her," Margaret said. "I want to ask her why she'd gotten involved with Sean."

"She said in her newspaper interview that they'd sort of fallen into the affair after having known one another for years."

"Yeah, which is no help. What attracted her to Sean? Was he her first affair? If so, why decide to cheat at that point in her married life? If not, why was she still married to Ronald? Was Ronald also cheating? Did Ronald cheat first? I have a lot of questions for Nina."

Ted chuckled. "I got that. I can make a list of them for Brady, but I'm not going to give them to him until after he's provided us with updates on all of the suspects. I'm pretty certain the updates will raise a lot more questions."

"No doubt."

"That was about all that Brady said about Nina."

"Okay, what about Ruth? I'd love to ask her some of the same questions."

"Except Ruth was divorced, so she wasn't actually cheating on anyone."

"Then she might have expected Sean to leave Susie for her," Mona said.

Margaret nodded. "Maybe she did expect Sean to leave Susie for her," she said to Ted.

"Maybe. Again, Brady says he didn't really know Ruth before the murder. She was a nurse, working for a private medical practice, at the time that Sean died."

"So she knows about anatomy."

"That is true."

"According to the newspaper, though, it was a big knife that would have done serious damage, even if the killer hadn't stuck it in just the right spot."

"The paper got it right. It was a big knife and Brady told me that the killer didn't need to be terribly exact. 'Just the right spot' was actually a fairly large area, or so the medical examiner seemed to think."

Margaret shuddered. "I'm not going to want to sit anywhere without a solid wall behind me from now on."

"Brady did say that at the time of Ruth and Sean's affair, he was aware that they were involved. It's a small town. Apparently everyone was talking about it. He also said that he wasn't certain that Ruth knew that she was being discussed so widely."

"She sounded shocked by how much people were talking about her after Sean's death. But she'd lived in Harper Glen for her entire life. She must have known what the town was like."

"You'd have thought so."

"What about Ronald? What did Brady have to say about him?"

"Ronald works in banking. His father was a senior vice president with the local bank decades ago. Then the local bank was bought out by a larger bank for a nearby town. That group of banks was then bought out by an even larger banking organization a few years later. Ronald's father ended up taking early retirement and moving to Florida. Everyone in town knew that Ronald had been expected to follow in his father's footsteps. He got a degree in business administration and then got a job at the bank where his father worked just before the first merger."

"That all sounds quite complicated."

"And boring," Mona added.

Margaret nodded at her.

"It's relevant, though. Brady reckons that everyone in town expected Ronald to move up through the ranks in the same way his father had. Instead, he's still working at the same branch of the local bank where he started, or he was when Sean died, anyway. I did think that Brady might have slipped up and given me more information about Ronald than he'd intended, but when I asked him about it, he laughed and said that he'd meant that Ronald was still there when Sean died."

"Surely he wasn't still doing the same job that he'd taken when he'd first finished college."

"No, he wasn't. Brady said he'd moved up from assistant loan officer to assistant branch manager, but that that position was a long way from being a senior vice president for the entire banking organization."

"And was Ronald unhappy about his lack of progress?"

"According to Brady, Ronald is well aware of his shortcomings. He went into banking because it was expected of him, but it isn't something he enjoys, and he doesn't feel he's especially good at managing a business."

"What did he want to do with his life?"

"That's a good question and not one that I thought to ask."

"I feel like the poor man is taking loan applications and opening savings accounts while he secretly wants to be a writer or an actor or maybe a research biologist."

Ted laughed. "That's an interesting mix of job titles."

"It was just whatever came to mind."

"I'll ask Brady. He probably has no idea, but maybe he'll be curious enough to ask Ronald."

"What else did Brady say about Ronald? He didn't love his job, but did he love his wife?"

"Apparently. Brady knew Ronald a bit because he banked at the branch where Ronald worked. He said Ronald had pictures of Nina and their children on his desk. As far as Brady knew, Ronald was always faithful."

"I'm not sure this conversation is getting us anywhere," Margaret said.

"It's good to have background information on the suspects, even if it doesn't feel especially useful. It might prove a good deal more useful when we get updated information."

"Who haven't we talked about?"

"Rick."

"Oh, yes, Rick. I don't like him."

Ted chuckled. "Brady didn't say as much, but I don't think he likes him either. He said that when Rick came back to town and bought his business, he seemed to think that owning a business made him more important than most of the other people in town. That was bad enough, but when the business started to struggle, Brady said that Rick got bitter and angry at just about everyone."

"Oh dear."

"It was a small printing business, and when he first opened, apparently he got a lot of local business. Then the large chain company opened a shop and just about all of his customers started going there. Rick didn't care that they were cheaper and faster. He expected his customers to be loyal to him, regardless."

"But the local small businesses had to do what was best for their businesses."

"Exactly. Eventually Rick's company went under. Brady did say that Sean was one of the last businesses in town that was still using Rick's shop for his printing needs. Apparently, Sean didn't move his business elsewhere until Rick shut his doors."

"That was nice of him."

"And then he gave Rick a job, which Brady said surprised him."

"Why?"

"Brady reckoned that no one in town wanted to hire Rick. He was angry at everyone for not supporting his business. Apparently, he'd started drinking heavily as well."

"But Sean still gave him a chance."

"Which didn't end well. Brady said he wasn't at all surprised when Susie said that Rick had been unreliable. He said he hadn't expected Rick to stay at the pizza place for as long as he did."

"But does any of that lead to murder?"

"That's the question, of course. Brady reckoned that Rick hated Sean, even though Sean was probably the one person in town who'd tried to help him the most."

"It's a long way from hate to murder."

"Not long enough," Ted said.

Margaret sighed. "After this conversation, I'm even more eager to hear where everyone is now."

"Which is exactly how I felt after I talked to Brady. As I said, he's going to work on the updates. We should have them soon."

"He should make them a priority," Mona said.

"I suppose he's busy with other things," Margaret said.

"He is very busy, actually. There was a large drug bust at the high school the day before yesterday. A few teachers, one of the administrators, and dozens of students were arrested. He reckons he won't finish the paperwork involved before Christmas."

"So a ten-year-old cold case takes a backseat."

"Indeed. Even if we spot something huge that was missed in the initial investigation, it might be weeks before Brady has time to go and question the suspects again."

"At least we now know more about everyone. I'm not sure that what I've learned changes my opinion on anyone, but it's interesting to learn more."

"I've kept everyone in the same order on my list of suspects, but I expect that all to change once we find out where everyone is now."

"Yeah, maybe I'll leave my list alone until after that."

"I should go, but I don't want to."

Margaret looked at the clock and then sighed. "It is getting late."

"Yeah, and we both have to work in the morning."

"Except you're still at work. You should get the morning off."

"I wish it worked that way. Sadly, it does not."

"Maybe you should look for a new job," Margaret said. "And before you say anything, I'm teasing. I know you love your job."

"I do love my job, but that doesn't mean that I don't sometimes think about finding a new one. I met a guy, Jake, in Liverpool years ago who ended up leaving the police and going to work in private security. Then he started his own private security company. Last year, he made over a million pounds in profit."

"Wow."

"Yeah, and the last time I saw him, he told me that he'll have a job for me any time I want to change careers."

"Do you think you'd enjoy the work?"

"Maybe. I doubt I would find it as satisfying as police work, but I know I'd appreciate the hours, the time off, and the extra money."

"All of those things are nice, but you also need to at least not hate what you do for eight or nine hours every day."

"I know. And I don't think I'd hate it. Jake was talking about putting me in his security systems department. He said my job would be to go into homes and businesses and help identify the places where the sensors and alarms and things should go. It actually sounds quite interesting, just not as interesting as finding killers and putting them in prison."

"Let's hope Jake meant what he said about always having a job open for you. Maybe one day you'll be ready for the change."

"I did think, if we get married and have children, that a job like Jake's would be better than what I'm doing now. I'd work a regular nine-to-five schedule and get weekends and holidays off."

"We can talk about that more as we see where our relationship goes, but ultimately, it's going to be your decision. Against my better judgment, I've fallen in love with a police inspector. I can't very well blame him if he keeps working that job for the rest of his career."

Ted chuckled. "Against your better judgment? I think I've been insulted."

"You know what I meant."

"I do. And I love you, in spite of your cruel words."

"They weren't meant to be cruel, just honest."

Margaret heard a loud banging noise. She looked around the room.

Mona sighed. "It's on Ted's end," she said.

Margaret flushed and then nodded.

"I have to go," Ted said. "The constable watching the CCTV thinks he might have found something. I suspect he's just saying that so he can have a five-minute conversation with someone before he has to go back to watching the footage, but I'm going to take a look."

"Good luck. I hope he did find something and that it leads straight to the car thief."

"Me too, but not tonight. We can go and find him in the morning."

Margaret laughed. "Definitely in the morning."

She tapped the button to end the call and then sighed. "I can't expect him to change jobs for me."

"He wouldn't be changing jobs for you. He'd be changing jobs for your relationship and your children. There is a difference," Mona said.

"But the world needs good, smart, honest, hard-working police inspectors."

"And security companies need smart, honest, hard-working employees. You're borrowing trouble. Ted isn't going to do anything without a lot of thought and many conversations."

Margaret nodded. "I'll worry about it tomorrow."

"I need to think about everything he told us. I might need to rearrange my list of suspects."

"You think. I'm going to bed."

Katie followed Margaret into the bedroom. When Margaret climbed into bed a short while later, Katie was already asleep in her favorite spot at the foot of the bed.

10

When Margaret got to work the next morning, Joney and Rachel were talking in the lobby.

"There you are," Joney said. "We were just talking about the stolen cars."

Rachel nodded. "We were hoping you'd know more than what was in the local paper today."

"I haven't seen today's paper. Was there anything interesting in it?" Margaret asked.

Both women shook their heads.

"It was mostly just the same things that were published previously, but in a different order," Joney said. "Heather did her best to make it interesting, but there wasn't anything new there."

"I'm afraid I don't know anything about the cars," Margaret said. "Ted is part of the team that is investigating, but he couldn't tell me anything, even if there was news."

"Jeff Carlson, the guy whose car was stolen, sounds really upset," Rachel said. "He talks a lot about how he and his wife moved here because they thought that the island would be a good and safe place to raise their children."

"He's just shouting loudly in the hopes that no one reminds him that he left the car unlocked," Joney said. "It's a good thing he and his wife aren't still together. That's the sort of thing that a wife would definitely remind a husband about."

Rachel laughed. "I can totally see that. Hopefully, the theft will remind quite a lot of people to start locking their cars."

Joney nodded. "I never used to lock mine, but when I bought my new one a few years ago, the salesman advised me to start getting in the habit. He said new cars were more tempting than older ones and that the island wasn't as safe as it had been years ago."

"And whatever anyone thinks, cars do get stolen now and again," Rachel said. "Locking your car is always a good idea."

"Do the police have any theories as to why those two particular cars were taken?" Joney asked Margaret. "I mean, neither was new or even close to new. Is there something special about them? Are they easier to steal than other cars?"

Margaret shrugged. "If they are, Ted hasn't mentioned it, but that might not be something that the police would want the general public to know."

Rachel laughed. "That's very true. I'd hate to find out now that I'd bought a car that car thieves find easy to steal."

"The first car that was taken was locked, wasn't it?" Joney asked.

"It was," Margaret said. "Or at least, the owner said he was certain he'd locked it."

"But we all forget now and again," Joney said. "I try really hard to be careful, but I can't tell you how many times I've walked halfway across a car park only to turn around and walk back to my car to make certain that I locked it."

Rachel laughed. "I do that all the time, too. I have a remote, so I start pushing it as soon as I turn around. Usually I can zap it before I've walked too far back."

"Maybe the car thefts aren't related," Joney said. "Maybe the first one was stolen because someone wanted that particular make and model of car. Maybe the second one was taken by someone who was walking past and noticed that Jeff had left it unlocked."

"It's possible that the thefts aren't related," Margaret said. "But I do hate the idea of there being two car thieves on the island."

"I do, too," Joney said.

They talked for a bit longer about the thefts before Margaret looked at her watch. "I have some tests running. I need to go and check my results," she said.

"Is there any news on the murder investigation?" Rachel asked.

"Ted talked to Brady about the suspects. Brady told him more about each of them. I'll fill you in later."

"Let's go for lunch," Joney suggested.

"I can do that," Margaret said.

"Midday?" Rachel asked.

Margaret nodded before she walked through the door behind Joney's desk. In her office, she put her purse into a drawer and then switched on her computer. When it was ready to go, she checked her emails before heading back to her small lab. She spent most of the morning going through the results of her various tests.

"I'm ready for a break," she told Joney when she walked into the lobby a few minutes before noon.

"Aren't we all?" Joney asked. "I've had nothing but grumpy customers to deal with all morning."

"Oh dear. I am sorry."

Joney shrugged. "It comes with the job but it's quite unusual to have to deal with several in a row. We pride ourselves on getting the customers exactly what they want, quickly and efficiently."

"And they still complain?" Margaret asked.

Joney laughed. "Some of them complain just to see if they can get a discount, but others come up with all sorts of reasons to moan."

"Tell us about it over lunch," Rachel suggested. "I'm ready to go."

It didn't take the trio long to walk to the same restaurant where they'd eaten on Monday. Luckily, the waiter they had upset that day was nowhere to be seen. They ordered drinks and then lunch while Margaret told them what she could remember of her conversation with Ted the previous evening.

"All of that was interesting," Rachel said when she was finished. "But I'm not changing my list – not yet, anyway."

Joney nodded. "I'm tempted to move people around, but I'm not going to do so. I want to know what they've all been doing since the initial investigation. I suspect I'll want to move everyone once we have that information."

"Do you know when we'll get more from Brady?" Rachel asked.

Margaret shook her head. "Apparently, he's really busy, but he's hoping to put together an update in the next few days."

"If you get the information over the weekend, don't solve the case without us," Rachel said.

Margaret laughed. "I very much doubt that anyone is going to solve the case in a hurry. If it were that simple, Brady would have found the killer ten years ago."

"Ten years is a long time to keep a secret," Rachel said. "And it's a long time to live with guilt."

"I can't imagine it," Joney said. "I feel as if I'd end up confessing eventually. The guilt would just eat away at me."

Rachel nodded. "Especially if I were still living in the same small town where I'd murdered someone. I can't imagine still going to high school baseball games, knowing that I'd stabbed someone to death during a game."

"Maybe the killer enjoys keeping his or her secret," Joney said. "Maybe he or she gets a thrill every time he or she goes to the stadium."

"Or maybe the killer moved away to get away from the guilt," Margaret said.

"I think that's what I would do," Rachel said thoughtfully. "I think I'd move far away and try to forget that it had ever happened."

"So if someone involved in the case has moved away, he or she gets bumped up the suspect list," Joney said.

Rachel nodded. "Except for Susie."

"Why except for Susie?" Margaret asked.

"I can see her wanting to get away from the town where her husband died," Rachel explained. "Assuming she didn't kill him. Actually, even if she did, every part of the town must have constantly reminded her of him."

"She worked with him, lived with him, and slept with him," Joney said. "I agree with Rachel. I wouldn't be surprised if she'd moved away."

"Maybe she stayed and married Greg," Margaret said.

Both women made faces. Before the conversation resumed, the waiter delivered their lunches. As he walked away, Rachel shook her head.

"I know Sean wasn't perfect, but he was still better than Greg," she said.

"Why?" Margaret asked. "We've no reason to believe that Greg ever cheated on his wife."

Rachel shrugged. "I feel sorry for him, losing his wife that way, but I still didn't care for him. He was boring, but in a sort of creepy way."

"He was better than Rick," Joney said.

The other two women nodded.

"I think I'd marry a baseball bat before I'd marry Rick," Rachel said. "The newspaper didn't interview his ex-wife. I wonder if the police did."

"Probably," Margaret said after swallowing quickly. "She was at the game, wasn't she?"

"I don't remember, but it doesn't matter. Even if she wasn't spotted there, she might have been there," Rachel said.

"But they had a son on the team," Joney said. "She must have been there."

They talked for a bit longer about the case and the suspects. Over dessert, Margaret remembered what Joney had said earlier.

"You were going to tell us about the complaints you've been dealing with," she said to Joney.

Joney sighed and then scooped a large bite of brownie and ice cream. "People are just dumb," she said before she ate the bite.

Rachel laughed. "Try working on the sales end of things. I do everything I can to explain our products to customers and they still come back with dumb questions."

"One of the complaints I got today was that our window cleaner cleans too well," Joney said flatly.

Rachel and Margaret both laughed.

"Did you ask why they didn't want their windows too clean?" Rachel asked.

"I told them I didn't understand the complaint. They demanded to speak to Arthur and, of course, he insisted that we give them their money back."

"He's too nice," Rachel said. "If he were in charge of dealing with complaints, we'd go out of business in a month."

Joney nodded. "Which is why he doesn't usually get involved, but this time the man complaining happens to live next door to Arthur. When I told him that I didn't understand what he was complaining about, he told me that I had to let him talk to Arthur or he'd simply go next door and talk to Arthur's wife. And then he complained to Arthur about me."

"You know Arthur didn't take him seriously," Rachel said.

"Yeah, I know, but I still hate the idea of people complaining about me."

"But you can't just give people their money back every time they ring with a complaint," Rachel said. "We would seriously go out of business."

Joney grinned. "I didn't give the next guy his money back."

"What was his complaint?" Margaret asked.

"His case of cleaners had an extra bottle in it."

Margaret and Rachel simply stared at her for several seconds.

"Say that again," Rachel said eventually.

Joney chuckled. "I told you today was a bad day. Do you remember last month when we gave everyone a bottle of our newest product with their order as a promotion? He didn't want the free bottle of cleaner."

"Surely if it was free, he could have just given it away or thrown it away or something," Margaret said.

"I suggested both of those things. He wanted me to send someone over to take the extra bottle back."

"What did you do?" Margaret asked.

"I told him that I'll pick up the extra bottle the next time I'm near his shop. I told him that it's a very popular product and that I'd happily use it at home. Then he decided that he wanted to keep it after all."

"Was that it?" Margaret asked after her last bite of dessert.

Margaret shook her head. "The last one was the best. The guy rang to complain about the frozen beef stew he'd purchased last month."

Rachel frowned. "We don't sell frozen beef stew."

"I know that, but the, um, gentleman on the phone didn't want to believe me. He insisted that he'd taken our phone number right off the box from the stew. When I said that wasn't possible, he offered to bring me the box so that I could have a look for myself."

"That's worrying," Margaret said.

"He was in Scotland, so I wasn't too worried. I suggested that he take a photo of the packaging and send it to me so that I could see exactly which product was an issue. After some back and forth, he agreed."

"And it wasn't our packaging," Rachel guessed.

"Oh, it was our packaging, it just wasn't for beef stew. I'm not sure where he found the box, but it was for one of our commercial cleaning products. I don't know how he mixed that up with the box that his beef stew came in, either, but he had a box and he'd called the number on the back without paying much attention to what he was doing."

"And our number was on the box for the cleaning product," Margaret said.

Joney nodded. "And can I say, it took me far too long to persuade the man that he'd made a mistake. I really believe that he thought that if he shouted at me loudly enough that I'd admit that we'd put beef stew in our cleaning solution or something."

All three women laughed.

"And now I suppose we have to go back to work," Joney said after they'd paid their bills.

"Or we could run away to Paris and spend the afternoon shopping," Rachel suggested as they walked outside. "Or we could climb the Eiffel Tower."

"I would love to drop everything and fly to Paris," Margaret said.

"Wouldn't we all?" Rachel asked.

"It's the sort of thing that your aunt could have done whenever she'd wanted. I'm surprised she didn't travel a lot more," Joney said.

Margaret shrugged. "As I understand it, when she first arrived on the island, she didn't know how much she'd actually inherited. By the time she realized that she was a very wealthy woman, she'd already fallen in love with Daniel. That made traveling less tempting."

"What would you do if you suddenly inherited a fortune?" Rachel asked.

"I've no idea," Margaret said. "I'd probably be just as cautious as Aunt Fenella, though. My sister, Megan, would just start buying things. She'd probably spend every penny in a year or less."

"When are we going to get to meet Megan?" Rachel asked.

"Hopefully soon. She has a new man in her life, or she'd have been over sooner. As it is, she's hoping they can visit together in another month or two."

"You don't sound happy about that," Joney said.

Margaret shrugged. "I'm not sure I'm going to like the new man. Everything that Megan has said about him has raised red flags for me, but she just laughs off my concerns."

"Oh dear," Rachel said.

"You should have Ted do some detective work," Joney suggested as she unlocked the office door. "Maybe he can find out more about your sister's new boyfriend."

"I don't want to do anything that might upset Megan. She's old enough to make her own decisions when it comes to dating."

"Maybe you'll feel better about it once you meet him," Rachel said.

"Maybe. And if not, then at least Ted will get to meet him, too. If he has any suspicions, he can do some discreet checking without me even asking," Margaret said.

Joney patted her arm. "It's going to be okay."

"I hope so. Megan can be impulsive sometimes. It's difficult, living so far away from her."

"How old is she?" Rachel asked.

"Over thirty and old enough to take care of herself," Margaret replied with a shrug. "But I'm the older sister. That isn't going to change, no matter how old we get."

Margaret walked back to her office and spent the afternoon writing up the results of the tests she'd run the previous day. Then she got things ready for her next project. As she was leaving, she bumped into Arthur.

"I haven't seen you all week," he said with a smile. "Great work on the report you gave me yesterday, though. It's excellent."

"Thank you."

They talked about her next project for a few minutes before Arthur looked at his watch.

"I can't talk for long tonight. We have guests coming for dinner. The wife promised me that I can have some pudding if I come home early enough to help with everything."

Margaret laughed. "You go and get home then," she said. "I just need to wash my coffee mugs from today."

In the small staff room, she washed the mugs and then dried them and put them back in the cupboard. Then she headed for the lobby.

She waved to Joney, who was on the phone. The drive home didn't take long. Katie was pacing back and forth in front of the windows when Margaret arrived.

"What are you doing?" she asked the cat, who frowned before disappearing into Fenella's room.

Margaret walked into the kitchen and then stopped and stared at the mess that seemed to be everywhere. "You attacked the automatic feeder," she said softly. There were pieces of cat food liberally spread throughout the large kitchen. The feeder was on its side, its top only partially in place. The plastic holding tube was badly cracked. The electronics that made the flap open and close to distribute the food had been pulled out of their housing. There were wires pointing in every direction and Margaret could see three of the four batteries partly buried under a pile of kibble.

"Merrow," Katie said softly from the doorway.

"Is that supposed to be an apology? It's a long way from an adequate one. This wasn't an accident," Margaret replied.

Katie looked at her for a minute as if trying to judge just how much trouble she was in. As Margaret stared hard at her, she suddenly turned around and ran away.

Margaret sighed. "It could be worse. I'm not sure how, but it could be worse," she muttered as she tried to tiptoe around the crunchy piles to get to the cupboard that held cleaning supplies.

"I don't think she likes being left alone all day." Mona's voice floated through the air.

"Yes, well, she's going to have to get used to it. I have to work for a living. And for a while she might have to live without any lunch. I don't know when I'm going to have time to get another automatic feeder."

Margaret pulled out a broom and started trying to sweep everything into a pile.

"She probably didn't mean to cause so much trouble," Mona said as she appeared on a stool at the counter.

"She knew exactly what she was doing," Margaret countered. "She's a very smart animal."

Mona shrugged. "Destroying a feeder doesn't seem very smart to me."

"Except now she'll get both her breakfast and her lunch before I leave for the day. She'll probably eat it all in one sitting and make herself sick, but there isn't anything I can do about that."

"Maybe Elaine can come over and get lunch for her."

Margaret shook her head. "Aunt Fenella made arrangements with Mrs. Jacobson, which worked fine until Mrs. Jacobson wanted to go on vacation. I'm not going to give the key to Aunt Fenella's apartment to anyone else, not even Elaine."

"Shelly already has a key."

"Does she? It doesn't matter. I don't want to start asking Elaine for favors."

Mona chuckled. "Because you know she wouldn't hesitate to ask you to return the favor and she'd probably ask for something considerably more demanding than just getting lunch for a cat."

Margaret bent down and picked up the mangled feeder. She was pleased to discover that the fourth battery was still in place inside the unit. At least Katie hadn't swallowed a battery. After putting the broken machine and all its parts on the counter, she went back to work with the broom. When someone knocked a few minutes later, she'd gotten nearly all of the cat food into a reasonably neat pile.

"Who is that?" Margaret asked Mona.

"It's Ted."

"He's just in time to help with the cleaning."

Mona nodded and then slowly faded away.

Margaret walked to the door and let Ted into the apartment.

"I'm happy to see you," she said after their kiss. "Katie destroyed her automatic feeder today. Want to help sweep up the mess?"

Ted laughed. "You used to be happy to see me because you loved me."

"I still love you. I'll love you even more if you help clean up the mess in the kitchen."

"You're still wearing your work clothes. You go and change into something more comfortable while I tackle the mess in the kitchen."

"You don't have to be this nice."

Ted laughed and kissed her again. "I don't mind. Cleaning up some spilled cat food sounds like a weirdly relaxing chore. I need to unwind for a few minutes."

"I'll be in to help in just a few minutes," Margaret promised. She rushed into her bedroom and shut the door. It took only a minute for her to get out of her work clothes and into jeans and a T-shirt. As she headed toward the door, she noticed Katie sitting in the middle of her bathroom floor.

"You were very naughty," she said sternly.

Katie walked out of the bathroom, her head down and her tail tucked between her legs. She stopped in front of Margaret and made a soft, sad sound.

"You were very naughty," Margaret said again, her tone less harsh.

Katie looked up and then down again.

"Why did you destroy your feeder? What am I going to do with your lunch tomorrow?"

Katie looked up again and then sat down and put her chin on the floor with her paws on the top of her head. She squeezed her eyes shut and sighed.

"I'm going to have to buy another feeder, and I don't even know if I can get one on the island. Aunt Fenella bought that one somewhere, but I don't know where."

"Meewwww," Katie said sadly.

Margaret sighed. "I can't stay angry with you, even though I should. You're too cute."

Katie looked up hopefully. Margaret picked her up and gave her a cuddle. "I'm sorry that I have to work every day. And I'm sorry that

Mrs. Jacobson is on vacation. The feeder was there to keep you from starving while I'm out. It was for your own good."

"Mewwoooww," Katie said firmly.

Margaret walked out of her room. When she reached the kitchen, Ted was scooping cat food into a garbage bag.

"Did you want to try to keep any of this?" he asked. "I got a clean rubbish bag in case you did."

"I don't think so. I'd be worried that some small plastic part might have gotten mixed into the mess."

Ted nodded. "You're probably right. It's a shame to waste it, though."

"Yeah, but I'd never forgive myself if Katie swallowed a piece of plastic. And now that I've said that, you don't think she already swallowed any pieces, do you?"

Ted shook his head. "I pieced everything back together as best I could. I didn't find any missing pieces. I suppose it's possible she swallowed a tiny bit, but it seems to have broken into fairly large pieces. Maybe it's designed to break that way when a cat attacks."

Margaret sighed. "I'm going to have to keep a close eye on you, just in case," she said to Katie.

"I'm surprised you've forgiven her," Ted said with a chuckle.

"She's very cute. And it isn't her fault that Aunt Fenella went away or that I have to work every day or that Mrs. Jacobson is on vacation."

"That's true."

Margaret put Katie down and went to help Ted with the cleaning. Working together, they were able to get all of the food picked up in just a few minutes. Margaret grabbed a mop and gave the floor a good clean. While she was working, Ted took a look at the feeder.

"I might be able to put it back together," he said. "But I'm not sure that's a good idea. She'd probably just attack it again."

"So what can I do?" Margaret asked. "She needs lunch every day, and I can't get home to feed her."

"If you trust me with a key, I can probably manage to get here most days. It won't be at exactly the same time every day, but I should be able to visit between eleven and two or so."

"I don't want to inconvenience you."

"It's not an inconvenience. I nearly always get my lunch on the promenade. I often pop back to my flat while I'm down here. Dropping in here for five minutes won't be any additional bother."

"What happens when you're too busy to get here?"

Ted shrugged. "We could cross that bridge when we come to it. Or you can find someone else. I was just offering."

"I appreciate the offer. Maybe we could try it for a day or two."

"I'll plan to feed her tomorrow and Friday, anyway," Ted said, making a note on his phone. "And I'm declaring this thing dead," he added, nodding at the old feeder. "I didn't realize that some of the wires got broken. I'm not going to start trying to replace them."

"Neither am I," Margaret said as she walked to the desk. She found the envelope of spare keycards that Fenella had left her. After taking one out, she put the envelope back in the desk.

"Here you are," she said, handing it to Ted. "Are you sure you want to commit to feeding the badly behaving cat?"

Ted grinned. "I still love her. As I said, let's see how it goes. I should be able to manage for a few days, anyway. When does Mrs. Jacobson get back?"

"Not for another five weeks or so. I probably need to look for another automatic feeder."

"Where did this one come from?" Ted asked as he dumped the pieces into the garbage bag.

"Aunt Fenella bought it from somewhere. It was in her storage room on the ground floor."

"So maybe we should go and get some dinner and then try a few shops to see if we can find another one."

"Will anything be open after we've had dinner?"

"The DIY store will be. That was my first thought for a place to look."

Margaret nodded. "That sounds like a very romantic date night. Dinner and a trip around a Do-It-Yourself store. Let's go."

Ted grinned. "That sounded sarcastic."

"It wasn't meant to. I appreciate the offer. Katie isn't your cat."

"But she's yours, at least temporarily. I want to do what I can to help."

With the kitchen more or less returned to normal, Margaret poured out about half of Katie's normal dinner for her. "I'm sure she must have eaten some of the mess that she got everywhere, right?" she asked Ted as she measured out the food.

"Probably," he replied with a shrug.

A short while later, Margaret was ready to go.

"I hope she'll behave while we're out," she said to Ted as they walked out of the apartment.

"Surely she's worn out after battling the feeder all day. She should just curl up and sleep while we're out."

"Let's hope."

They had dinner at a nearby Italian restaurant and then Ted drove them to the large hardware store on the outskirts of Douglas. While they didn't find any cat feeders, Margaret enjoyed spending some time looking at the various kitchen and bathroom displays. She and Ted pretended that they were building a dream house and talked about everything from countertops to flooring to cupboard hardware.

"That was fun," Ted said in the car on the way back to Margaret's apartment. "I still think the darker grey quartz was a better choice."

Margaret shook her head. "It was twice the price of the lighter grey one. I will admit that I liked it better, but not two times better."

"But it's a dream home. There aren't any budgets in a dream home."

"Even if we had an unlimited budget, I wouldn't want to waste money. The darker grey was not two times nicer than the lighter grey."

They were still debating the two countertops when Ted parked near Promenade View.

"Do you want to come up for a while?" Margaret asked.

He nodded. "I want to be certain that Katie is happy with me. I'm going to be feeding her for a few days."

When they got to the apartment, Margaret went into her room to change. When she emerged, she found Ted sitting on a couch with Katie on his lap.

"I think she's happy with you," she said dryly.

Ted laughed. "She's incredibly sweet."

"Think of the kibble. You swept up kibble for ages."

"But she's purring."

Margaret shook her head. "If we do have children, I hope you won't be this soft on them."

"I probably will be, if they're as cute as Katie."

"Maybe our children won't be cute at all."

Ted took her hand and pulled her down onto the couch next to him. "Our children are going to be the cutest children on the whole island," he said before he kissed her.

An hour later, after some mindless television, Margaret walked Ted to the door.

"I'll see you tomorrow night around six," he told her. "And I'll text you and let you know when I've fed Katie."

"You're the best."

"Don't ever forget that," he said with a chuckle.

11

"Ted will be here to feed you around noon," Margaret said to Katie the next morning. "And don't you dare complain if he's late. You could have had your lunch at exactly noon if you hadn't killed your automatic feeder."

Katie didn't even look up from her spot in the sun.

Margaret sighed. "I hope you'll be suitably appreciative when Ted comes over. He's doing me a huge favor, looking after you."

After being ignored again, Margaret grabbed her purse and her car keys and headed for the door.

"Try not to destroy anything today," she added before she let herself out of the apartment.

"Good morning," Joney said when Margaret walked into the office a short while later.

"Good morning," Margaret replied.

"Is there any news on anything?" Joney asked.

Margaret shook her head. "Brady is supposed to be sending the updates soon for the case in Ohio. And the local paper is going to be running their updates next week."

"I don't want to wait until next week."

Margaret laughed. "Neither do I. I hope Brady sends something soon."

"If you get an update over the weekend, you'll have to ring me and Rachel and let us know."

"I can do that."

"As for today, do you want to have lunch together again?"

Margaret hesitated. While she very much enjoyed having lunch with her new work colleagues, she hadn't really planned on eating café meals every day. She'd had only a single paycheck so far from her new job and she really needed to work harder at sticking to her budget.

"Or we could order pizza and stay here," Joney suggested before Margaret replied. "We have a credit at the pizza place down the street that we need to use up, actually. We ordered a bunch of food from them for a business meeting. To thank us, they gave us a credit for a couple of large pizzas and some salad and garlic bread. I've been meaning to order it for ages, but we keep going out every day."

"Pizza sounds good, maybe because we keep talking about Sean's business."

Joney nodded. "I was thinking about pizza last night. I was re-reading the newspaper articles about the murder, and I kept wondering whose pizza really was better."

"Surely that's a matter of personal taste."

"Yeah, okay, I was wondering which pizza I'd like better, then."

"I wonder if both restaurants are still open."

"Oh, that's a good point. Maybe Susie shut the restaurant and moved to Alaska or something."

"Alaska?"

"It was the first thing that came to mind. Do many Americans move to Alaska?"

Margaret shook her head. "I'm told it's a beautiful state, but it's cold and dark for much of the year. I know someone who lives there. It takes a very special sort of person to live with the cold and the darkness."

"What do you like on your pizza?"

"Vegetables."

Joney laughed. "Very good. I'll get one with lots of veggies. And one with just cheese. And I'll see what Rachel and Arthur and Stan want. I think we get three or four pizzas, which is more than we can eat, but someone can take home the leftovers."

"Sounds good."

"I'll have them deliver around midday. We can eat in the staff room."

"That also sounds good."

In her office, Margaret fired up her computer and then looked back through her notes. She needed to do some research before she did any additional testing. When she finally took a break, it was nearly noon. She stood up and stretched and then checked her emails. She was still clearing away the junk emails when Joney knocked on her door.

"The pizza is here," she said.

"Great. I need a break."

Margaret hit delete a few more times and then got up and headed to the staff room. Rachel and Arthur were already there, sitting at the table with plates full of pizza, garlic bread, and salad. Joney was filling a plate for herself. Margaret grabbed a plate and began to fill it.

"I was just telling Arthur about your murder investigation," Rachel said as Margaret sat down at the table.

"It isn't my investigation," Margaret said with a grin.

Arthur chuckled. "It sounds quite interesting. As we're eating pizza, I can't help but wonder if the poor man was killed by his pie-baking rival."

"That's certainly one possibility," Margaret said.

"If he did it, he must have thought that Sean's restaurant would go out of business if Sean died," Joney said.

"I'm not sure that's how it would have worked, though," Margaret said. "If Susie inherited the shop, and she should have, really, then why wouldn't she keep it going? She worked there too, after all."

"Maybe the other pizza shop owner, whose name I've completely forgotten, was having an affair with Susie," Arthur said.

"His name is Greg," Margaret said. "And I suppose that's possible, but if they were involved, no one knew about it at the time of the murder."

"If they're together now, that will be suspicious," Rachel said.

Everyone nodded.

Margaret frowned. "You know what's been bothering me?" she asked. "How did Sean manage to fall asleep at the game? I appreciate that the game wasn't at all exciting, but he was sitting on hard wooden bleachers and surrounded by people. Could you sleep under those circumstances?"

Rachel shrugged. "I can't really sleep anywhere but tucked up in my bed, but I had a friend at uni who could sleep anywhere. She'd just put her head down and be out cold in seconds."

"I have been known to fall asleep in my chair in front of the telly," Arthur said. "But I can't imagine sleeping at a baseball game."

Joney nodded. "From the pictures, it didn't look as if the bleachers were all that sturdy. I suspect every time anyone moved, the entire structure shook. I can't imagine sleeping through that."

"He did wake up when their team scored," Rachel said. "Presumably the crowd made a lot of noise at that point."

"Presumably," Margaret said. "It was just a thought. My brain has been trying to process everything while I've been busy trying to think about other things."

They chatted about the case with Arthur while they enjoyed their meal. Then Margaret helped Joney clean up the staff room before she went back to work. She'd just walked into her office when her phone buzzed.

"Katie has been fed and snuggled and given one small treat," the text from Ted read. "She seemed happy to see me and very grateful for lunch."

"Thank you so much!" Margaret texted back.

"No problem. I should be able to do tomorrow, too."

"See you later?"

"I certainly hope so."

Margaret sat down at her desk. More research led to her setting up a couple of tests to run overnight before she was done for the day. Stan waved as she was walking through the production area.

"I hear I missed a nice lunch today," he said when Margaret stopped.

"Joney got pizza and salad for everyone."

"I was sorry I already had plans."

After a short conversation, Margaret walked back to her office, gathered up her things, and headed for home. She waved to Joney on her way through the lobby. Joney waved back and then went back to her telephone conversation.

"I'm home," Margaret announced as she walked through her apartment door a short while later.

Mona looked up from one of the couches. Katie jumped off Mona's lap and ran into Fenella's bedroom.

"Has she been causing trouble again?" Margaret asked, frowning after the animal.

"I don't believe so," Mona said. "She was very polite to Ted when he was here."

"I should hope so. I am going to have to get another automatic feeder, though. I can't keep relying on Ted to get here at lunch time every day."

"He'll do his best, but work will probably be a problem at least some days."

Margaret nodded. "He's only a temporary solution to the problem."

"Speak of the devil," Mona said as someone knocked on the door.

Margaret opened it and greeted Ted with a kiss.

"Hello," he said when it ended. "How are you?"

"I'm fine. Surprisingly hungry, considering I had a large lunch."

"I'm starving. I brought a sandwich here with me when I came to feed Katie. I loved eating it while watching the water, but it seems to have been a very long time ago."

"Let me give Katie her dinner and then we can go out somewhere."

Ted nodded. "We'll want to eat quickly. Brady said he'll be sending the updates later today. I want to be back here to discuss them."

"Surely we can talk about them anywhere," Margaret said.

"I suppose so, but your flat is one of my favorite places in the world."

Margaret looked around the beautiful room. "Mine, too. Give me five minutes to get ready and feed Katie."

"I can feed Katie while you change."

She gave him a grateful smile before heading into her bedroom.

When she walked back out a few minutes later, Ted was standing at the door.

"I'm not going to check my emails again until we get back from dinner," he told her. "I'm afraid if the updates come through, I'll be too distracted to eat."

"Let's go somewhere nearby and fast," Margaret suggested as they rode the elevator to the ground floor.

Ted nodded. "I was thinking maybe we could just get pizza or Chinese food and take it back to your flat."

"Not pizza," Margaret laughed. "I had pizza for lunch."

"Chinese? Indian? Or do you want to get sandwiches from the sandwich shop?"

"Let's get Indian. We haven't done that for a while."

There was an excellent Indian restaurant only a short walk away. There, Ted ordered far more food than Margaret thought they could eat. He got everything to go. It didn't take them long to put the order together. Ted and Margaret were on their way back to her flat less than twenty minutes after they'd left.

Ted carried the boxes of food into the kitchen. Margaret got out plates and utensils. A few minutes later, they were sitting across from each other at the table, eating.

"Delicious," Margaret said after a few bites. "Indian food over here tastes very different from Indian food in America."

"Really? I suppose that makes sense, in a way, since I'm certain it tastes different from actual food in India, too."

Margaret nodded. "I hope Brady delivers. I'm really eager to find out where everyone is now."

"While we wait, let's talk about where we think people are," Ted suggested. "It will be interesting to see how our predictions compare to the reality."

"Where do you want to start?" Margaret asked as Mona walked into the room.

She sat down between Margaret and Ted, notebook in hand.

"I really hope that Susie is a good deal happier now," Ted said. "I hope she took over the restaurant and made it even more successful than it had been when Sean was alive."

"That would be nice. Maybe she's found a nice guy, too, one that treats her better than Sean did."

"I would never wish anything awful on anyone, but I'm less concerned about where Nina is now," Ted said with a small shrug.

"I would expect she's divorced, at least," Margaret said. "I can't imagine why Ronald would have stayed with her after everything that happened."

"He stayed with her even though he knew she was cheating. I'm not sure why the murder would make any real difference."

Margaret sighed. "It just feels as if it ought to make a difference."

"So you think Nina is single now?"

"Maybe, or maybe she found someone else. I don't think she's still with Ronald, anyway."

"And what about Ronald?"

"I hope he's found happiness somewhere."

"Maybe he and Susie got together."

Margaret frowned. "I hope not. I'd rather Susie found herself someone who wasn't connected to the case in any way."

"I can understand that," Ted said.

"I just don't want Ronald and Nina to still be together, not unless they got some counseling and worked on their marriage."

"Maybe they did. They had children to consider."

"They won't have done any such thing," Mona said. "But I won't be surprised if they're still together, regardless."

Margaret frowned at her. *Poor Ronald*, she thought.

"Perhaps he's happy enough with things as they are."

Or maybe he murdered Sean and now Nina is afraid to leave him.

Mona chuckled. "I suppose that's possible," she said, sounding as if she didn't think much of the idea.

"Who else?" Margaret asked Ted.

"Ruth?" Ted said. "I hope she's found someone else or learned to live happily on her own."

Margaret nodded. "She seemed really unhappy. I'd almost rather she'd be happy on her own. She didn't have a great track record when it came to picking men to date."

"What about Rick?"

"I hope he's come to realize that he isn't as wonderful as he thought he was. Hopefully he's found another job and is working hard at it."

"Why do I doubt any of that has happened?" Ted asked.

Margaret sighed. "Because Rick didn't seem like the type to learn from his mistakes?"

"Who have I missed? Just Greg?"

"I think so. I'm not sure how I feel about Greg. I suppose I hope his business is still doing well, regardless of what happened to Sean's business."

Ted nodded. "Assuming he didn't kill Sean, I hope he's doing well."

Margaret grinned. "We could put that caveat with everyone. I want them all to be doing well, aside from the person who killed Sean."

"Yeah, but life often isn't fair."

"The one thing that's been bothering me is that Sean was asleep," Margaret said as she put their dishes into the dishwasher.

Ted was busy packing up the leftovers. He paused and then shrugged. "Some people can sleep anywhere."

"Yes, I know, but was Sean one of those people?"

"He must have been, otherwise someone would have commented on how odd it was."

"But I don't think the newspapers asked anyone that question."

"Even if they didn't, Brady must have asked everyone."

Margaret nodded, but she wasn't convinced. "I know you don't have access to the police reports, but you do have access to Brady. Could you just ask him about that?"

Ted nodded. He pulled out his notebook and made a note. "We're going to have lots of questions for him after we get the updates, but I'll include that one."

"I already had lots of questions. I hope the updates answer some of them."

"I have your list of questions for Nina and also your question about Ronald and what he'd wanted to do with his life. Is that all?"

"I think so, although the questions for Nina also apply to Ruth, really."

Ted added that to his notes. "I'm not certain any of your questions will help solve the murder, but they should tell us more about the suspects."

"Will Brady be able to repeat the answers he gets to you?"

"I don't know. He can't tell me anything he learns from police interviews, so maybe not."

Margaret sighed. "When did you last check your emails?"

Ted laughed. "About two minutes ago. Let's have some pudding or take a walk on the promenade, or maybe both."

"All I have here is a few cookies. We could get ice cream and then walk on the promenade," Margaret suggested.

Ted nodded. "Let's do that. Anything is better than sitting around and waiting for the email to arrive."

Margaret put on her shoes and grabbed her handbag. Ted was right behind her when they reached the door. She turned the handle and pulled. The door didn't open.

"That's odd," she said, trying again.

Ted frowned. "That's worrying," he said. "It might be a glitch in the locking mechanism, but it's also a serious fire hazard."

Margaret tried the door again before rummaging through her bag to find her keycard. She held it against the back of the lock. Nothing happened.

"Maybe Ted should check his emails," Mona said from the kitchen doorway.

Margaret frowned at her. "I remember Aunt Fenella saying that this happened once in a while," she said. "She told me to leave it for a minute or two and then try again."

Ted shrugged and then sat down on the nearest couch. He pulled out his phone and tapped on the screen. "Or we could just stay here and read through Brady's email," he said excitedly a moment later.

"I'd really like to know that we aren't trapped in here, though," Margaret said. She tried the door again. It opened normally.

Ted shrugged. "You should have someone from the maintenance department take a look at your locking mechanism. I know it only took a minute or two to clear, but those minutes could be life-threatening in case of a fire."

"I'll do that," Margaret said, glaring at Mona.

Mona walked over and sat next to Ted.

"Why don't we talk in the kitchen?" Margaret suggested. "We could have a few cookies and some tea or coffee while you read what Brady sent."

Ted followed her into the kitchen. Margaret swallowed a laugh as she watched Mona slowly fade from view. Mona reappeared in the kitchen a moment later, sitting on the chair next to the one that Ted had taken.

"Tea? Coffee? Something cold?" Margaret offered.

"Just make a pot of tea and get on with it," Mona snapped.

Margaret hid a grin as she piled chocolate-coated cookies onto a plate.

"Tea sounds good," Ted said. "Do you want any help?"

"I can manage. You can start reading if you want."

"I'm going to start by skimming the entire thing, just in case there are any surprises in there. If he only managed to send us part of the information or something, I'd like to know that in advance."

Margaret nodded before turning her attention to making tea. When she sat down opposite Ted a few minutes later, he was smiling.

"It looks as if Brady covered everyone," he said. "I skimmed too quickly to make sense of what he's said, but it does look as if everyone is there."

"Go ahead then, where does he start?" Margaret asked as she took a cookie.

"He starts with Susie."

Margaret waited while Ted took a sip of tea.

"This will go faster if I don't have to keep asking questions," she said as he put his cup down.

He chuckled. "Sorry, I got distracted by the tea. Let's see what he has to say about Susie."

He scrolled down his phone screen and then looked up at Margaret.

"She's still living in Harper Glen. She's still running the restaurant. She's also still single."

"Is she happy? Is the restaurant still successful? Has she dated any of the other suspects since the murder?"

Ted shrugged. "I can tell you that the restaurant is still successful. Brady reckons it does as much business as it did when Sean was alive, maybe more. Apparently, Susie can be just as generous as he was, but people are less inclined to ask her for help because they all know about Sean's untimely death."

"Is the pizza there still better than Greg's?"

"In Brady's opinion, yes. Apparently, Susie had all the recipes, so nothing has really changed."

"I suppose that's good."

"He says that as far as he can tell, Susie's life isn't all that different now to how it was before Sean's death. She's single, but she seems to live the exact same way she did when she and Sean were married."

"Does that mean she doesn't date?"

Ted scrolled down his screen. "Ah, here it is. Apparently, she hasn't been out with anyone since Sean's death. Brady reckons she either still misses Sean or she's realized that she's happier on her own."

"He treated her so badly, I can't say that I'd blame her for wanting to stay single."

"Do you have any questions about her based on the update?"

Margaret frowned. "I'm trying to decide if she's benefited from Sean's death or not. I think not having to be married to the man is a benefit, but she might not feel the same way."

"Brady does say that Sean had a few life insurance policies that paid out to Susie. Combined, they gave her enough money to pay off the mortgages on both the restaurant and her house. That would suggest that even if the business isn't doing as well, she's still making more profit than they did when Sean was alive."

"Which does give her a motive, then, aside from wanting him dead because he was cheating."

Ted nodded. "Brady talks about Nina and Ronald next."

"At the same time? Does that mean that they're still married?"

Ted shook his head. "Apparently, they got divorced within a year of Sean's death, and it would have been sooner if Ronald could have pushed the paperwork through faster."

"So Ronald filed for divorce?"

"He did. Brady says that Nina seemed so shocked and upset about Sean's death that for months she didn't even seem to realize that Ronald was divorcing her. She didn't get herself an attorney or ask for anything in the divorce. Brady says Ronald ended up insisting on giving her half of the house and a lump sum of money because he felt so bad about everything."

"He's too nice."

"Probably, but from what Brady says, he's quite happy now."

"Oh? Tell me more."

"After the divorce was final, they sold the house and Ronald took a year-long sabbatical from work to go traveling. When he got back to Harper Glen, he brought his new wife with him."

"His new wife?" Margaret and Mona both echoed.

Ted grinned. "Apparently, he met her in Paris, but she's actually French Canadian by birth. She'd been living in Paris for a few years and thinking about moving back to Canada. Ronald managed to persuade her to move to Harper Glen with him instead."

"And they're happy together?"

"From what Brady says, yes. She's a few years older than he is, but apparently she's stunningly beautiful. She owns an import and export business that she runs from Harper Glen now. She and Ronald bought a huge house on the outskirts of town, and they live there with a couple of live-in staff."

"Live-in staff? How luxurious."

"How dreadful," Mona said. "Imagine never being truly alone. Max used to offer to hire someone to live with me and take care of my needs, but I always turned him down."

Ted shrugged. "I'm not certain I'd be comfortable living with people who were being paid to take care of me."

"It isn't likely to be a decision you'll ever have to make," Margaret said.

Ted laughed. "On a police inspector's salary, you're right about that."

"I make decent money at Park's, but not enough to have staff, live-in or otherwise."

"Well, Ronald and his wife have staff. Apparently, they hired a couple. He acts as their chauffer, gardener, and general handyman while his wife cooks and cleans for Ronald and Amelie."

"Amelie? I love that name."

"It's very pretty."

"So Ronald is better off because of Sean's death, but I'm not sure that strengthens his motive. He couldn't have known that Nina would react that way if Sean was murdered."

"Unless killing Sean was what Ronald needed to do in order to empower himself," Mona said.

Margaret stared at her. "*Empower himself?*" she thought.

Mona shrugged. "He probably didn't realize it at the time, but maybe killing Sean made him feel like the master of his own destiny for the first time."

"Maybe," Margaret said doubtfully.

"Maybe what?" Ted asked.

"Sorry, I was thinking out loud," Margaret said as Mona laughed. "I was just wondering if killing Sean gave Ronald more self-confidence, but then I thought otherwise."

"It's possible, but I think it's more likely that Sean's untimely death made Ronald realize that his life was passing by far too quickly. It probably brought on something of a midlife crisis in the man."

Margaret nodded. "So where is Nina now? You said Ronald gave her half of the house and a lump sum."

"He did. She used the proceeds from the sale of the house to buy herself a much smaller house on the opposite side of town. She took a short leave of absence from teaching in the early days after the murder, but eventually went back to it. Brady says that she's been living quietly ever since. He reckons he hasn't heard a single rumor about her in the past ten years."

"Maybe she'd just become more discreet," Mona said.

"Is it possible that she's simply using more discretion?" Margaret asked.

Ted shook his head. "Brady admits that he's been keeping a fairly close eye on the main suspects in the case. He reckons he'd have heard about it if Nina was seeing anyone."

"Who is next, then?" Margaret asked as Mona made a note.

"He talks about Greg next. Apparently, he's still running his restaurant and keeping his head down."

"Is that suspicious?"

Ted shrugged. "Evidently, right after the murder, he offered to buy Susie out. The whole town was talking about it, but according to Brady's sources, he didn't offer nearly enough. Brady was told that Susie more or less laughed in his face when he made the offer."

"Surely he must have known what the business was properly worth."

"Maybe, but maybe he was hoping that Susie didn't."

"So he tried to cheat a grief-stricken widow out of the business that her husband had worked so hard to build."

"That's one way of putting it."

"Is there any other way to put it?"

Ted grinned. "Remember, this is just what Brady heard through the grapevine. It's possible that Greg offered Susie fair market value for the business, but she still declined."

"He needs to ask Susie about the offer."

"Why?"

"What if Greg thought he'd get the business for a really low price if Sean was dead? What if that thought was enough to convince him to kill Sean?"

Ted made a note in his phone. "So ask Susie about the offer that Greg made."

"And maybe ask Greg, too. Not about the offer, exactly, but about why he thought Susie would sell the business to him. Maybe someone told him that Susie wanted to sell the business and was willing to take a low price but couldn't because of Sean."

"Surely, if that were the case, then Greg would have mentioned the conversation when he was questioned," Ted said.

"Not if that conversation was the reason why Greg killed Sean."

Ted nodded. "I'm starting to follow your logic now. Maybe someone wanted to cause some trouble for whatever reason, so he or she told Greg that Susie wanted to get rid of the business but couldn't. Maybe that someone thought that Greg would go and offer to buy

Susie's half of the business or something. It's a bit of a leap to think that the person was trying to get Sean killed."

Margaret nodded. "It won't be easy to find the person, though, if that person now knows that his or her words led to Sean's murder."

"I'm going to run the idea past Brady, anyway. He can decide if he wants to do anything with it."

"Who does that leave?"

"Rick and Ruth."

"Please don't tell me that they ended up together."

Ted laughed. "I didn't mean to imply that. No, they did not end up together."

"So where are they now?"

"Rick moved to Cleveland about a year after the murder. He got a job with a large chain printing company there and is now the district manager for the company, responsible for all of their stores in Ohio and Pennsylvania, including the one that put his little shop out of business."

"Wow, I'm not sure what to say to that."

Ted grinned. "Brady says that he's happy that Rick was finally able to stop blaming everyone else for his problems and start working toward finding solutions. He reckons that the shock of the murder made Rick snap out of what was probably depression."

"I can see that," Margaret said. "He's definitely better off since Sean's murder. Does that mean he had a solid reason for killing him, though?"

"I don't think so," Ted said. "He couldn't have known how he'd feel after Sean's death."

Margaret shrugged. "I hope Ruth is happy now."

"Ruth got remarried about a year after Sean's death," Ted said. "She married a man called Trevor Smith who moved to Harper Glen about six months after Sean died."

"What does Brady say about Trevor?" Mona asked.

It took Margaret a moment to realize why Ted hadn't replied. "What does Brady say about Trevor?"

"He's actually a police detective," Ted said.

"I didn't see that coming," Mona said.

Margaret nodded. "So he and Brady work together?"

"They do. Brady says that Trevor is good at his job and a good judge of character. Based on his marriage to Ruth, he's moved Ruth to the bottom of his list."

"Where was she before?"

Ted shrugged. "I don't think he said."

"But now he thinks she's innocent. Interesting."

"It is interesting."

"And she's better off since Sean's death, too. It seems as if everyone is better off, really."

"The murder sent shockwaves through the community. It made some people realize that life is short and motivated them to do something more with their lives. None of that helps us find the killer, though," Ted said.

Margaret nodded. "We have a list of questions for Brady. Nothing he told you is confidential, right?"

Ted grinned. "You want to share it with the intrepid investigators at Park's?"

"I would like to. They're all eager to hear where everyone is now."

"Go ahead and tell them everything we talked about tonight. Now that we've worked through the entire email, we should talk more, too."

"Give me a minute to think about everything Brady said," Margaret replied. She got up and walked to the counter. While she was making herself another cup of tea, Ted's phone rang.

"Ted Hart," he said into the device.

A moment later, he said, "I'll be right there," and then put the phone down.

"That isn't good news," Margaret said.

"Another car has been stolen. I'll tell you about it tomorrow. We'll talk about Sean, too. I'll probably send Brady a reply before I go to bed, but that will depend on how long I'm out working on the stolen car case."

Margaret walked him to the door and then gave him a quick kiss. "Good luck," she said.

He nodded. "I hope it helps. Love you."

"Love you, too."

She watched him walk to the elevators and then waved as the doors shut in front of him. When she walked back into the kitchen, she smiled at Mona.

"I suppose you want to talk about the suspects," she said.

Mona shook her head. "I have an appointment elsewhere. We'll talk tomorrow," she said before she disappeared in a cloud of purple smoke.

Margaret looked at Katie. "Do you want to talk about the suspects?" she asked.

Katie shook her head and then walked away. Margaret sighed and followed her into the living room. They settled in to watch television together until bedtime.

12

"Good morning," Joney said when Margaret arrived at work the next day. "Please tell me you have updates on the murder investigation. Barring that, I'd love to hear more about the car that was stolen last night. This victim isn't talking to Heather, so I know nothing more than a car was stolen in Douglas."

"That's more than I knew," Margaret laughed. "Ted didn't mention where the car was taken from when he got the call last night."

"Well, that's disappointing."

"Ah, but I do have updates on the suspects in the murder investigation."

"Yes!" Joney said, clapping her hands together. "Is it too soon to take our lunch break?"

Margaret laughed again. "I'm afraid so. I have some tests running in the lab that have to be sorted out. I'll be back at noon."

"I'll be watching the clock."

Margaret was still chuckling as she walked to her office. Then she made her way to her lab and got to work. It was a quarter past twelve when she walked back into the lobby. Arthur, Rachel, and Joney were all waiting for her.

"Where should we go for lunch?" Joney asked as she got to her feet.

"Fridays are supposed to be our day to go somewhere other than the local cafés," Rachel said.

Joney nodded. "What about that little place down the street? I don't think Margaret has been there yet."

"Perfect," Rachel said. "It's only a five-minute drive."

They all piled into Arthur's luxury sedan for the short journey. Once they were all seated with drinks in front of them, Joney looked at Margaret.

"Go on then, tell us everything."

"I'll tell you everything that Ted told me. Then we can talk about what it all means," Margaret said.

Before she could begin, the waiter came back to take their orders. Once that was done, Margaret told them everything she could remember from the conversation the previous evening. When she was finished, she sat back and took a long drink of soda.

"Wow," Rachel said. "I don't know that any of that helps with the murder investigation, but it was fascinating."

Joney nodded. "Is it just me, or does it seem as if everyone is better off without Sean? That sounds really mean, but that's sort of how it felt."

"I said that last night," Margaret told her. "But before we could discuss it, Ted got called in to work."

"Let's talk about each of the suspects in turn," Arthur said. "And keep in mind that I'm late to the party. I only read the original newspaper interviews last night."

"Here we are," the waiter said, putting Joney's lunch in front of her. He quickly distributed the rest of the meals and checked that they had everything before walking away.

"Let's start with Susie," Joney said after her first bite. "She might not be happier, but she's better off financially."

Margaret nodded. "Brady didn't say that she was happy. He said that her life really hasn't changed."

"I hope she's happier," Rachel said.

"I think we all do," Joney said. "But does the fact that nothing has changed mean that she killed him?"

"I'd suggest the opposite," Rachel said. "I think, if she'd killed him, she would have made a lot of changes. Surely, she didn't kill him just to keep doing what she'd been doing for years?"

"Unless she loved everything about her life except the fact that he was in it," Joney said.

Rachel frowned and then nodded. "You could be right about that, I suppose."

"I don't think she did it," Arthur said. "I'm certain she was angry with him for cheating, but I can't see her killing him over it."

"What about Nina?" Joney asked. "Can you see her killing him?"

"I struggled to come up with a motive for Nina," Arthur said. "If she was tired of being involved with the man, she could have just ended things. I can't see any reason why she would have wanted him dead."

"She's probably the person who seems the least happy now that he's gone," Rachel said.

"Brady reported that she's been living quietly in a small house on the outskirts of town since the divorce," Margaret said.

"I wasn't surprised that Ronald divorced her, but I was surprised that she's stayed single," Joney said.

Margaret nodded. "It seems as if Sean's death upset her a great deal."

"Or maybe it's the guilt, eating away at her," Arthur suggested.

"I suppose that's possible," Joney said. "I can't imagine how it would feel to kill someone."

"If she did kill him, why did she want him dead?" Margaret asked. "I think figuring that out might be the key to working out why she's so unhappy now."

"If she didn't kill him, why is she unhappy now?" Rachel asked.

"Maybe she really loved him," Joney said.

"Maybe, but it's been ten years. Surely, even if she'd been madly in love with him, she'd have moved on by now," Rachel argued.

"It sounds as if you think she killed him," Arthur said.

Rachel shrugged. "I'm just speculating, really. What if you thought you had a good reason to kill someone, so you stabbed them to death and then discovered that you didn't really want them dead?"

"You'd probably go into shock and barely even notice when your husband divorced you," Joney said.

Rachel nodded. "I'm not suggesting that I've solved the murder. It's just interesting, that's all."

Margaret nodded. "It is interesting."

"On the other hand, Nina's former husband seems to have benefitted enormously from the murder," Joney said.

"To be fair, Sean didn't have to die in order for Ronald to divorce Nina," Margaret said.

"I guess one question is how much less did the divorce cost Ronald because Nina was still in shock from the murder?" Arthur said.

"He did give her half of the house and a lump sum," Margaret said.

"But what might she have been able to get if she'd fought back?" Joney asked.

Margaret shrugged. "I've no idea."

"Regardless, it seems as if the murder shook him into action," Rachel said. "From what we've been told, he wasn't even considering divorcing Nina before the murder."

"Which is when he should have been thinking about it – while Nina was cheating on him," Joney said. "Once Sean was dead, Nina wasn't cheating any longer."

"It must have been hard for him to watch her mourn for her dead lover, though," Arthur said.

Margaret nodded. "That might have been more difficult than watching her cheat. Maybe he told himself that she was just having a bit of meaningless fun. Maybe it wasn't until Sean was dead that he understood how much Sean had meant to Nina."

"Maybe Ronald did know exactly how much Sean meant to Nina. Maybe that's why Ronald killed him," Rachel said.

"Also a possibility," Margaret admitted.

"I can't understand why Greg would have made a low offer if he wanted to buy the business from Susie after Sean's death," Joney said after a moment. "I mean, if he wanted the business, he should have been prepared to pay the fair market price."

Rachel nodded. "But maybe he's a jerk who thought that Susie didn't know what the business was worth. Or maybe he thought he could get away with making a low offer because Susie was too upset about her husband's murder to pay proper attention to what he was offering."

"Either way, he's not a nice person," Joney said. "But is he a killer?"

"I wondered if someone had told him that Susie wanted to sell the business at any price," Margaret said. "Maybe that conversation drove him to murder."

"What a horrible thought, especially since it wasn't true," Rachel said.

"Maybe it was true," Joney said. "Maybe Susie did want to sell before Sean died. Maybe it was only after his death that she decided she wanted to keep the business for herself."

"In that case, I hope that wasn't the motive for the murder," Rachel said. "Imagine how disappointing it would be to kill someone for nothing."

Margaret shuddered. "What a horrible thought."

"Pudding for anyone?" the waiter asked as he cleared away their empty plates.

"Do you still have the chocolate ice cream cake?" Joney asked.

The waiter nodded.

"Chocolate ice cream cake?" Margaret repeated questioningly.

"It's thin layers of vanilla ice cream between thin layers of chocolate cake," the waiter told her. "We top it with hot fudge and whipped cream."

"That sounds amazing," Margaret said. "I'm sorry I ate so much lunch now."

"We can package the cake for takeaway, but you'd need to put it in a freezer fairly quickly," he replied. "And that wouldn't be good for the hot fudge."

"I'm having the cake," Joney said.

"Me too," Rachel said.

"Okay, I'm convinced," Arthur said.

Margaret sighed. "Make it four," she told the waiter.

As he walked away, her phone buzzed. She smiled as she read the screen.

"Katie has been fed. She has been petted and scratched and told how wonderful she is. She has also been given a few treats. I'm starting to understand why she killed her automatic feeder."

It took only a moment to send a quick "thank you" reply.

"Let's talk about Rick," Rachel said as Margaret put her phone away. "He really turned his life around, didn't he?"

"He did," Margaret agreed.

"But was that because Sean's death made him realize that life is short, or because he felt so guilty about killing Sean that he decided that he needed to do something with his life to make amends?" Joney asked.

"Or did something else happen to make him decide to change?" Rachel suggested.

"That's also possible," Margaret said.

"Did Brady say whether Rick is married or involved with anyone now?" Joney asked.

Margaret thought back to the conversation from the previous evening. "I don't think he did. And now I really want to know."

"You said he moved to Cleveland about a year after Sean's death. Maybe he'd met someone during that year. Or maybe something else happened that made him want to make a change," Joney said.

Margaret nodded. "I'll have Ted ask Brady if he knows why Rick suddenly changed his life. It might have been the murder, but it might have been something else entirely."

"And find out if he's single or seeing someone," Rachel added.

"I will," Margaret promised, making a note for herself.

"Which just leaves Ruth," Joney said. "Who is now married to a police detective and is possibly above suspicion."

"Just because Brady doesn't think she did it doesn't mean I agree," Rachel said stoutly.

"So you still think she's a suspect?" Margaret asked.

"Of course she's still a suspect," Rachel said. "But I will admit that she's moved down my list a bit. Brady is there. He knows all of the suspects personally. If he doesn't think she killed Sean, he's probably right."

"I'm inclined to agree," Joney said. "I'm actually quite happy that she found someone else. I still want to know if she's ever spoken to her oversharing friend again, though."

"I'll ask Ted to ask Brady," Margaret said.

"So where does that leave us?" Arthur asked. "Should we make a list of suspects?"

"Ice cream cakes for everyone," the waiter said. He put plates in front of each of them. As he walked away, Margaret counted the thin layers.

"Twelve layers of deliciousness," she said with a happy sigh before she picked up her fork.

"Who is at the top of everyone's list, then?" Joney asked as everyone ate.

Margaret shrugged. "That's a really tough question. I'm leaning toward Greg, but that might be because I'm angry at him for trying to cheat Susie out of a fair price for her business."

Joney nodded. "I'm with you on that. Let's put him at the top of the list."

"Then maybe Nina next," Rachel suggested. "Mostly because of how she reacted to his death."

"I'll agree with both of those," Arthur said. "I want to put Rick next. Maybe killing Sean was the catalyst that got him to act."

"What a horrible thought," Joney said.

Arthur shrugged. "We don't know why he changed otherwise."

"Okay, he can be third on the list," Rachel said. "Let's put Ronald next, then Susie, and lastly, Ruth. I'd happily switch Ruth and Susie, really. I don't think Susie killed her husband."

"But Brady doesn't think Ruth did it," Joney said. "And he's an expert at this sort of thing."

"Okay, leave Ruth last and Susie just above her," Rachel said. "Are we all in agreement?"

The others nodded. Rachel grinned at Margaret.

"You can tell Ted to tell Brady that we've talked it through and reached our conclusions based on next to nothing. He really ought to arrest Greg immediately."

Margaret laughed. "I'll let Ted know."

They chatted for a bit longer about the case while they finished their cake, then they headed back to the office. Margaret spent the afternoon working on a report about her latest tests. Every Friday the entire team went to a nearby pub for a drink after work. Margaret joined the others for the short walk just after five.

"We solved your murder over lunch; let's solve the car thefts over happy hour," Rachel said as they took seats around a corner table.

"We could do it if we knew more," Joney said. "The most recent victim wouldn't talk to the newspaper."

"He changed his mind," Rachel said. "I read the article on the website before we came here." She glanced at Arthur. "After five, of course, when I was no longer working hard."

Arthur laughed. "You know I'm really strict about such things."

Rachel nodded. "It really was after five, though."

"What did the article say?" Margaret asked.

"The man whose car was stolen is Joe Ball," Rachel said. "He drove home from work, parked his car on the street near his house, and went inside. When he came back out half an hour later, it was gone."

"Where does Joe live?" Joney asked. "Central Douglas?"

"No, he's farther out." Rachel named a street.

Joney frowned. "Don't the houses there have driveways and garages? Why did he park on the street?"

"He said in the interview that he knew he was going right back out again, so he thought it would be easier to leave the car on the street," Rachel replied.

"I can understand not putting it away in a garage, but I can't see why he couldn't put it on the driveway," Arthur said.

Rachel shrugged. "Heather asked him about it a couple of times. He just kept repeating the same thing over and over again."

"That's odd," Joney said.

"What sort of car did he have?" Margaret asked.

"Unlike the previous two, Joe's car was new only two years ago. He told Heather that he's still making payments on it," Rachel replied.

Margaret frowned. "What happens to his payments if the car isn't recovered?"

"Presumably, his car insurance would pay off the balance," Rachel said. "He'd be left without a car, though, and he'd probably be out of pocket because he'll have been making payments for the past two years."

Arthur nodded. "The car might be worth a bit more than he still owes, but new cars lose a lot of their value as soon as they're driven off the lot."

"What else did you learn from the paper's website?" Joney asked Rachel.

"Not much. Joe insisted that he'd locked the car, but Heather got him to admit that it was remotely possible that he'd forgotten. He also said that he'd left a jacket and some other things in the back of the car. He was vague when Heather asked him to list the other things, though."

"He probably isn't certain," Arthur said. "There are all manner of things in the back of my car. A jacket, a box of tissues, one of my wife's shoes, a snow brush that I've never had to use. There are probably other things, too."

"Why only one of your wife's shoes?" Rachel asked.

Arthur laughed. "She changed out of her high heels after an event once and left both shoes in the back of my car. A few days later, she remembered that they were there, but she could only find one of them. She thinks the other one slid under the seats and got stuck. Anyway, she took out the one that she'd found and decided to look for the other one later. And then we both forgot all about it until right now. I shall have to go hunting for it this weekend."

"I have a lot of stuff in the back of my car, too," Stan said. "There may even be a few toys left over from when the children were small. I've been driving the same car for fifteen years now. Stuff just seems to accumulate."

"Did Heather say anything about Joe? What does he do for a living? Is he married? She must have been able to get some information out of him," Joney said.

Rachel shrugged. "He works for one of the banks. He moved to the island about a year ago to work for them. He's single and isn't entirely certain he likes the island, but until his car was stolen, he was enjoying living somewhere safer than London, where he'd been before."

"I'd bet he didn't leave things in his car when he parked it in London," Arthur said.

Everyone laughed.

While they finished their drinks, they talked for a while longer about cars and the things that people leave in them. Then they all walked back to the office together to get their cars.

"See you all on Monday," Rachel said. "Ring me if Brady solves the case between now and then," she told Margaret.

"I can't see that happening, but I'll ring you all," Margaret promised. "Unless it happens on Sunday night."

"I suppose that's fair," Rachel said, laughing.

Margaret waved to everyone as she drove out of the parking lot. When she reached her apartment building, she spotted Ted's car parked outside. When she emerged from the elevator on the top floor, he was leaning against the wall outside of her door.

"You have a key," she reminded him as she approached.

He nodded. "But that's so that I can get Katie her lunch, not so that I can just let myself in whenever I want."

After a quick kiss, Margaret opened her door.

"You can just let yourself in, though," she said. "But maybe text me and let me know that you've done so. Otherwise, I might not realize that you're here and start screaming when I see you."

Ted chuckled. "Or maybe I'll just wait outside the door for you to get home."

"That's probably safer," Margaret said with a laugh.

"What do you want to do for dinner?" Ted asked.

"Anything, really."

"This is going to sound odd, but there's a restaurant I didn't know existed not far from here that I'd really like to try."

"Okay."

"That's it? Just 'okay'? I was expecting questions."

Margaret grinned at him. "And you're dying to tell me more, so go ahead."

"I wouldn't put it that way, but I'm going to tell you anyway."

Margaret laughed. "Darling, tell me about the restaurant you want to try."

Ted grinned broadly. "If you insist. You know last night I got called away because of another stolen car."

Margaret nodded.

"On my way to the victim's house, I passed this little restaurant that I didn't know was there. It's called Like Home and the sign said, 'Homemade Food with a Twist,' which intrigued me."

"Okay, now I'm intrigued, too."

"So let's go there."

Margaret changed out of her work clothes while Ted got Katie her dinner. Then they headed down to Ted's car.

"Can you tell me anything about the third stolen car?" she asked as Ted pulled away from the promenade.

"Not really. The victim gave Heather an interview, though."

"Yeah, Rachel was telling us some of what he said when we were at the pub."

"He didn't tell me much more than he told Heather. He probably left the car unlocked. People often do."

"Maybe they'll be more careful now that three cars have been stolen."

"Maybe."

Ted pulled his car into the small parking lot in front of the restaurant. Margaret read the sign and then shrugged.

"It could be good," she said, trying not to sound doubtful.

The building was small, and the exterior needed a coat of paint. The windows looked streaky, as if someone had cleaned them badly some days earlier.

Ted frowned. "It looked better after dark. We can go somewhere else."

"We're here. We may as well try it."

"Are you certain you want to go in there?"

Margaret laughed. "If it doesn't look clean inside, we'll just order toast or something that feels safe."

Ted shook his head. "If it doesn't look clean inside, I'll get the station to ring me with an emergency."

"That works for me."

They walked across the parking lot. Ted pulled on the door.

Margaret took a deep breath and then walked into the building.

"This is not what I was expecting," Ted said in Margaret's ear.

She nodded. They'd walked into a small foyer. The carpet looked new and the walls had clearly been painted recently. A young woman greeted them with a smile.

"Good evening. Table for two?" she asked.

Ted nodded.

"Right this way," she said, picking up two menus and then walking through the door behind the hostess stand.

Ted and Margaret followed her into a small dining room. The floor was tiled and again, the walls looked as if they'd just recently been painted. Everything appeared to be spotlessly clean. There were no more than a dozen tables, but only two of them had customers sitting at them.

"Is this okay?" the woman asked as she stopped at a table for two against a wall.

"This is fine," Ted told her.

"Great. Your server will be right with you." She put the menus on the table and walked away as Margaret and Ted took seats.

"This is much nicer than I was expecting," Margaret said in a whisper.

Ted nodded. "I'd feel better if it were busier, though."

Margaret nodded. "It does feel quite empty in here."

She picked up her menu and read through the various options. Everything on it seemed to be what she would consider comfort food. "It all sounds good," she said to Ted.

"We've eaten here a dozen times since they opened and we've never had a bad meal," a man a few tables away said.

The woman with him nodded. "We're enjoying coming here as much as we can before everyone else on the island finds out about it and it gets busy."

Both members of the couple on the other side of the small room nodded.

"The chicken casserole is my favorite," the man said. "I'd eat it every day if I could."

Ted grinned. "Maybe this was a good choice after all."

A moment later, the woman who'd seated them returned.

"Okay, so I'm Debbie and now I'm your server, "she said with a grin. "It was supposed to be my sister, but she had to run home to see to her son. He fell and banged his head on something, and her husband is panicking."

"Oh dear. I hope he's okay," Margaret said.

"Oh, he'll be fine. He's seven and he's totally fearless. That means he gets banged up a lot. He never gets badly hurt, though. Last week he almost broke his arm, but it ended up just being a bit of a sprain. The week before that, he knocked out a tooth, but the dentist said it was about to fall out anyway. He's accident-prone, but he leads a charmed life."

Margaret and Ted both laughed.

"So are you ready to order? Do you want to order drinks first? I can't believe I've forgotten how to do this properly. Can I get you something to drink?" Debbie asked, looking a bit flustered.

They ordered soft drinks.

"What's the best thing on the menu?" Ted asked her as she wrote down their drink order.

"Ah, that's a tough question. My favorite is the beef stew, but my sister would say the chicken casserole. It's our dad in the kitchen. He raised us after our mum passed away when I was only a baby. He didn't know how to cook anything when she died, so he bought a bunch of recipe books and taught himself how to make lots of different things."

"Wow, good for him," Margaret said.

Debbie nodded. "After a while, he realized that he loved to cook, and he started talking about quitting his job and going to work in a restaurant. He never did it, though, because he wanted to be home with us as much as he could, and restaurants are open on nights and weekends. It wasn't until my sister and I both graduated from uni that he finally felt as if he could chase his own dreams. He started working as an assistant chef at one of the restaurants on the promenade, but when his father passed away, he inherited almost enough to get his own place. My sister and I both contributed our savings to make this place a reality. Now we all work here and we're all hoping we aren't going to go broke, but even if we do, we're all really proud of ourselves."

"You should be," Ted said. "Congratulations."

She shrugged. "Let me get your drinks. And since my sister isn't here, I recommend the beef stew."

Everyone in the small room chuckled as the woman disappeared through a door on the back wall of the small room.

"The beef stew is excellent," the man at the next table said. "They serve it with some herb bread that is just wonderful."

"That does sound good," Margaret said.

Ted nodded. "But so does the chicken casserole."

"Which comes with dumplings," the man told them. "They're sort of a bit spicy, but light as a feather."

"Let's get one of each and share," Margaret suggested.

Ted nodded. "That's a better idea than my idea."

"What was your idea?" Margaret asked.

"I was just going to order both," he said with a chuckle.

"Oh, don't do that," one of the women said. "Your server is also the pastry chef. She does amazing puddings."

"Dad doesn't like to make puddings," Debbie said as she emerged from the kitchen with drinks for Ted and Margaret. "I started making them as soon as I was old enough to read the recipes. I don't like to cook, but I love to bake."

Ted and Margaret ordered their meals.

"It won't be long," Debbie promised before she disappeared through the door again.

A moment later, a man walked through the door from the foyer. He looked around and then seated himself at a table across the room from Margaret and Ted. As he sat down with his back to the rest of the room, Ted squeezed Margaret's hand.

"Joe Ball," he mouthed at her.

"The third victim?" she whispered back.

He nodded. Debbie was back a moment later.

"Joe, I didn't know you were here," she said as she approached his table.

"I just got here."

"What can I get you, then?"

He shrugged. "I'm celebrating tonight."

"Celebrating?"

"Don't you read the local paper's website?"

"I do, but not while I'm at work."

Joe laughed. "My car got stolen last night."

"And you're laughing?"

He shrugged. "I'm behind on my payments. Now I don't have to worry about making them any longer."

"But what will you do without a car?"

"I'll be fine. I can walk to work, and I can walk here. Where else do I need to go?"

He ordered a cup of coffee and the chicken casserole. As Debbie walked away, Margaret looked at Ted.

"He's quite happy that his car is gone," she said in a low voice.

Ted nodded. "Which isn't exactly what he said last night."

"Interesting."

A few minutes later, another couple walked into the restaurant. It was obvious that everyone else in the building knew them. They said a few words to everyone before selecting a table.

"Hey," Debbie said when she emerged from the back and saw them. "How are you guys tonight?"

In the small room, everyone got to hear about the woman's migraine that had finally gone and the man's back problems that didn't seem to be improving. Debbie took their order and then checked that Ted and Margaret didn't need anything else to drink.

"Your food will be right out," she promised before she walked away. She was back only a few minutes later, with two steaming bowls.

"Beef stew and chicken casserole," she said as she put them on the table. "Our herb spice bread goes with the beef stew," she added as she put a plate with a small loaf of bread down. "Can I get you anything else right now?"

"No, thanks. It all looks and smells wonderful," Margaret said.

Debbie grinned. "Shout if you need anything."

Ted picked up his fork and took a bite of beef stew. Margaret tried the chicken casserole.

"It's really good," Ted said.

"This is delicious," Margaret told him. She cut a slice from the small loaf of bread and took a bite. "And this is so good I can't even tell you," she said with a small moan.

Ted cut a slice and tried a bite. "I think I have a new favorite restaurant," he said.

Margaret nodded. "No wonder everyone in here is a regular."

As she took another bite, another man walked in from the foyer. He looked around the room and then smiled nastily.

"I knew I'd find you here," he said to Joe. "How much longer are you going to be using my garage?"

13

Ted frowned and stopped eating.

Joe looked up from his phone and sighed. "I told you that I was going to need to use it for a week or two."

"Yeah, it's been a week or nearly," the man snapped.

"You said I could use it for a fortnight. I have another week."

"Something has come up. I need it tonight."

Joe shook his head. "I put some stuff in there. I can't relocate it by tonight."

"You're going to have to. I need to get into my garage."

"I've paid you for the use of the garage for a fortnight."

"Yeah, but the stuff I'm getting tonight is worth more than what you've paid me. I need to get it tucked away before anyone takes any interest in it, if you know what I mean."

Ted and Margaret exchanged glances.

"How much space do you need? I mean, I'm not using the entire garage," Joe said. "Maybe we can find a compromise."

The other man shrugged. "We might be able to compromise. I'm not trying to be difficult, but things change, you know?"

Joe nodded. "I know what you mean, but I'm sure we can make it work. Do you want to meet me at the garage in an hour or so? You can see what I've put in it, and then we can talk."

The other man hesitated for a moment. "Yeah, we can do that."

"Do you want to join me for dinner?" Joe asked.

The man frowned and then shook his head. "The wife is expecting me. I'll see you at the garage in an hour."

Ted pulled out his phone and sent a text message. Margaret cut herself another slice of bread while he was busy.

"I'll see you there," Joe said as the man turned around to leave.

"Don't be late," the man snapped.

Joe chuckled. "You know I have to have pudding."

The man turned around and grinned at Joe. "You can't eat here and not have pudding," he agreed before spinning back around and exiting the room.

"We might have to skip pudding," Ted said to Margaret.

"Can we get something to go?" she asked.

"For takeaway, you mean?"

Margaret nodded. "That."

"I suppose we could. We need to be out of here before Joe leaves, though. Ideally well before, so I can take you home before I follow him."

"You don't have to take me home. I'll stay in the car and just watch."

Ted shrugged. "We'll see how things go. For now, eat up."

Margaret didn't need any encouragement to keep eating. The food was excellent. When Debbie next walked past, Ted asked for pudding menus. She gave them the menus as she cleared away their empty plates. Joe was still waiting for his dinner.

"I want a piece of the chocolate brownie pie," Margaret said. "I'm not sure what it is, but it sounds delicious."

"'Warm brownie baked inside a chocolate cookie crust,'" Ted read from the menu. "That does sound good."

"Are you getting the same thing?"

He shook his head. "I thought I'd get a slice of Bakewell tart."

Debbie was back a moment later to take their order. Ted didn't say anything about having the desserts to go, so Margaret didn't mention it.

A few minutes later, Debbie delivered their desserts before taking Joe his dinner.

Margaret took a bite of her pie and sighed happily. "I want this every day for the rest of my life," she said.

Ted grinned. "This is excellent, too. Do you want a bite?"

"No, thanks. I'm not a huge fan of almonds. Or were you just offering because you want a bite of mine?"

"I wouldn't say no to trying a bite of yours."

Margaret chuckled and then pushed her plate toward him. "You're very lucky that I'm quite full. You may have a small bite."

Debbie was back a few minutes later. "What else can I get for you?" she asked as she cleared away the dessert plates.

"Just the bill, please," Ted said.

She nodded. "It won't be a minute," she promised before she walked over and had a short conversation with Joe.

He hadn't quite finished his dinner, but that didn't stop him from ordering a slice of Victoria sponge for dessert. Ted had his wallet out when Debbie returned. He quickly counted out what was needed for the check and handed it to her.

"We will definitely be back," he told her.

Debbie grinned. "Tell a friend," she suggested.

"I'm going to tell all of my friends," Ted replied. "Or maybe just a select few, actually. I'd hate for it to get too busy in here."

Debbie laughed. "We need it to get busier, but not too much busier. Especially not if my sister is going to rush home every time her husband rings."

Ted kept his head down and Margaret between him and Joe as the pair left the restaurant. When they got outside, they climbed into Ted's car.

"What now?" Margaret asked.

"Now I should take you home, but I don't want to risk missing Joe when he leaves."

"I promise to do exactly as I'm told."

Ted chuckled. "You just have to stay in the car. I have a sneaking suspicion I know exactly what we're going to find in Joe's friend's garage."

"Three stolen cars?"

"That seems quite likely. I was able to get a constable here in time to follow the friend. It seems he owns a large commercial garage on a nearby industrial estate. The constable reckons that there is room for half a dozen cars inside the garage."

"So plenty of room for the cars Joe has stolen and whatever stolen property his friend is taking possession of tonight."

"We don't know for certain that he's going to be taking possession of stolen property," Ted said.

Margaret laughed. "It sure sounded like it to me."

Ted nodded. "And to me. Someone is investigating now. Joe's friend, Bruce, made a quick stop at the garage and then went home, presumably to get his dinner. Someone will let me know if and when he leaves the house again."

"This is exciting and also scary."

"Do you want me to take you home?"

"Not if it means you might miss something."

Ted looked as if he wanted to argue, but then he sighed. "And there's Joe. It looks as if he got his pudding to take away."

The man had just walked out of the building, carrying a small box that was just the right size for a piece of cake or pie. He walked across the parking lot and then turned to follow the sidewalk.

"How long will it take him to walk to the garage?" Margaret asked.

"It's probably a fifteen-minute walk away," Ted said. "I thought he might get a taxi, but I suppose he could walk."

"We aren't going to try to follow him on foot, are we?"

"No, but he is," Ted said, nodding toward the man who'd just stepped out of the shadows.

Margaret recognized him as one of the constables she'd met at a recent party. He was wearing dark clothes and carrying a leash. The leash was attached to a very large brown dog who looked excited to be going for an early evening walk. They followed the sidewalk past the restaurant in the same direction that Joe had gone.

"What now?" Margaret asked as Ted started his engine.

"Now we're going to drive over to the garage. The constable will let us know where Joe goes. We need to try to find a place to park where we can see and hear as much as possible."

Margaret didn't dare look around as Ted pulled out of the parking lot and turned left. Somewhere behind them, Joe was being followed by a huge dog and an experienced constable. The drive to the garage didn't take long. It was next to a small warehouse that had several parking spaces outside. Ted pulled his car into one of them.

"And now we just sit here?" Margaret asked.

Ted shook his head. "We're too obvious in the car. We need to get out of sight."

"How do we do that?"

"We're going to take a stroll around the garage. The constable who followed Bruce here said that there are several windows at the back. We might be able to stand next to one of them and at least see what's happening inside."

"Why would you put windows in a garage where you plan to store stolen property?" Margaret asked in a whisper as they got out of the car.

Ted looked around the deserted industrial park. "Bruce didn't have the garage built – it was already here. He's been renting it for about six months now. I suspect it works well enough for his purposes. There isn't anything behind the garage except empty fields."

They walked along the side of the building and then slowly began to make their way along its back. There were only a few windows, and they were spread out across the expanse of the building. As they passed the first one, Margaret saw that it was covered in a thick film.

Ted nodded toward it. "That will stop people from seeing in, but still let in some light."

"Are they all covered?" Margaret asked.

"We're going to find out."

There were four windows in total, and they were all covered in the thick film. When they reached the other end of the building, Margaret frowned.

"Now what? We won't be able to see anything from back here."

"You aren't supposed to be looking," Ted said with a small chuckle.

Margaret flushed. "You know what I meant."

"I did. You meant exactly what you said," Ted teased. "Let's see what's along this side of the building."

Halfway along the side of the building, they found another window. It was small, but there was no film across it.

"It looks as if Bruce missed this one," Ted whispered.

Margaret peered into the dark garage. "I can't see anything."

Ted nodded. "But once Bruce turns on some lights, we should be able to see a lot more."

"Will he be able to see us, though?"

"Not if we're careful."

They spent the next half hour sitting on the ground waiting to see what was going to happen next.

"Thank goodness it's June," Margaret said as a cool breeze blew past them.

Ted nodded. "I should have taken you home. We had plenty of time."

"But we didn't know that we had plenty of time."

"No, but you really aren't..." He stopped when his phone buzzed silently. He read the screen and grinned. "It's showtime," he said. "Bruce just turned into the industrial estate. Joe was waiting for him at the entrance. They should be here soon."

A few minutes later, Margaret saw headlights approaching. She shrank back against the building, trying to make herself invisible. The car stopped and she heard a door slam. A moment later, lights went on inside the garage. Margaret got up and peeked in the window before immediately dropping back down to the ground.

"There are three cars in there," she told Ted. "And I'm pretty sure one of them is Tim's."

Ted did his own quick look through the window before he sat back down next to Margaret. As he sat down, Margaret could hear voices drifting toward them from the parking spaces in front of the warehouse.

"Stolen cars aren't easy to get rid of." Margaret was pretty sure that was Bruce's voice.

"I get that, but they have to be worth something." *And that has to be Joe,* she thought.

"Not much. Maybe a couple of hundred pounds each."

"Maybe a couple of hundred for the oldest one, but the second one is newer and the third is practically new."

"Yeah, but we have two choices with stolen cars. We can try to get them off the island to sell them, or we can just break them up for parts. The older two are only good for parts. It isn't worth the risk or expense to try to get them off the island. We can try to get the third one away. It's got some value across, but the expense of getting it there will eat up any profit on our end."

There was a short silence before Joe spoke again.

"I'll take a thousand for all three."

"Six hundred."

"Eight hundred."

"Seven hundred, and I won't go any higher."

Joe sighed. "I should argue, but I really want to be rid of them. I had no idea it would be so difficult to shift them."

"I assume it's easier back in London."

"I don't know. I never stole cars back in London."

"No? How'd you learn to do it, then?"

Joe laughed. "You can learn everything online these days."

"Yeah? Well, you should have done more research while you were on there. Stealing cars is a dumb idea on the island."

"Yeah, I found that out, but it doesn't matter. I just needed to get rid of mine, really."

"One of them is yours?"

"Yeah, didn't you know?"

"Nope. You stole your own car?"

"Yeah."

"Why?"

"I'm three months behind on the payments. Now the insurance will pay out and clear my debt. Once that happens, I can buy another new one."

"So why take three?"

"So that the police don't suspect me of being involved, of course. If mine was the only car that was taken, they might suspect me."

"You should have taken other cars like yours – newer ones."

"I would have, but they're a lot harder to steal. The videos online only showed me how to take older cars, like the first one I took. I got lucky with the second, because the owner left it unlocked with the keys inside."

"People are dumb."

Joe laughed. "You can say that again."

"Ah, here comes my delivery. Thanks for staying to help."

"No problem. I'm happy to do it."

Margaret could see the large truck that was slowly approaching the garage. It drove inside. She and Ted both stood up and peered through the window.

"And that looks very much like stolen property," Ted said as Joe, Bruce, and a third man began to unload boxes off the back of the truck.

"What now?" Margaret asked as she sat back down.

"Now the fun starts," Ted said. He tapped on his phone screen. Less than thirty seconds later, she could hear sirens.

Someone inside the garage shouted an expletive. Margaret got back up and watched as Joe ran toward the open garage door.

Bruce and the third man seemed to be trying to put everything back into the truck. As Joe ran away, the first marked police car arrived. There were three more behind that one. They parked across the entrance to the garage as the two men inside exchanged glances and then shrugged.

"Let's go," Ted said, getting to his feet.

He and Margaret walked to the front of the building. Bruce and his associate were standing next to the truck. As soon as Bruce saw Ted, he started talking.

"Ah, you must be a police inspector, then. I can explain everything," he said.

"Go ahead, then," Ted said.

"I'm Bruce King. This is my garage. I came down tonight to check on it, and while I was here, this man drove his truck into the garage." He nodded at the man next to him. "I tried to tell him that he was in the wrong place, but he wouldn't listen."

Ted looked at the other man. "Is that true?" he asked.

The other man looked at Bruce and then shook his head. "He hired me to pick up a truck at the Sea Terminal and drive it here. I don't know what's in it. I'm just doing a job."

Ted looked around the garage. "Mr. King, I think we have another problem," he said. "The cars in this garage, the garage that you said was yours, have all been reported stolen."

Bruce frowned. "Ah, yes, I can explain that, too. I recently allowed a friend of mine to use the garage. He said he needed a place to keep a few cars for a week or two. I never for one moment imagined that he was going to be stealing those cars."

"And your friend's name is?" Ted asked.

"Joe Ball," Bruce said.

Margaret sighed. *No honor among thieves*, she thought. It wasn't that she'd wanted Bruce to lie, but he might have at least pretended that he didn't want to get his friend in trouble before he told Ted Joe's name.

Another car pulled up. Mark Hammersmith climbed out. He was another Douglas-based inspector and one of Ted's friends.

"What do we have here, then?" he asked Ted.

"Three stolen cars for a start," Ted replied.

Mark sighed. "Bruce, Bruce, Bruce, what did I tell you about stealing cars?"

"Mark, you should know me well enough to know that I would never steal a car on this island. There isn't any profit in it," Bruce said.

Mark chuckled. "So where did they come from?"

"My friend, Joe Ball, put them here. I believe he was simply trying to get out of having his own car repossessed."

"I might believe all of that, but what about the truck?" Mark asked.

"I believe the driver is a bit lost," Bruce said. "Isn't that right?" he asked the driver.

The man stared at him for a moment. "Er, maybe."

Mark walked over to the truck. The back was still open. He looked at the boxes inside. "It's a shipment of designer handbags," he said. "Still in their original packaging. They were probably on their way to a shop at Tynwald Mills."

"Perhaps the driver's sat nav got confused," Bruce said.

Mark grinned. "That's one possibility," he said. He turned around and looked at the constables. "Take them both to the station. We'll get things sorted there."

"Mark, please. I have other things to do tonight," Bruce protested.

"I did, too," Mark said. "But now I'm stuck with this, so you're stuck with me."

He turned to the nearest constable. "Take him in. I'll be there shortly."

As the two men were escorted out of the garage, Mark walked over to Ted.

"It's a good thing most criminals do stupid things, isn't it?" Mark asked.

Ted chuckled. "Joe will be sorry he didn't pay more attention to the other diners in the restaurant tonight."

"It was foolish of both of them to have that sort of conversation in a public place," Mark said.

"And now we've cracked the car theft case and made two bonus arrests."

Mark laughed. "Bruce gets arrested at least twice a year. He'll probably get a few months inside for this one, but he'll be back out and back to his old tricks in no time. I suspect this associate is from across. He'll just get shipped back."

"What about Joe?" Margaret asked.

"The cars have been recovered. He could get some jail time, but he probably won't. His biggest problem will be that his car will probably get repossessed," Mark said.

"Except he works for one of the banks," Ted said. "And most of them have strict codes of conduct for their staff. He might find himself out of a job when word gets out."

"Maybe no one will find out," Margaret said.

"Hello, hello," a loud voice said. "What do we have here?" Heather walked toward them, a huge smile on her face.

"Good evening," Mark said. "No comment."

Heather laughed. "Those are the three cars that were stolen in Douglas in the past week. You must be delighted to have found them. Was this your excellent detective work, Inspector Hammersmith?"

"No comment," Mark said.

"In that case, I'm going to assume that it was the work of Inspector Hart. I am surprised to see his girlfriend here, though. Have you joined the police now, Ms. Woods?"

Margaret sighed. "No comment."

Heather laughed. "Does anyone want to talk about the truck full of stolen property sitting in between the stolen cars? I don't suppose you'll tell me who owns the garage, will you? I can find out, but that will take time."

"You should probably get started, then," Mark said.

Heather shook her head. "You should want this story told properly. If you won't comment, then I'll simply have to speculate wildly."

"You do that," Mark said. "I can't wait to read the result."

Heather glared at him for a moment. "It will be on the website within the hour," she snapped before she turned and walked away.

Mark shook his head. "I miss the good old days when Dan Ross was the only annoying reporter on the island. He wouldn't have bothered to come down here at this hour of the night. He'd have just rung me later and asked what had happened."

"And you would have just said no comment," Margaret guessed.

Mark shrugged. "I might have given him a bit of information, depending on how the investigation was progressing. I always tried to work with him when I could, but now he's reporting on lost puppies and school sports days while Heather gets all the really interesting stories."

"One of these days she's going to get that really big story that will get her a job with one of the big papers across," Ted said. "I keep hoping it will be soon."

Mark nodded. "And here's the crime scene team, ready to start dusting for prints and searching for evidence. We should get out of the way."

As they walked back toward Mark's car, Ted told him everything that had happened while he and Margaret had been at the site. He'd just finished when Ted's phone buzzed.

"Joe was picked up at home and taken to the station. He was told that we just had a few more questions about last night," he told Mark after he'd read the screen.

Mark grinned. "I'm looking forward to talking to him."

"Yeah, I'd really like to be there."

Mark looked at Margaret. "Take her home and then meet me at the station. We can talk to him together," he told Ted.

"I'll be there in half an hour."

Mark shrugged. "Take your time. I don't mind keeping Joe waiting for a bit."

As Mark got into his car and drove away, Margaret and Ted walked back to his car.

"That was interesting," Margaret said as he started the engine.

"Indeed. I'm sorry to just be taking you home and leaving you, but I do want to be there when Joe is questioned."

"I understand. I'd love to be a fly on the wall for that myself."

"If you can turn into a fly, I'd be more than happy to include you."

"I don't think I'd want to be able to turn myself into a fly. I'd probably get stuck in a spider's web in the first two minutes. I hate spiders."

Back at Promenade View, Ted walked Margaret to her door. He kissed her several times just inside her apartment.

"I really do have to go," he said between kisses.

"Yes, I know," she replied eventually.

"I'll see you tomorrow," he said. "It's Saturday, and I shouldn't have to work. Let's plan on spending the day together."

"After you sleep in, right?"

Ted laughed. "I'm going to have a late night tonight. I will want to lie in. I'll be here around midday. We can get lunch and then maybe go to Port Erin to walk on the beach or something."

"That sounds good. I'll see you around noon tomorrow."

"And who knows, maybe I'll have something back from Brady by then. He said he was going to start interviewing all of the suspects again immediately. Maybe our line of questioning has already led to a confession."

Margaret laughed. "That would be good news, but I can't see it happening. The killer has gotten away with it for ten years. He or she isn't going to confess now."

Ted shrugged. "Maybe someone else will start talking. Maybe someone else knows more than he or she admitted ten years ago."

"Maybe you should go."

She kissed him one more time and then opened the door and almost pushed him out. He chuckled.

"I love you," he said.

"I love you, too."

She watched him walk to the elevators before shutting the door. As she switched on the lights, she noticed a small ball that was slowly bouncing across the floor. Every time it bounced, it got slightly larger. By the time it was right in front of Margaret, it was nearly as tall as she was. After a loud clapping noise, the ball cracked and then fell to the ground in pieces. Mona was standing inside, looking somewhere shaken up.

"The bounces were harder than you'd been expecting," Margaret guessed.

"You remember how much I disliked rolling," Mona said. "This was supposed to be better. I'm not certain it was." She stepped out of the remains of the ball and then looked at the floor. A few snaps of her fingers made the pieces of ball disappear.

"Tell me about the car thief, then," Mona said as she sank down onto the nearest chair.

"What makes you think I know anything about the car thief?" Margaret asked.

"It's all over the newspaper website. Heather even mentioned that she'd seen you at the scene where the cars were all found."

Margaret frowned. She grabbed her laptop and opened it.

"I hope Ted won't be in any trouble," she said after she'd read the article.

"He'll be able to smooth things over with the Chief Constable," Mona said. "He did find the stolen cars, after all. But how did he manage that?"

"For once, he was simply in the right place at the right time."

Margaret told her great aunt about their dinner and the overheard conversation. Then she told her everything that had happened at Bruce's garage.

"Next time something that exciting is happening, let me know," Mona said. "I would love to have been there."

"How do I let you know?"

Mona frowned. "That is a problem, isn't it? You can't exactly shout my name in front of anyone. I'm certain I can come up with something, though. I just need to think about it for a short while."

"What did Aunt Fenella do when she was caught up in such things?"

"Your Aunt Fenella did her best to avoid such things. And Daniel would never have included her the way that Ted included you. He would have put her in a taxi and sent her home while he went off to the garage."

"I'm glad Ted didn't think to do that."

"We were going to talk about the suspects in the murder investigation," Mona said.

Margaret yawned. "I'm too tired to think any more tonight. We can talk tomorrow morning."

"I might have plans for tomorrow morning."

"Do you?"

"Not yet, but you never know what might come up."

Margaret laughed. "Let's not worry about it for tonight. I need some sleep. If you're here in the morning, we can talk. Otherwise, it will keep for another time."

Mona frowned. "Are you quite certain you're too tired to talk tonight? I could do most of the talking. You could simply listen."

"I'm sorry, but I'm exhausted. You can talk to Katie, though, if you can find her."

"She's in Fenella's room, sleeping on her bed."

"She's smarter than I am."

Mona sighed. "I'll see you tomorrow," she said. She waved her arm and then seemed to turn into a Mona-shaped collection of flower petals. As Margaret reached a hand toward them, they began to drop to the floor. As each one touched the ground, it vanished in a tiny puff of smoke.

"Now that's how you make an exit," Margaret said as the last of the petals vanished.

14

When Katie woke Margaret on Saturday morning, it took her a moment to realize where she was.

"I was dreaming that I was in the US," she told Katie as she filled her food bowl. "When you started tapping on my nose, in my dream I thought it was my ex-boyfriend trying to wake me. He never woke me by tapping on my nose, but nothing makes sense in dreams."

"Merroowww," Katie said.

"I'm much happier here. I'm actually really glad you woke me. I don't want to spend any time with that man, not even in my dreams."

"Mewww," Katie replied before she started eating.

Margaret started a pot of coffee and then headed for the shower. After getting dressed and having a healthy breakfast, she went grocery shopping and did a load of laundry. She was just putting her clean clothes away when someone knocked on her door.

"Good morning," Ted said, pulling her close.

"It's very nearly afternoon," Margaret replied when he released her.

Ted chuckled. "I suppose you've been up for hours, doing all sorts of useful things."

"I have, yes."

"And I just rolled out of bed half an hour ago."

"But you were up late, dealing with Joe and Bruce."

"That didn't actually take all that long. They both did their best to blame the other one for everything that happened. Mark and I took their statements, did some paperwork, and I was home before midnight."

"So you just slept late because you could."

"I slept late because after I got home, I got an email from Brady. After I read it, I rang him."

"Oh? And that kept you up? Tell me everything."

"Let's talk over lunch. I'm starving."

"We could have sandwiches here. That won't take long."

"I could take you somewhere nice."

"I went grocery shopping this morning and bought lots of sandwich fillings. I'm going to start taking lunch to work at least once or twice a week. That will be better for my health and my wallet. But that means I have lots here for sandwiches."

"In that case, let's stay here. I'll make it up to you at dinner."

It didn't take the pair long to put together sandwiches. Margaret added some salad and an apple to her plate. Ted opted for a banana. After getting them each a cold drink, Margaret sat down opposite Ted at the kitchen table.

Where is Mona? she wondered. *Now would be a good time to have a phone number for her.*

As Ted cleared his throat, Mona suddenly appeared. She looked as if she'd just woken up. Her hair was sticking out in every direction, and she appeared to be wearing pajamas. Margaret stared at her for a moment.

"Oh, dear. This won't do," Mona said. She waved her hand and vanished.

"So Brady has been talking to the suspects again," Ted said.

"I'm here now," Mona said, reappearing in the chair between Ted and Margaret. She was dressed in a summery dress and heels and her hair and makeup were perfect. She pulled a notebook out of thin air and snapped her fingers to conjure up a pen. "Ready," she said, smiling at Margaret.

"And what has he learned?" Margaret asked.

"I'm not certain he's learned anything, but he's had some interesting conversations. You wondered about Sean's dropping off to sleep at the game. When Brady asked Nina about that, she shrugged and said that Sean could sleep just about anywhere. What was interesting is that when he asked Susie about it, she said that she'd never known Sean to fall asleep in public in all the years they were together."

"Why didn't she say something about that when he died?" Margaret asked.

Ted nodded. "Brady asked her that. She said she didn't think it really mattered. Whether Sean had been sleeping or not, he was still dead."

"But he was sleeping. The question is, why?"

"Exactly. Brady is kicking himself for not asking that question at the time. He's going to go back through the postmortem, but he doesn't think that any tests were run to see if Sean had drugs in his system. The cause of death was obvious. It's unlikely tests that would have been considered unnecessary were run."

Margaret sighed. "Did Brady ask anyone else if Sean was prone to sleeping in odd places?"

"He did. Greg said he'd seen Sean fall asleep at games before. He was the only one who said it, though. Everyone else said it wasn't normal. Nearly everyone also talked about what a boring game it was, though. While it wasn't normal behavior for Sean, no one who saw him napping at the game found it odd or worrying."

"So it's possible that Sean was drugged before he was stabbed. I suppose that would be true even if he hadn't fallen asleep during the game, though. I'm surprised they didn't test for drugs."

"As I said, the cause of death was obvious."

"So either Susie is telling the truth and it seems likely that Sean was drugged, or Nina is telling the truth and he might or might not have been drugged. Does that get us any closer to finding the killer?"

Ted shrugged. "Brady kept the conversations informal. That means he can share what was said with us, but it also means that he couldn't push too hard. He's planning on bringing each of the suspects in for a formal interview over the weekend."

"So he just asked them all about Sean's sleeping habits?"

"He asked Nina about her relationship with Sean, again, just informally. She said that she'd never cheated before and that she'd never planned to cheat, but that the more she got to know Sean, the more she found herself falling in love with him."

"They'd known each other for years before the affair, right?"

Ted nodded. "They'd all grown up in Harper Glen."

"I don't believe it," Mona said. "You don't suddenly fall in love with someone you've known your entire life. She had a reason for starting the affair."

"Maybe she just wanted free pizza," Margaret said.

Ted frowned. "Pardon?"

"I was just trying to imagine why she'd suddenly start an affair with someone she'd known for her entire life," Margaret said, ignoring Mona's laughter. "Maybe she wanted free pizza."

"I suppose that's one possibility," Ted said.

"What about Ruth? She'd known Sean her entire life, too, right?"

Ted nodded. "But she started seeing him after her marriage fell apart. She told Brady that being with Sean made her feel young and beautiful again."

"And has she forgiven her friend who talked to the paper?"

"Brady didn't ask her that question, but he did say that he sees the two of them out and about in town now and again. They have lunch together or go out shopping, so it seems as if they're still friends."

"How very odd," Margaret murmured.

"Brady also talked to Ronald, just casually, when he bumped into him somewhere. He asked him what Ronald had wanted to do with his life, if he hadn't had to please his parents. Ronald just laughed and said that he'd been so thoroughly indoctrinated in their dreams that he'd never given it a single thought."

"How awful."

Ted nodded. "We're going to be better parents than that when we have kids."

Margaret flushed. "I certainly hope so."

"Brady also managed to bump into Rick. Apparently, he doesn't come back to Harper Glen very often, but he's in the area at the moment dealing with some management issues at the store there."

"Did Rick have anything interesting to say?"

"Brady asked him about turning his life around. Apparently, Rick admitted that Sean's murder was the catalyst for him. The idea that someone could end another person's life so easily frightened him into taking a long, hard look at his own life. He realized that if he died suddenly, no one would have anything good to say about him. He said he wasn't even certain that anyone would be sorry that he'd died, so he decided to do what he could to fix the situation."

"Does Brady believe him?"

Ted shrugged. "Brady doesn't know what to think. All of our questions are making him take another look at the case. He spent the last few days talking to everyone informally, but after we talked last night, he said he was eager to have formal interviews with each suspect again."

"Why? I feel as if we're just going around in circles at the moment."

"He said he just has a feeling that he's getting closer to the solution. He's planning to start each new interview by saying that he's having some additional tests run on the samples that were taken from the body at the postmortem."

"Can he do that?"

"Tell the suspects that or actually have some tests run?"

Margaret laughed. "Both, really."

"The police in the US are allowed to lie when questioning suspects," Ted said. "In this instance, Brady isn't trying to coerce a confession, he's simply trying to see if the idea makes anyone nervous. As for the second part, no, he can't actually have any additional tests run. No samples were saved from Sean's postmortem."

"Nina gave him a brownie," Margaret said.

Ted nodded. "I'm fairly certain that's where Brady is now focusing his efforts. I think your question made him start to wonder if maybe Nina drugged the man."

"But whatever she gave him didn't kill him. Why drug him?"

"Maybe to make it easier for herself to kill him."

Margaret frowned. "I suppose that makes sense, but if I were going to go all the trouble to drug someone I wanted dead, I think I'd just poison him and be done with it."

Ted grinned. "Good to know."

"Maybe Nina had another reason for wanting Sean to sleep through the game," Mona said.

"Why else might Nina have wanted Sean to sleep through the game?" Margaret asked Ted.

"Maybe she'd fallen out of love with him and simply didn't want to talk to him," Ted said.

"Maybe she wanted to talk to someone else but didn't want Sean to hear the conversation."

"The only other person nearby was Greg," Ted said.

Margaret frowned. "Has anyone tried to work out the relationship between Greg and Nina? Is it possible that there's something there?"

"I can ask Brady to see what he can find."

"Perhaps she was very public about her affair with Sean to distract from the affair she wanted to keep quiet," Mona said.

"If she was involved with Greg, why haven't they gotten together now?" Margaret asked. "He's single, and she's been single for years."

"Maybe Greg is no longer interested. Or maybe Greg killed Sean and that's made Nina no longer interested in having a relationship with him."

"I wouldn't want to be involved with a murderer," Margaret said with a shiver.

"If she ended things with Greg following Sean's death, that suggests that she knows that Greg killed Sean," Mona said.

"But we don't have any reason to believe that Nina and Greg had an affair," Margaret said.

"It's an interesting idea, though. I'm going to suggest it to Brady. Again, the police can lie to suspects. Maybe he can tell Nina that someone saw them together."

"Is that everything?" Margaret asked.

Ted shrugged. "I think so. I'm going to ring Brady now and tell him where our thoughts are going. He might just laugh at us, but hopefully he'll take us seriously. Then we can go and spend the afternoon doing something fun."

Ted walked into the living room to make his phone call. While he was talking, Margaret cleared away the lunch dishes and tidied up the kitchen. When Ted came back, he was smiling.

"I caught Brady before he'd left his house for the day. Apparently, his thoughts have been running along the same lines, so he was already planning to start his day by having Nina brought in for an interview. He's going to talk to Greg and Ronald today, too."

"I want to be a fly on the wall," Margaret said.

"Would you settle for listening in?"

"What? Seriously?"

Ted grinned. "He's going to have to get permission from each of the people he interviews, but he's going to ask if any of them mind if the conversation is shared live with law enforcement colleagues around the world. We'll only be able to listen, not speak, which will be frustrating if we don't care for his interview techniques, but it's something."

"But I'm not a law enforcement colleague."

"Don't worry. Brady will do everything in the right way to make it all legal. We just have to be ready for three o'clock."

"Three o'clock today?"

"That's when Nina is coming in for her interview. That's our time, not US time. It will still be morning in the US."

Margaret looked at the clock. "What do you want to do for two hours, then?"

"Why don't we just walk into town and do some window shopping? We can decide later whether we want to listen to the interview from my flat or yours."

"The views are better here," Mona said quickly.

"I have an apartment full of food," Margaret said. "When did you last go grocery shopping?"

Ted laughed. "Good point. We could have tap water and crackers in my flat."

"Let's come back here, then."

They walked into the town center and looked in a few store windows, but neither of them was all that interested in shopping.

"Let's head back," Margaret suggested not much after two. "I can't stop thinking about what's coming."

Ted nodded. "I keep worrying that Nina is going to refuse to allow us to listen to the conversation."

"I hope not. I feel as if we're getting somewhere."

"Yeah, and I'm tired of being on the outside looking in. I want to hear her answers for myself."

"It's frustrating for me, just reading newspaper articles and getting secondhand information. It must be a lot more so for you, since this is your job."

"Let's just agree that we're both frustrated," Ted said as they reached Margaret's building. "And let's talk about snacks. I feel as if lunch was a long time ago."

In her apartment, Margaret got out cheese and crackers, chips, grapes, and pretzel sticks. Ted poured them each a glass of white wine and then filled a plate for himself. Margaret selected a few things and then sat down at the table next to him. Mona was still in her seat at the table. As Margaret sat down, she noticed that her great aunt now had a glass of wine and a plate full of fruit in front of her.

"Do you have a favorite painting?" Margaret asked Ted.

He looked surprised. "I've never really thought about it. Why?"

She shrugged. "I'm just trying to make conversation."

They were still talking about art when Ted's phone buzzed a short while later.

"Ah, Brady, hello," Ted said. "I'm putting you on speaker."

"Very good. Nina has just arrived at the station. She'll be brought to me here, in the interview room, in a moment. The first thing I'm going to do is ask for her permission to share the conversation. If she refuses, I'll have to disconnect."

"That's fine. We understand."

"You need to mute yourselves now, please."

"I will," Ted said, tapping a button on the phone.

After a moment, Margaret looked at Ted. "Are we muted?"

He shrugged. "The phone says we are. Hello?"

"I guess we're muted," Margaret said with a grin.

A minute ticked past slowly while Margaret watched the second hand go around. As it began another revolution, she heard what sounded like a door opening and closing.

"Ah, Nina, thanks for coming in," Brady's voice was loud and clear.

"I was surprised to get the request," a woman's voice replied. "We just talked about Sean a few days ago in Shopper Mart."

"That was just an informal chat. I'm now working on conducting a new round of formal interviews with all of the witnesses. I've been discussing the case with a few colleagues around the world, and they've given me some different perspectives on the murder."

"Really? How interesting."

"She sounds bored," Margaret whispered.

Ted nodded.

"Just a few formalities," Brady said. He read out her rights and then asked her for permission to record the conversation, slipping the part about sharing the conversation live with others into the chat as if it were perfectly normal. Nina didn't seem to notice.

"Yes, fine, whatever," she said impatiently when he was finished.

"I don't want to keep you too long, so let's get started," Brady said. "When we spoke informally, we talked about Sean falling asleep at the game. Can you repeat what you told me about that, please."

"What I told you? I don't remember what I told you, but Sean could sleep anywhere. He often fell asleep on me when we were at dinner or watching television."

"And do you stand by that statement even if I tell you that Sean's widow doesn't agree?"

There was a short silence. "She's probably just trying to cause trouble. She hates me, of course."

"Why would saying that her husband didn't often fall asleep in public cause you any trouble?" Brady asked.

Another silence. "Because she knows that I said he was sleeping at the stadium that night. Maybe she thinks that I'm lying to cover up for the murderer or something."

"Are you lying to cover up for the murderer?"

Nina laughed, but it sounded forced. "Of course not."

"I should tell you that since the issue has been raised, we're now working on getting some of the samples from the postmortem tested."

"What does that mean?"

"It means that we're going to be testing the samples that were taken to see if there were any traces of drugs in Sean's system the night he died."

"He took drugs, though."

This time it was Brady who was silent for a moment. "Are you saying that Sean was taking illegal substances at the time of his death?"

"I don't know anything for sure."

"She's going to start backpedaling fast," Margaret said.

Ted nodded.

"But you think he was taking drugs?"

"He might have been. He was under a lot of stress at work and at home. He was trapped in an unhappy marriage. He and Susie fought constantly. It wouldn't surprise me to hear that he was taking something to make life more bearable."

"Would you care to speculate what we might find when we test those samples, then?"

"I've no idea. If he was taking something, it clearly made him drowsy, though."

"So now you're suggesting that he fell asleep at the stadium because he'd been taking drugs, not because it was just his nature?"

"I thought it was just his nature, but he was probably taking drugs from the time we started seeing one another. If Susie says he wasn't usually like that, then maybe he'd changed in the weeks and months before his death."

Margaret could hear Brady shuffling papers. "The postmortem does state that there was no sign that the deceased was a habitual drug user."

"How long do you have to take drugs before it becomes a habit?" Nina asked.

"That's a good question. So let me make sure I understand what you're saying. You won't be surprised if we find evidence that Sean had taken some sort of drug or drugs on the night he died."

"It's possible."

"What did Sean eat or drink during the game?"

"You can't possibly expect me to be able to answer that question. It was ten years ago. I can't remember what I had to eat for lunch yesterday."

"I can refresh your memory by telling you what you said on the night of the murder."

"That would be a good start."

After a few more pages were flipped, Brady spoke again.

"You said that Sean brought a water bottle with him and that he drank from it periodically during both of the games. He also brought a small bag of chips and a chocolate bar, which he ate during the middle school game. That was all that he had, aside from a brownie that you gave him between games."

"So maybe there was something in the water. It could have been alcohol, rather than drugs."

Brady shuffled papers again. "The contents of the water bottle were tested. It held nothing but water. The empty wrappers from the chips and the chocolate were also tested. Again, nothing out of the ordinary was found. If we do find drugs in the man's system, we'll have to talk about what was in the brownie you gave him."

"Maybe his wife gave him something. Maybe she was hoping he'd fall asleep and miss the game."

"They can do a lot with testing these days. We might be able to work out how long the drugs had been in his system before he died."

"The brownie wasn't mine."

"What do you mean?"

"I mean, I was selling cakes and brownies and things at the bake sale between the games. When the second game started, I grabbed a few leftover brownies and took them back to my seat to give to Sean. I'm not even sure where they came from."

"When you were originally questioned, you said that you gave Sean some of your leftover brownies."

"I was distraught. I also never imagined that the brownies I'd given him had been drugged. Such a thing never even crossed my mind."

"You had an assistant at the bake sale, didn't you?"

"Yes." Nina named another woman.

"I'm going to speak to her about the brownies. Maybe she'll remember where they came from."

"She won't. And even if she thinks she does, you know you can't possibly believe her, not after all this time."

"Was anyone else at the game acting oddly? If an entire batch of brownies had been laced with something, I'd have expected several people in the crowd to react."

"I didn't notice, but maybe only a few of the brownies were actually drugged. Maybe someone was trying to cause trouble or something. Whoever did it probably didn't expect the person who ate the brownies to just fall asleep in his seat."

"We'll have to see what Sean was actually given and when. Let's talk about something else."

"Sure, but I hope it won't take long. I have a hair appointment at noon."

"It won't take long if you answer my questions quickly," Brady said with a small chuckle. "I just want to hear about your relationship with Greg Owens."

The silence seemed to stretch for a very long time. Margaret looked at the clock and watched the second hand count over thirty seconds before Nina spoke again.

"Sorry, I wasn't expecting that question. I'm not sure what you mean, really. Greg and I are friends, in the same way that I'm friends with just about everyone in town. I don't see him as often as I did when our children were in school together, but I do eat at his restaurant probably once a month or more."

"What if I told you that a witness has come forward to say that he saw you and Greg kissing in a parking lot the week before Sean's murder?"

Nina's laugh sounded weak. "I'd say your witness is lying."

"I can't imagine why he would lie."

"Maybe because he wants to get me into trouble for some reason. I can't imagine why he would, but maybe he killed Sean and is trying to pin the blame on me. That's only one possibility, of course. There are others."

"So you're denying that you and Greg have ever been more than just friends?"

There was a short pause. "At one time we were closer than we are now," Nina said eventually. "It's possible that someone saw us together and misunderstood our friendship. We used to hug and even kiss occasionally. It was just friendly affection."

"And this was during the same time you were involved with Sean?"

"Probably. Like I said, it was just friendly. It didn't mean anything."

"You said in your initial statement that Sean gave one of the brownies to Greg. Did he seem to be behaving differently after he'd eaten it?"

"Sorry, the change of subject threw me," Nina said after a minute. "I don't remember Greg eating one of the brownies. If you say that he did, I believe you, but I also don't remember him behaving differently to normal."

"But Sean fell asleep, which wasn't normal, and that didn't worry you?"

"Sean had been working hard lately. I knew he was really tired."

"And had Greg also been working hard?"

"Sure, they both worked hard. Running a small business is difficult."

"I'm sure it is, which makes it surprising that Greg wanted to buy Sean's restaurant."

"Greg wanted Sean's recipes more than anything else."

"He must have been disappointed when Susie wouldn't sell the business to him, then."

"Sure, but his mistake there was offering her too little. She knew he was trying to take advantage of her grief, so when he came back with a more reasonable offer, she refused to even consider it."

"It sounds as if you know quite a lot about Greg's business."

"Like I said, we're friends."

"I'm going to ask you to wait for a short while. I have to interview someone else, but when I'm finished with him, I expect I'll have more questions for you."

"Can't I come back another time? Like I said, I have a hair appointment."

"I'm sorry, but I'd prefer to get this done today. You can wait in the room next door. I hope my next interview won't take long."

Nina protested a bit more, but eventually Margaret heard the sound of chairs being pushed back.

"I'll just show you into the next room before my next witness arrives," Brady said.

Margaret heard the door open. Someone gasped.

"Collins, you were supposed to wait to bring him in until I let you know I was ready," Brady said angrily.

"Sorry, we must have gotten our signals crossed," another voice said.

"Mr. Owens, if you'd like to take a seat, I'll just get Ms. Hicks settled and then be back to speak to you," Brady said.

"You're interviewing Greg next?" Nina asked.

"Right this way, please," Brady said.

As the background noise got louder, Margaret looked at Ted.

"She's guilty of something," she said.

Ted nodded. "If nothing else, I suspect she gave Sean a brownie with something in it that made him fall asleep. The question is, did she then stick a knife in him?"

"She sounded worried when she saw Greg."

"She did. I'm wondering if they worked together on the murder and now she's worried that he's going to start talking."

"She has every right to be worried," Mona said.

A minute later, they heard Brady going through Greg's rights with him. Then he went over the recording and listening items. Greg didn't seem to be paying much attention.

"Do you know how busy my restaurant is at lunchtime?" he demanded after agreeing that he understood everything that Brady had said.

"I'm sorry if the timing isn't convenient, but certain things have just been brought to my attention, and I need to discuss them with you."

"Nothing you've just learned about a ten-year-old murder investigation is worth dragging me in here during one of my busiest times of day."

"I'm sorry you feel that way. Let's see if we can get through my questions fairly quickly then."

Greg sighed. "Very quickly."

"When you were questioned right after the murder, why didn't you tell us that you were also having an affair with Nina Hicks?" Brady asked.

Mona inhaled sharply. Margaret and Ted exchanged glances.

15

After an awkward moment, Greg chuckled. "Did she tell you that?"

"Why do you think that?" Brady countered.

"Clearly, you've worked out that Nina killed Sean. No doubt she's trying to find a way to shift the blame elsewhere."

"What makes you think that Nina killed Sean?"

"You said yourself that new information has come to light. That suggests that you've learned something significant. If Nina is now claiming that she and I had an affair, that suggests that you think Nina killed Sean."

"I'm not sure I follow your logic, but it wasn't Nina who told me about the affair."

"Oh? Then someone else is lying to you. Interesting."

"The person who told me doesn't have any reason to lie about it."

"That's also interesting. Why would someone choose to lie unnecessarily? Are you quite certain the other person has no reason to lie? If it were, say, Susie Payne, for example, she might be trying to damage my reputation in an attempt to destroy my business. We are rivals, after all."

Brady chuckled. "It isn't Susie Payne. It's someone who has no reason to lie and someone for whom I have a great deal of respect."

"I can't do anything about what you choose to believe."

"So let's talk about brownies."

"Brownies?"

"Yes, on the night that Sean Payne died, Nina ran a bake sale during the break between the two baseball games. When she returned to her seat, she brought a plate with brownies on it back with her."

"If you say so. It's been ten years."

"According to your initial statement, you ate one of the brownies."

"I'm sure it was very nice, too. Are we done?"

"How did you feel after you ate the brownie?"

"Seriously? You're asking me to remember how I felt ten years ago after eating a brownie?"

"If you can't remember, then that suggests that the brownie didn't have any ill effect on you."

"Are you suggesting that Sean was poisoned? I thought it was clearly established that he'd been stabbed."

"We have reason to believe that there was something in the brownies that didn't belong there."

"Brownies supplied by Nina. So she poisoned him and then stuck the knife in to be sure he was dead?"

"But you don't remember feeling unwell after eating one of the brownies."

Greg sighed. "I remember getting up and down from my seat several times after I ate the brownie. Maybe it upset my stomach. Maybe it just made me restless. Maybe it was nothing to do with the brownie. Perhaps Sean was allergic to something, and Nina took advantage of that and baked that something into the brownies knowing it would kill him but not harm anyone else."

"That's an interesting idea. Why did you offer Susie so little for the restaurant after Sean's death?"

"I made what I thought was a fair offer. I'd been given misleading information about the level of profits they were achieving. Once I was given the correct information, I went back to Susie with a revised offer, but she refused to speak to me a second time."

"Who gave you that misleading information?"

"I can't see why that matters."

"It matters if that information was being given to others, maybe even given to someone who murdered Sean because of it."

"I never thought of that," Greg said after a moment. "But I can see your point. Someone was telling people that Sean's business was failing. Anyone could have decided it would be smart to get rid of Sean and then buy the business for below market value."

"So who told you the business was failing?"

"He's going to blame Nina," Mona said.

Margaret nodded.

Ted gave her a quizzical look.

"He's going to blame Nina," Margaret said.

"It was Nina," Greg said. "We were close friends at the time. Someone must have seen us together and thought it was more than that, but we were simply friends."

"And she told you that Sean's business was failing?"

"She said that he was miserable, that his marriage was over, that his business was failing, and that he wanted more than anything to get out of Harper Glen. I was getting ready to make him an offer for the business right before he died, actually."

"Interesting. So Nina lied to you."

"I prefer to believe that she simply misunderstood Sean. His business had suffered a small downturn, but it was much less significant than Nina seemed to think."

"Why would Nina want to kill Sean?"

"That's a complicated question. Before today, I never would have even given the idea a single thought. At the time of his death, I thought Nina was in love with him."

"But just a few minutes ago you accused her of poisoning and stabbing him."

"This conversation is opening my eyes to many things."

"Oh?"

"I thought Nina and I were good friends. I trusted her when she told me that Sean's business was failing. I was too trusting, but I never doubted her motives – not before today, anyway."

"And what do you think now?"

"I don't know what to think. I'm worried, though. I'm worried that Nina killed Sean in a misguided attempt to help me. Perhaps she thought that I would be more likely to convince Susie to sell me the business if Sean was out of the way."

"You must have been very close friends if you think Nina would have killed someone for you."

"Ah, yes, well, the thing is, I always suspected that she wanted to be more than friends, if you know what I mean. She used to say that she thought we'd be good together. I didn't pay much attention. Having lost my first wife, I'm not really interested in getting married again."

Brady sighed. "I need to go and have a quick word with someone. I'll be right back."

Margaret heard the chair being pushed back. A moment later, she heard a door open and close.

"Are you guys still there?" Brady asked.

"We are," Ted said after he tapped on the phone to unmute the call.

"Let's see what Nina has to say to all of this," Brady said. "Please mute again."

Another door opened and closed.

"Sorry to have kept you waiting," Brady said. "I've just been having a very interesting conversation with Greg."

"Really? That surprises me. The man is dull as dishwater."

"So why were you having an affair with him?"

"It wasn't really an affair, just a bit of fun."

"And why did you tell him that Sean's business was failing?"

"I never told him that."

"He says you did. He also suggested that thinking that the business was failing gave you a motive for Sean's murder."

There was a short silence before Nina laughed. "That doesn't even make sense."

"He suggested that you killed Sean because you thought it would be easy to persuade Susie to sell the business to him."

"That's crazy."

"Maybe. If we find evidence that there was something in the brownies, we'll have to give the idea some consideration."

"Greg gave me the brownies."

"Now we're getting somewhere," Mona said.

"Greg gave you the brownies?" Brady repeated questioningly.

Nina sighed. "It was such a simple plan, really. Greg was the one who complicated things."

"Why don't you tell me the whole story?"

"I want immunity from prosecution if I tell you everything."

"I can't promise you immunity, but I will testify in court that you were very cooperative."

"Ten years after the fact," Margaret muttered.

"I started seeing Sean. Greg was supposed to get involved with Susie. He tried, but she wasn't interested. I did my best to make things difficult, flaunting our relationship everywhere, but Susie didn't seem to care."

"Why?"

"Why what? Oh, the original plan was to break up Sean and Susie. Greg was supposed to convince Susie to sell him her share of the restaurant. Really, all Greg needed was a few hours to copy down Sean's recipes, and then it didn't matter what happened to Sean's business after that."

"So this was all about getting Sean's recipes?"

"It was about driving Sean out of business and making me and Greg rich. Once we had Sean's recipes, he wouldn't have been able to compete against us. Greg already had the best pasta sauce, but we needed Sean's pizza sauce and crust recipes. With those, we would have been unstoppable."

"I'm surprised you didn't just ask Sean for the recipes once you were involved with him."

"Oh, I did, repeatedly. He always just laughed at me. He knew his recipes were his business."

"So what was the plan?" Brady asked.

"Greg was supposed to get close to Susie, talk her into leaving Sean, and then convince her to sell her share of the business to him. Unfortunately, Susie wasn't interested. Then Greg got the idea that we could discredit Sean, make him look like a bad person – one that no one would want to do business with. We were already openly having an affair, but Greg decided that we should give him some drugs. People would have been outraged if they thought Sean was taking drugs."

"So he gave you a brownie full of something to give Sean at the game."

"Yeah, and then Sean ate it and just went to sleep," Nina said with a sigh.

"So you stabbed him."

"No!" Nina shouted. "I don't know who stabbed him, but it wasn't me."

"Perhaps it was Greg."

Nina sighed. "I've been wondering that for ten years. I keep telling myself that he didn't have any reason to kill Sean, but neither did anyone else. Maybe he thought he'd have a better chance at getting his hands on the business if he only had to deal with Susie."

"If buying the business was so important to him, why did he make such a low offer after Sean's death?"

"Because he's a greedy idiot," Nina snapped. "He thought the grieving widow would take the money and leave town. Instead, she laughed in his face and then refused to speak to him again. After all of our hard work, we ended up with nothing."

"I'm going to need to ask you a lot more questions," Brady said. "I'm just going to get someone to take notes. I'll be right back."

Margaret listened as one door opened and closed and then a second one.

"Just a few more questions, Mr. Owens," Brady said.

"I do have better things to do," Greg snapped.

"I've been told that you supplied the brownies that Sean ate."

There was a long pause before Greg spoke again. "Sometimes it's best not to try to plan things," he said. "I'm not good at planning things. Something always goes wrong. I should have learned that years ago. Things went wrong then, and I'm still paying the consequences."

"Years ago?"

"I spent months tinkering with my wife's car, getting the brake line to leak ever so slowly. I was so tired of being a husband and a father. I knew if I timed things just right, she'd be driving on snow and ice when the brakes finally failed. And she was. And they did. And she died. But the baby, he survived, and I was left having to raise him on my own. I'd have been better off if I hadn't done anything."

"I'm going to need to get someone in here to take notes," Brady said.

"And then Nina and I worked together on a plan," Greg continued. "It was her idea. She said I didn't have to be the number two pizza place in town. I could be number one if I had the right recipes. And she said she knew how to get them. It wasn't my fault Susie wasn't interested in me. There wasn't anything I could do about that, but I could improve on the plan. I thought I had improved on the plan. Everything worked perfectly. Sean went to sleep. I stabbed him. He died. I offered Susie what Nina said was a fair price for the restaurant. And she laughed at me."

"That must have been upsetting."

Greg chuckled. "I should have expected it, shouldn't I? Every time I kill someone, my life gets worse instead of better. It doesn't seem fair. You'd think after three murders, I'd be better at it."

"Three?"

"Ah, well, maybe we shouldn't go there," Greg said.

"I'll be right back," Brady said.

The door opened and closed.

"I'm sorry, but I'm going to have to switch this off now," Brady said. "I want everything from here on to be done strictly by the book."

Ted quickly unmuted the call. "No worries. Thanks for letting us listen in. Let us know who the third victim was," he said.

"Will do."

The phone clicked and then went silent. Margaret stared at Ted.

"That was quite awful," she said after a minute.

"It was," he agreed.

"But we solved the case," Mona said. "I think I'll go dancing tonight." She floated out of her chair, straight up toward the ceiling before seeming to fly right through it and vanishing.

Okay, that was an exit, Margaret thought.

"I think a walk on the promenade might help," Ted said after another minute.

"I hope that will clear my head," Margaret said.

They walked in silence for several minutes before Margaret spoke.

"I hope they both go to jail for a long time."

Ted nodded. "It's difficult to know which of them was behind the original plan, but they both should bear some blame for Sean's death."

"I do think that was all Greg, though."

"It seems so. He also admitted to killing his wife and someone else, so Brady has a lot to work through there."

"And everyone said he was boring."

As they walked, they talked through everything that they'd heard. Margaret was still feeling somewhat in shock when they got back to her apartment.

"Dinner?" Ted asked.

"It's later than I realized. We should get something."

"How about something simple for tonight and we'll go out for a nice meal tomorrow night?"

"That works for me. After we eat, I have to call everyone from work and let them know what happened."

"Maybe you'd better wait until we have confirmation from Brady that the information is being released to the public."

They went to the closest Chinese restaurant for dinner and then walked back to Margaret's apartment. There, they watched television and talked about human nature.

***

The next day, Brady called to let them know that there was going to be a press conference later in the day.

"Basically, Greg has confessed to killing Sean, his wife, and his father. Nina has admitted to working with Greg to try to steal Sean's recipes," he told them. "Thank you for all of your help."

"We were happy to help," Ted replied. "When the dust settles, maybe you can help me with one of my cases."

On Sunday afternoon, Margaret called everyone from the office and told them what had happened.

"We were right," Joney said. "I'm proud of us."

"We solved it first," Rachel said. "When can we start working on the next case?"

Margaret laughed. "Maybe there won't be a next case," she said.

"Of course there will," Mona's voice echoed around her. "And I'll be there to help solve it yet again."

MURDER AT COLLINS AIRFIELD

A MARGARET AND MONA GHOSTLY COZY

Release date: November 8, 2024

When Margaret Woods is woken out of a deep sleep by the sound of a fire alarm, she has no idea that an arsonist has struck in her apartment building. It isn't long, though, before the entire island is talking about the fire and who might have been behind it.

Meanwhile, Ted is working on another cold case. This time, though, there's a connection to the island. Joel Ward died in Canada thirty-five years ago, but he'd had a house on the island, and many of the suspects in the investigation still live there.

Margaret finds herself tangled up in two more investigations. Mona seems to be doing her best to make sure that Margaret meets every suspect in both cases. If that isn't enough, Margaret is busy at her new job, and increasingly worried about her sister, Megan.

A SNEAK PEEK AT MURDER AT COLLINS AIRFIELD
A MARGARET AND MONA GHOSTLY COZY

Release date: November 8, 2024

Please excuse any typos or minor errors. I have not yet completed final edits on this title.

Chapter One

"What is that noise?" Margaret asked as she sat up in bed. It was dark and the clock told her that it was two o'clock in the morning. Katie mewed softly as she climbed up the bed toward Margaret.

"It's the fire alarm," Mona's voice was quiet but still managed to be heard over the incessant ringing sound. "There's a fire. You need to get out of the building."

Margaret was still half asleep as she got out of bed. She pulled on a pair of jeans and a T-shirt and brushed her hair into a ponytail. Then she picked up Katie and held her close.

"It's going to be okay," she told the tiny cat. "We're going to be just fine."

She walked out of her bedroom and into the living room of the large luxury apartment she was currently calling home. Her purse was where she'd left it on the table near the door. After checking that the keycard for the apartment was in the bag, she opened her door. Several of her neighbors were standing in the corridor, looking confused.

"Are we supposed to evacuate?" one of them asked Margaret.

Before Margaret could reply, the doors on one of the elevators at the end of the hall slid open. The fireman inside stepped out.

"Everyone needs to leave the building," he said. "It's precautionary. We're working to get the fire under control. But we want you all to be safe. Please use the stairs if you can. If you can't manage the stairs, please let me know."

He began to knock loudly on apartment doors. "There's a fire. You need to evacuate the building," he shouted loudly as he made his way down the corridor.

Margaret and the others headed for the stairs. In her haste, Margaret had forgotten to put Katie in her carrier. She looked down at the cat, who was smaller than average, and sighed.

"You're going to be good and stay with me, right?" she whispered.

Katie snuggled against her and squeezed her eyes shut. Margaret glanced at her purse. It was large enough to tuck Katie inside if absolutely necessary. The walk down from the sixth floor seemed to take forever. The shrieking siren kept blasting her ears. When they reached the ground floor, a pair of firefighters urged them to exit the building as quickly as possible.

"Please cross the road to the promenade and remain there until the building is cleared," they were told. "We're working to contain the fire. Please let someone know if you know that there are people remaining in the building."

Margaret followed the small crowd out of the building and across the street. The entire area was lit up by the flashing lights of fire trucks, police cars, and an ambulance. On the promenade, people in everything from evening wear to pajamas were huddled together in small clusters, all silently staring at the building they'd just left. Margaret smiled and nodded at a few people as she found a spot to stand near the edge of the crowd.

"You're Margaret Woods, aren't you?" a woman asked a few minutes later.

Margaret looked over at the woman. She appeared to be somewhere around fifty. She was wearing pajamas, with a bathrobe over the top, and a pair of slippers.

"I am," Margaret admitted.

The other woman nodded. "I thought so. I've seen you going in and out of the building before. I was always going to say hello, but I didn't want to bother you."

"Hello," Margaret said after an awkward pause.

The woman laughed. "I'm American, too, you see. I was always going to introduce myself to your aunt as well, but I never worked up the nerve."

"I'm sure Aunt Fenella would have loved to have met you."

"Maybe. I thought about it when she first arrived on the island, but at that point everyone on the island wanted to meet her. She'd just inherited a huge fortune. Everyone wanted to be her friend."

Margaret nodded. "Except when she first arrived, Aunt Fenella had no idea that she'd inherited a fortune. She was just happy to have an apartment to call home."

"Really? I suppose I'd imagined that she knew all about her Aunt Mona Kelly."

"She'd only met Mona a few times over the years, when Mona traveled to the US to visit her sister, Aunt Fenella's mother. I don't think any of Mona's US family knew just how wealthy Mona was."

"Maybe you'd have visited her if you'd known."

Margaret laughed. "I suspect some of the family would have visited, certainly."

"That came out a bit more rudely than I intended."

"It's fine. It's three o'clock in the morning."

"Everyone on the island knew Mona, and we all knew she was incredibly wealthy, too. She captured Maxwell Martin's heart when she was eighteen, and he showered her with expensive presents for decades."

Margaret nodded. She knew there was quite a lot more to the story than that, but it seemed easier to keep it simple.

"Every time I walk past Mona's car in the parking garage, I'm jealous," the woman continued. "I've always wondered if she really loved Max or just loved his money. There were all sorts of rumors and stories about her and other men."

"And it all happened before I arrived on the island."

"Of course." The woman shook her head. "I'm making a right mess of this. I'm Marcia Baker. I moved to the island twenty-five years ago when I married a man I'd met through a weird set of circumstances."

"Oh? Now you have to tell me more."

Marcia laughed. "I was in my mid-twenties, working as a veterinary assistant in Iowa. Someone brought in a cat that didn't have a tail. The man claimed that it was a Manx cat. My boss, the vet, asked me to see what I could learn about Manx cats, so I did some research. The internet didn't have as much useful information in those days, of course."

Margaret nodded. "And it sounds as if that was lucky for you."

Marcia nodded. "It really was. I found a few books at the local library, but they weren't much help. The vet told me to try calling a vet here on the island. Our little patient had some issues with her tail nub, you see, and we weren't certain how best to deal with it."

"So you called a vet on the island?"

"That was the plan," Marcia said, laughing again. "What I actually did was call the wrong number."

"Oh dear."

"Yeah. When the guy answered, I said I needed information about Manx cats. He said he'd do his best. I just started asking away, never even thinking to check that I had the right person."

Margaret laughed. "And was he able to help much?"

"Oh, he tried. He answered all of my questions, but it quickly became obvious that he didn't really know anything about cats."

Marcia stopped as another ambulance pulled up in front of the building.

"I hope that doesn't mean that someone got hurt in the fire," Margaret said.

"The paramedics aren't rushing inside, so that suggests that they are here just in case they're needed," Marcia said.

Margaret sighed. "Let's hope they aren't needed, then. But you were telling me about your phone conversation."

"Oh, yeah, so I asked a bunch of questions and got answers that I knew were wrong. When I confronted the guy, he said it was obvious that I was American, but even so, it seemed odd that I would just call a random Manx person and expect that person to know a great deal about cats, Manx or otherwise."

"He wasn't wrong," Margaret said with a chuckle.

Marcia nodded. "I got angry with him and said that I'd assumed that a vet on the island would know more about Manx cats than I did. He replied that he expected one would and then offered to find me a phone number for one. That was when I finally realized that I'd called the wrong number. I was so flustered that I simply hung up on him."

"I can understand that."

"Then I called the right number, which was only one number off the number I'd called in error. They were very helpful. We quickly discovered that our patient wasn't a Manx cat at all. Actually, we discovered that our patient's owner was taking ordinary kittens and removing their tails in an attempt to sell them as Manx."

"How awful."

"Yeah, it was pretty bad. The guy ended up getting banned from owning animals for the rest of his life, which he totally deserved."

Margaret nodded and gave Katie a pat. "How could anyone hurt a kitten?"

"So the next day, after I'd shared everything that I'd learned with my boss and he'd called the police to report the abuse, I called the wrong number again. I wanted to apologize for my mistake. And honestly, I wanted to talk to the guy again. He had a very sexy voice, and I loved his accent."

"I think a lot of Americans find British accents attractive."

Marcia grinned. "I understand you've already found yourself a boyfriend. Ted Hart is a very handsome man, accent or no accent."

Margaret felt color rush into her cheeks. "I am seeing Ted Hart," she acknowledged. "And he is very handsome."

"And he's a police inspector. Your aunt married a police inspector from the Douglas unit. I suppose it's only natural that Ted was one of the first people you met when you came to the island."

Margaret nodded. *Except Aunt Fenella didn't introduce us to Ted. We met Ted because we found a dead body,* she thought.

"But where was I? Oh, yes, I called the wrong number again to apologize. I explained the mix-up and then we started talking, and talking, and talking. We ended up chatting for over an hour. By the end of the call, he'd asked for my number and said that he might call me one day. As it happened, 'one day' turned out to be the next day."

Margaret laughed. "How romantic."

"Yeah, I was dating a guy back in Iowa, but I ended things with him as soon as I started talking to Rick. We talked every day for a month and then my boss got the bill for the calls I'd made to the island and Rick got the bill for the calls he'd been making to me. After that, we switched to email."

"Phone calls used to be so expensive, especially international calls."

Marcia nodded. "Anyway, we emailed back and forth for a few months before Rick suggested exchanging photos. By that time my family was convinced that Rick was either a sixty-year-old man who was hoping I was underage or a sixteen-year-old boy who was hoping for naughty pictures."

Margaret laughed. "I can understand their concerns."

"I could, too, but this was years ago, before people were using the internet for all things nasty and criminal. It never crossed my mind to lie to Rick about anything, and fortunately, he didn't think to lie, either. When we finally did exchange photos, he looked exactly like what I'd been expecting, all long hair and crooked teeth. My goodness, but he was gorgeous."

"The Isle of Man is a long way away from Iowa."

"It is, indeed, but after we'd seen photos, we decided we wanted to meet in person. I wasn't sure about coming to the island and he wasn't interested in spending time in Iowa, so we decided to meet in London. I've never been more afraid of anything than I was of flying to London on my own."

"You should have brought a friend."

"I should have, but I couldn't find one that wanted to come along. My mother cried buckets at the airport. She was convinced that Rick was going to kill me in my sleep while I was here. He'd booked us a hotel in London and paid for two separate rooms so that I wouldn't think he was just trying to get me into bed. At least, that's what he'd told me. When I got on the plane, I was trusting him to be at the airport and trusting that he'd actually booked a hotel like he'd said."

"What happened next?" Margaret asked as a few firefighters walked out of the building.

The two women watched them stop just outside the door for a conversation.

"Oh, it was all drama," Marcia said with a laugh. "I got off the plane, stumbled my way through immigration with my brand-new passport and then wandered accidentally into the red channel at customs. When they asked me what I wanted to declare, I just stared at them. Eventually, someone kindly took pity on me and sent me over to the green channel. Once that ordeal was over, I walked out into the biggest airport I'd ever seen and simply froze. It seemed as if there were thousands of people going in every direction, and I had no idea which way to go."

"Big city airports are terrifying."

"They really are. Eventually, I followed the crowd toward an exit. I kept scanning faces, trying to spot Rick, but I couldn't see him anywhere. I finally found a bench and just sat down, clutching my suitcase, while I tried to think."

"Did you have a cell phone?"

"No. Even if I'd had one, I doubt it would have worked in the UK."

"Sometimes I forget how fast technology has moved."

"It's astonishing, really."

"So what did you do?"

"I was mentally adding up the credit limits on my various credit cards, trying to work out how much I could afford to spend on a hotel room, when I heard my name. You know those announcements when they say 'so-and-so, pick up a white courtesy phone?' It was one of those announcements. And I was so dumb, that I sat there, thinking that they were paging a different Marcia Masterson."

Margaret laughed. "I can see me doing that."

"Eventually, it crossed my mind that Rick might be looking for me and that maybe the page was for me, so I found a courtesy phone. When I told them my name, they told me that Rick was looking for me and told me where to find him. He wasn't even that far away, and he was holding a sign with my name on it. I really don't know how I missed him when I got off the plane, but I found him."

"And was it love at first sight?"

Marcia laughed. "Maybe for him. I wasn't so sure. My mother's warnings were still ringing in my ears, of course, so I took it very slowly. We got a taxi to the hotel, where we did have separate rooms. I took a quick shower and changed before we went out for lunch. Everything felt odd. The language was more or less the same, but everything felt very different. It was like falling into another reality or something. It's hard to explain."

"I understand, though. I felt the same way the first time I traveled to the island. Actually, I still feel that way a lot of the time."

Marcia nodded. "It's weird, isn't it? The UK is as much a foreign country as France or Kenya or Afghanistan, but because the language is the same, we expect it to feel like the US."

"And sometimes it does, but usually it feels very different."

"Of course, I've been here for a long time now. I can't imagine moving back to the US now."

"But what happened in London that first day?"

"We had lunch and then we walked around the city. We walked past Buckingham Palace, and we took the tube other places. I was exhausted and jet-lagged, but I didn't want to stop. I only had a week, and I wanted to see everything."

"I can understand that."

"I was falling asleep on my feet when we got back to the hotel. We went to our rooms to change for dinner, and I truly did fall asleep. And I was completely out, too. When Rick knocked on the door a short while later, I didn't hear him. He knocked. He tried calling the room. I was out cold. Luckily, he'd asked for two keys for each room when he'd checked in, so he let himself in to check on me. When he realized that I was just sleeping he went out and got himself some dinner. Then he came back with sandwiches, chips, chocolates, and a cold drink for me. He left them in my room with a note, telling me to eat when I got hungry and sleep as much as I needed to sleep and that he'd be back in the morning."

"How very kind."

Marcia nodded. "He was very kind. I have no idea what time it was when I finally did wake up, but I was starving. I ate everything Rick had left and then went right back to bed. I woke up at seven the next morning feeling almost back to normal."

A police car rolled to a stop near the women. They both took a few steps away from the vehicle before Marcia continued talking.

"Rick spent the rest of the week showing me everything wonderful about London and even a bit farther afield. We ate at fancy restaurants, went for tea one afternoon, and just generally had an amazing time. By day three, we only needed one hotel room. On my last evening in London, Rick proposed."

"That was fast."

"We'd been talking for months, on the telephone and over email. I know it sounds fast, but it didn't feel fast. It felt just right. I said yes and then flew home and started making plans."

"But you'd never been to the island."

"I know, but Rick promised me that we could move anywhere in the world if I didn't like the island. I agreed to give it a year before I asked to move elsewhere."

"I suppose that's fair enough."

"My mother did everything in her power to convince me not to marry Rick. When she realized that wasn't going to work, she started trying to convince me to make him move to the US instead of me moving here. The problem with that plan was that he had a great job and already owned a house. I liked my job, but it didn't pay great, and I was still living with my parents. Moving to the island just made more sense."

"What was Rick doing for work then?"

"He worked in the insurance industry. I didn't realize when we met just how successful he was. I was just happy that he had a job and a house. It wasn't until after we were married, and I actually moved to the island, that I discovered that his house was what I would consider a mansion."

Margaret grinned. "What a lovely surprise."

"It was lovely, especially since he had a housekeeper who took care of the place and him. I had no idea."

"Did you get married in the US, then?"

"Oh, yes. My mother wasn't letting me leave Iowa without a ring on my finger," Marcia said with a laugh. "She'd been planning my wedding since the day I was born. I have two older brothers, and she'd been hoping for a girl every time. Anyway, she planned just about everything, and she and my father paid for it all, so I couldn't really complain. We got married less than a year after I'd dialed that wrong number. And then I moved to the island."

"Did you fall in love with it immediately?"

"Sadly, no. I cried myself to sleep every night for the first three months. I didn't know anyone. Rick was working all day. Our poor housekeeper was wonderful, but she didn't have time to entertain me. She had to cook and clean and run errands for Rick. I was terrified of driving on the wrong side of the road. And I'd never lived away from my parents before, either. It was all overwhelming."

"I'm surprised you stayed."

"I was crazy in love with Rick. That was the only reason I stayed. In those early months, I just kept counting down the days until that year I'd promised him would be up. Then Rick persuaded me to take some driving lessons. And he bought me a car. And I started to go out and about a little bit. Even that didn't help much, though. What really helped was when I started taking classes at the college. I'd dropped out of college after a year when I decided that I'd rather work than have to take one more test."

Margaret laughed. "I loved college, but my sister, Megan, was a lot like you. She only stayed in school because my parents bribed her to do so. She's glad they did now, but at the time she was really tired of studying and tests and writing papers and everything."

"When I'd first arrived on the island, I'd assumed I was going to have to get a job, but once I discovered that Rick was earning enough to support us both, I realized I had a lot more options than I'd expected. He was the one who suggested that I should go back to school. And that was a smart idea."

"What did you study?"

"Business management. I only took a few classes, actually. What made it so wonderful for me was that I made a few friends. And those wonderful friends made time in their lives to show me the island and help me fall in love with its uniqueness and its history."

"It really does have a wonderfully rich history."

"It does and the more I learned about it, the more fascinated I became. I ended up taking every history course the college offered and then taking classes through the Open University to learn more about European history generally, but that all came later. What mattered in the short term was that I realized that I wanted to stay on the island, at least for longer than that single year."

"And here you are twenty-five years later."

Marcia nodded. "Rick and I talked about moving several times, but we never did. He was ten years older than me, so we talked a lot about moving once he was ready to retire. I never found a full-time job, but I do a lot of research and teach an occasional class at the college."

"That sounds interesting."

"I have brochures in my apartment if you're interested in taking a class or two on the island's history. I teach college classes, but I also teach short courses for adults with more general interest."

"I'd love a brochure."

"I'll slip one under your door."

"You keep your paws off it," Margaret said to Katie, who was fast asleep in her arms.

"When did you move into Promenade View?" Margaret asked.

Marcia sighed. "Rick and I were still talking about his retirement in the weeks before his fifty-eighth birthday. Two days after that birthday, he had a massive heart attack and died in his office. I was devastated when they came and told me."

"I'm so sorry."

"He was the love of my life. We never had children. It wasn't a conscious choice, it simply never happened. Suddenly, I was all alone in the world."

"And a very rich widow," the man standing nearby said.

Marcia laughed loudly. "Everyone on the island knows everyone else's business," she said. "I don't know that I'd say 'very rich' but Rick definitely left me well provided for. It only took me a few months to decide to sell the house."

"I'm sure it was a difficult decision," Margaret said.

"Yes and no. It was always far too large for us. Rick and I talked about it all the time. He'd bought it because it was the sort of property that men in his position were expected to own. He'd also always assumed that he'd have a wife and children one day to fill some of the rooms. Once we were married, we both assumed we'd have children one day. Eventually, it became obvious that I wasn't going to get pregnant, but by that time I'd come to love the house. So we stayed there, even though it was ridiculous to have eight bedrooms when Rick and I always shared one. The only time we truly appreciated the space was when my parents came to visit."

Margaret laughed at the face that Marcia made. "That bad?"

"My mother struggled with the cultural differences. My father always had a deep distrust of foreigners, so being surrounded by them made him edgy. And neither of them felt comfortable having a housekeeper. My mother wanted to make her own breakfast every day and keep her own room tidy. After their first visit, we used to give the housekeeper time off while my parents were here. That was easier on everyone."

"So you sold the house and bought an apartment in Promenade View?"

"I sat down with my advocate, and we had a long talk about what I wanted to do next. In the end, buying an apartment in Douglas made the most sense. I also bought my parents' house back in Iowa. They both passed away a few years ago. The house was left to me and my brothers in equal shares. One of my brothers moved in and took care of maintenance, but then he was offered a job in the next town over. He wanted to sell the house so he could afford to buy something in his new town. My other brother lives in Alaska and has no interest in ever going back to Iowa. I couldn't bear to let the house go, though, so I bought out their shares."

"Do you go back often?"

Marcia laughed. "I went back to sign all the papers when I bought the house. It hadn't been long since Rick's sudden passing and I was seriously considering moving back to the US. After a month in Iowa, I realized that I didn't want to live there any longer. I listed the house with a property management company, and they were able to find tenants almost immediately. When their lease is up, if they don't renew, I'll probably go back for a month or two. If they do renew, I'll postpone the trip for another year."

"So the island is home."

"It's where I feel closest to Rick, which is important to me. I tried dating a bit when I was in Iowa, but we can save those stories for another day. I haven't ruled out the possibility of meeting someone else, but finding someone isn't a priority."

"I'm single," the man next to them said.

"No, he isn't," the woman on his other side said. "We've been married for thirty years."

"She's rich," the man said in a pretend whisper to his wife.

She rolled her eyes. "She's also smart and pretty and twenty years younger than you. You don't have a chance."

The man looked at Marcia. "I don't even know her," he said, nodding toward his wife.

Marcia laughed. "If I were you, I'd hold on tight to her."

He looked at his wife and chuckled. "She's still pretty, and she's smart. Sometimes I forget how lucky I am."

"I'll have to start reminding you more often," his wife said.

"We've all heard all sorts of rumors about you," Marcia said to Margaret. "What made you decide to move to the island?"

"Megan and I came to visit Aunt Fenella in December," Margaret told her. "We'd been talking about coming to see her since she moved to the island, but we were both busy with work and other things. And then my ten-year relationship ended, and I started re-evaluating my life. I decided I wanted to change everything, so I quit my job and sold my house. Megan had just started a year-long sabbatical from her job, so it was the perfect time to visit Aunt Fenella. I decided that I'd sort my life out when I got back after the visit."

"And you fell in love with the island on that visit?"

Margaret looked around and then back at Marcia. "I did, rather. I'd never been to the island before, but as soon as I arrived it felt like home in an odd way. Since I was single, unemployed, and homeless, moving here was an easy decision to make."

Marcia laughed. "You seem to have landed on your feet for an unemployed, homeless person."

"I was all of those things by choice, except maybe single. Things have worked out better than I worried they might, too. Aunt Fenella offered me the use of her apartment while she's off on her honeymoon for the next year. I have to look after Katie, but that seems a small price to pay."

"Meroow," the small cat in Margaret's arms murmured.

"She's adorable. I've been thinking about getting a cat, but I'm afraid that seems too spinsterish."

"One cat is probably okay," Margaret said with a small chuckle.

"Did I hear that you're working for a local company now?" Marcia asked.

Margaret nodded. "Park's Cleaning Supplies. I was lucky that they found that they needed a chemical engineer not long after I arrived on the island."

"So you're working for Park's, living in your aunt's apartment, taking care of her cat, and dating Ted Hart. It sounds as if your life has changed a lot in the past few months," Marcia said.

"It has changed completely, and I'm so much happier here than I was in the US."

"I'm really glad to hear that. I'm also glad to hear an American accent. I miss them sometimes."

"They're all over the telly," the man next to her said.

Marcia nodded. "But that isn't really the same. I can't talk to the telly about the things I miss about the US."

"What do you miss?" Margaret asked.

Marcia named a few food items that had Margaret nodding.

"I was shocked that I couldn't get any of those things over here," Margaret said.

"And I miss space," Marcia added. "The US is just huge. You can get in your car and drive for hours and hours and hours and still be in the same state. Or you can drive for days and cross through several different states. Houses are bigger. Cars are bigger. Cities and towns spread out in every direction. There's just a lot more space."

"Maybe you should have kept your mansion," the man said.

Marcia laughed. "Maybe I should have at that."

"Here we go," the man said, nodding toward the front of the building.

A man in a dark suit had just walked out through the glass doors. He walked across the promenade and stopped in front of the crowd.

"What's going on?" someone shouted.

"When can we go back inside?" another voice yelled.

"In case you didn't know," Marcia whispered to Margaret. "That's the Chief Fire Officer."

ALSO BY DIANA XARISSA

The Isle of Man Ghostly Cozy Mysteries

Arrivals and Arrests

Boats and Bad Guys

Cars and Cold Cases

Dogs and Danger

Encounters and Enemies

Friends and Frauds

Guests and Guilt

Hop-tu-Naa and Homicide

Invitations and Investigations

Joy and Jealousy

Kittens and Killers

Letters and Lawsuits

Marsupials and Murder

Neighbors and Nightmares

Orchestras and Obsessions

Proposals and Poison

Questions and Quarrels

Roses and Revenge

Secrets and Suspects

Theaters and Threats

Umbrellas and Undertakers

Visitors and Victims

Weddings and Witnesses

Xylophones and X-Rays

Yachts and Yelps

Zephyrs and Zombies

The Margaret and Mona Ghostly Cozies

Murder at Atkins Farm
Murder at Barker Stadium
Murder at Collins Airfield

The Isle of Man Cozy Mysteries

Aunt Bessie Assumes
Aunt Bessie Believes
Aunt Bessie Considers
Aunt Bessie Decides
Aunt Bessie Enjoys
Aunt Bessie Finds
Aunt Bessie Goes
Aunt Bessie's Holiday
Aunt Bessie Invites
Aunt Bessie Joins
Aunt Bessie Knows
Aunt Bessie Likes
Aunt Bessie Meets
Aunt Bessie Needs
Aunt Bessie Observes
Aunt Bessie Provides
Aunt Bessie Questions
Aunt Bessie Remembers
Aunt Bessie Solves
Aunt Bessie Tries
Aunt Bessie Understands
Aunt Bessie Volunteers

Aunt Bessie Wonders
Aunt Bessie's X-Ray
Aunt Bessie Yearns
Aunt Bessie Zeroes In

The Aunt Bessie Cold Case Mysteries

The Adams File
The Bernhard File
The Carter File
The Durand File
The Evans File
The Flowers File
The Goodman File
The Howard File
The Irving File
The Jordan File
The Keller File
The Lawrence File
The Moss File
The Newton File

The Markham Sisters Cozy Mystery Novellas

The Appleton Case
The Bennett Case
The Chalmers Case
The Donaldson Case
The Ellsworth Case
The Fenton Case
The Green Case
The Hampton Case

The Irwin Case
The Jackson Case
The Kingston Case
The Lawley Case
The Moody Case
The Norman Case
The Osborne Case
The Patrone Case
The Quinton Case
The Rhodes Case
The Somerset Case
The Tanner Case
The Underwood Case
The Vernon Case
The Walters Case
The Xanders Case
The Young Case
The Zachery Case

The Janet Markham Bennett Cozy Thrillers

The Armstrong Assignment
The Blake Assignment
The Carlson Assignment
The Doyle Assignment
The Everest Assignment
The Farnsley Assignment
The George Assignment
The Hamilton Assignment
The Ingram Assignment
The Jacobs Assignment

The Knox Assignment
The Lock Assignment
The Miles Assignment
The Nichols Assignment

The Sunset Lodge Mysteries

The Body in the Annex
The Body in the Boathouse
The Body in the Cottage
The Body in the Dunk Tank
The Body in the Elevator
The Body in the Fountain
The Body in the Greenhouse

The Lady Elizabeth Cozies in Space

Alibis in Alpha Sector
Bodies in Beta Sector
Corpses in Chaos Sector
Danger in Delta Sector
Enemies in Energy Sector

The Midlife Crisis Mysteries

Anxious in Nevada
Bewildered in Florida
Confused in Pennsylvania
Dazed in Colorado
Exhausted in Ohio

The Isle of Man Romances

Island Escape

Island Inheritance

Island Heritage

Island Christmas

The Later in Life Love Stories

Second Chances

Second Act

Second Thoughts

Second Degree

Second Best

Second Nature

Second Place

Second Dance

BOOKPLATES ARE NOW AVAILABLE

Would you like a signed bookplate for this book?

I now have bookplates (stickers) that I can personalize, sign, and send to you. It's the next best thing to getting a signed copy!

Send an email to diana@dianaxarissa.com with your mailing address (I promise not to use it for anything else, ever) and how you'd like your bookplate personalized and I'll sign one and send it to you.

There is no charge for a bookplate, but there is a limit of one per person.

ABOUT THE AUTHOR

Diana has been self-publishing since 2013, and she feels surprised and delighted to have found readers who enjoy the stories and characters that she imagines. Always an avid reader, she still loves nothing more than getting lost in fictional worlds, her own or others!

After being raised in Erie, Pennsylvania, and studying history at Allegheny College in Meadville, Pennsylvania, Diana pursued a career in college administration. She was living and working in Washington, DC, when she met her future husband, an Englishman who was visiting the city.

Following her marriage, Diana moved to Derbyshire. A short while later, she and her husband relocated to the Isle of Man. After ten years on the island, during which Diana earned a Master's degree in the island's history, they made the decision to relocate again, this time to the US.

Now living near Buffalo, New York, Diana and her husband live with their daughter, a student at the University at Buffalo. Their son is now living and working just outside of Boston, Massachusetts, giving Diana an excuse to travel now and again.

Diana also writes mystery/thrillers set in the not-too-distant future as Diana X. Dunn and Young Adult fiction as D.X. Dunn.

She is always happy to hear from readers. You can write to her at:

Diana Xarissa Dunn
PO Box 72
Clarence, NY 14031.

Find Diana at: DianaXarissa.com
E-mail: Diana@dianaxarissa.com

Printed in Great Britain
by Amazon